# An Ancient Calling

# An Ancient Calling

ALVIN J. KITZMANN

THE
MIDDLE WINDOW
PUBLISHING CO.

ARVADA, CO

**An Ancient Calling**

Published by
The Middle Window Publishing Co
Arvada, CO

Library of Congress Control Number: 2014957955
Kitzmann, Alvin J, Author

An Ancient Calling
Alvin Kitzmann

ISBN: 978-0-692-34070-7

FICTION / Historical

QUANTITY PURCHASES: Companies, professional groups, clubs, and other
organizations may qualify for special terms when ordering quantities of this title.

For information email
info@themiddlewindowpublishingco.com.

*An Ancient Calling*

is dedicated foremost to my wife, Jean,
who watched as my story unfolded, and believed.
Whose love and patience had no bounds.

To our Scottish mothers,
Who were never able to go home.

And to one very special teacher, Ms. Evelyn W.,
who took the time to sit with a student
and do what she did best:
teach.

# Scotland

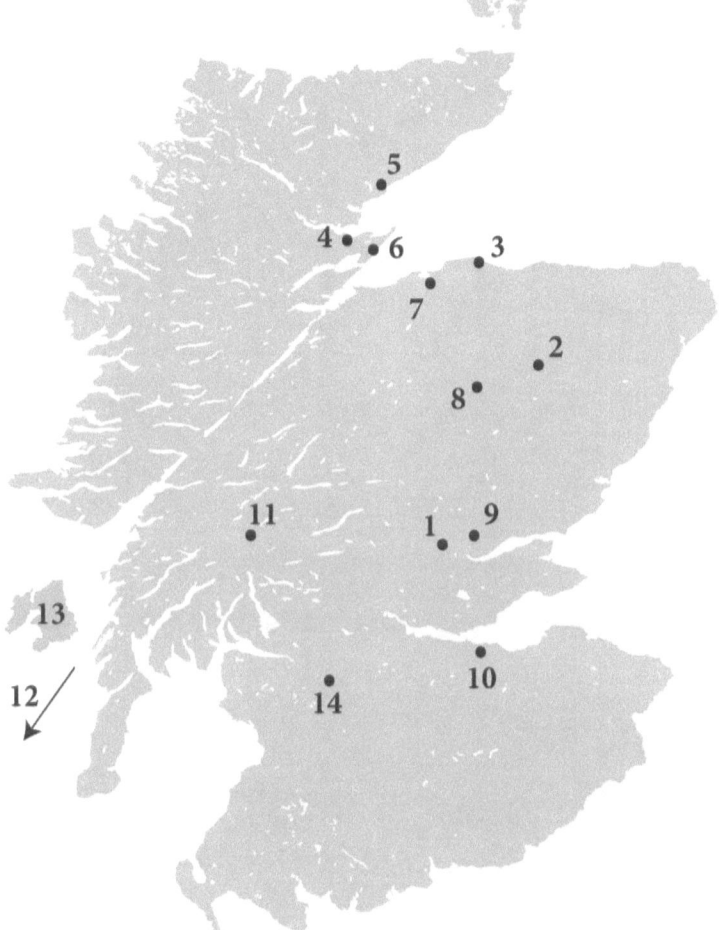

1. Methven
2. Kildrummy Castle
3. Lossiemouth
4. Tain
5. Brora
6. Bailintore
7. Kinloss
8. Loch Builg
9. Scone
10. Edinburgh
11. Strathfillan
12. Ireland
13. Islay
14. Glasgow
15. Orkneys

# ONE

## 1975 A Reversal of Fate

The room smelled of a light antiseptic, the fluorescent light casting a washed-out shade of yellow as it flickered with a dull hum. The Beatles' song "Let It Be" played softly in the background. Aaron, sitting on the examining table, self-consciously crossed his arms as he had done for the last few months. They had, like the rest of his body, taken on the same yellow hue as the room. He had no clue what was causing this, but tried to comfort his thoughts with his wife's gentle admonishments.

"Positives, Aaron," she would remind him. But he wasn't always. He pushed his thoughts to his beautiful Elizabeth, and the decisions he had made since his days in the Army. And now, being in the capable hands of his doctor, *Yes, positives*, Aaron reminded himself once more.

Raised on a farm and the youngest of nine children, he soon learned that life wasn't always fair, that some brothers were there to delegate the worst chores, and most often with fists. That is,

11

he smiled wryly, when they could find him. Learning *those* ropes quickly, Aaron became a master of hiding. When he wasn't whiling away what little hours the farm allowed a young boy, he would often search out the one brother that he did love, his brother Hugh. Working together, Hugh would share his love of politics, and his desire to serve his country. "We'll buddy up," Hugh told his younger brother, filling Aaron with hope. "I hear they are offering that if you ask. And as long as my number don't get called for the draft, I won't enlist, and we can serve together." Aaron dreamt of this, and also for the ticket it would provide to get him off the farm. Sadly, Hugh's number was called, and now, as Aaron sat on the doctor's table, he tried to push his thoughts back towards a positive direction. Yes, he could be occasionally negative, but then, couldn't everyone to some extent? Aaron smiled. No, not everyone. Now that he met and married Elizabeth, he realized, not everyone.

And now, after serving two tours of duty in Vietnam, and then marrying his beautiful wife, every day was a blessing. "Yes, Elizabeth, positives," he said to himself. "Our lives are good."

He had even taken his sergeant's advice, once he said that he wanted out.

"Consider computers, Aaron," he'd said, "and use the Army to get your degree. Hell, you've earned it, as much as any man." His sergeant had then stood and shook Aaron's hand. "You were a quality soldier. I'm sure you will do well."

Receiving his discharge, Aaron left California and returned to his home state of Colorado. Recalling his sergeant's words, he enrolled at Colorado State University in Fort Collins, where he earned half of his Bachelor of Science degree in just over eighteen months.

*God, that was a beautiful day,* Aaron reflected. He had just received his most recent grades, passing all, and decided to take a walk along North College Ave. Going east on Mulberry to Riverside Drive, he followed the road where all the trucks headed west to US 287, and then north to Laramie, each seeking to save a few miles bypassing Cheyenne. Walking towards 'Jefferson Station,' as his buddies called it, he saw a quaint restaurant that invited him in with a pleasant small town atmosphere. *What the hell*, he recalled, opening the door. The thought of a cool glass of milk, a slice of apple pie with a scoop of ice cream, all seemed appealing. He looked down at the four dollars he pulled out from his pocket, and went inside. Yes, the simple things. He loved them—always had—but more so since his tour in Vietnam had ended.

It was then that he caught his first glimpse of Elizabeth, setting a table in what he guessed was her section. She wore no ring, and she was gorgeous. Aaron reached into his pocket for half of his money, and pushed it into the hostess's hand. Aaron nodded subtly in the direction of the waitress and asked, "Is she seeing anyone?"

Looking at Aaron appraisingly, his tall frame squared by even stronger shoulders, she asked, "Farm boy?"

Aaron smiled, replying softly, "That obvious, huh?" Then nodding his head, "Yes'm. Most all my life. If it's possible, I'd like to sit in her section?"

His hostess— her nametag revealed she was Cynthia—guided him to a table in the section closest to the window, and handed him his menu.

"Then you got yourself a ticket, farm boy. Her name's Elizabeth, and she's not one for the hippie types. She'll be with you shortly."

The song "Loco-motion" was playing on a tabletop jukebox four tables up. Tapping each of the chairs to the melody as she walked away, Cynthia turned back and smiled. "How about the military? You serve?" she asked.

Aaron held up two fingers, and replied "Twice." Cynthia smiled, happy for her friend at what she thought might be a nice match.

Aaron watched as she approached Elizabeth and happily informed her of the young man sitting in her section, pretending to look over his menu. Cynthia's head nodded, then a furtive glance by Elizabeth, and then another by both of them. Elizabeth tried to hide her smile as she walked up to the young man seated in her section, feeling slightly set up. She looked at Aaron appraisingly.

"So, Cynthia tells me you served. In 'Nam?"

"Yes'm. Two tours with the 196th," Aaron replied.

Elizabeth laughed, and pulling out a chair, asked, "Did I just hear a "Yes'm?"

Aaron smiled and nodded. "Yes ma'am, you did. It's pretty much the way my parents, momma especially, raised us. It was always, 'Yes ma'am, no ma'am, thank ya, please.'"

Elizabeth giggled. "I'll bet you just blended right in!"

"I did," Aaron replied. "There were a lot of farm boys besides myself. Most of us were trying to learn the Army way of life and grow up. We did both, eventually."

"Did you enlist, or were you drafted?"

"Enlisted. I re-upped in '70 and stayed for the cleanup. They brought us home in '72. I've been out now for two and a half years."

Elizabeth smiled. "Cynthia said you grew up on a farm. Was it near here?"

"Yes'm," Aaron replied. "And no, it's not far. An hour east at the most, near the town of Kersey. I lived there all my life until I enlisted."

Cynthia was right; there was something about this man that she liked. She listened intently as Aaron gave a brief story of his life. She nodded her head at the parts she could relate to, listening intently as he talked about his upbringing and his family's beliefs. It was obvious by his shorter hair that he made no attempt to blend in with the current, barefoot life-style that had become prevalent on campus over the last seven years.

"My brother and I used to talk about politics for hours as we did our chores. We didn't always agree with the decisions our country made, or the presidents that were chosen," Aaron said, "but we respect the office. That's what led to our deciding to join the Army. And it was never about Vietnam. It was about our country, where you can have an opinion totally opposite of someone else's, and be heard. This is why we enlisted. We joined for what we believed in." Aaron hesitated. "I was supposed to go with my older brother, Hugh, the one I was closest to, but his number was called and he couldn't wait."

Elizabeth listened intently, and said, "I guess it's my turn?"

Aaron laughed, and smiling with encouragement, let her begin.

"I was an only child, and began working before the age of five. For as long as I can remember, I would get up before dawn to help with the cows then go to school, only to do it once more before I could start my homework. I'd go to bed, exhausted, and do it all over again the next day. I used to beg my mother for a brother or sister." Elizabeth stopped to wipe away a tear and after a few moments, began anew.

"But, then my mother and baby brother died as she was giving birth. I guess one should watch out for what they wish? I know my prayers had nothing to do with my mother's death, but my father took it hard. He began working non-stop. I had to work harder and I kept up my prayers, but this time I toned them down, asking only for someone to make our dinner." Elizabeth stopped again and looked at the man she had just met. Aaron reached across to hold her hand.

15

She felt his warmth, smiled, and continued. "It was when I turned eighteen that I knew I had to make a decision. Like you, I knew I had to get off the farm, and the only way to do that was to break my father's heart. He's stubborn, and feels that life is now, which is a polar opposite to how my mother felt. She used to sit me on her lap, and start sharing our Scottish lineage for hundreds of years. That's when he would get up, saying he had things to do in the dairy. I don't know if he was just interested in the here and now, as he said, or if it was for another reason. Momma said he lost someone dear to him in Korea." Elizabeth was quiet a moment, then continued. "My family has been in every war since my great grandparents came to the States. Some were hurt, like my father, who had his leg burned terribly in Korea, or my grandfather's brother, who served in WWI, only to lose his life from the Spanish Flu."

Aaron squeezed her hand supportively. "War is never pretty. I left behind a few quality friends in 'Nam as well." Aaron tried to lighten the conversation that seemed to pull them down the last few minutes. "Did I hear Scotland? Is that where your family got their fighting spirit?"

"Daddy just says I'm obstinate," Elizabeth replied, doing her best to smile, but it came out as a sad one at best.

"That was six months ago," she said. "We've not spoken since, though I'm sure one day we will again. We love one another too much not to. We're just both cut from the same stubborn piece of tartan!"

Elizabeth then changed the subject. "Have you seen our dairy?" she asked. "On the northeast corner of I-25 and Highway 14? North of the service station?"

Aaron shrugged his shoulders and shook his head no. "I go from class to home, repeat, five days a week, and study nights and week-ends. This is as far from the campus that I've been in the last few months. I doubt I'd remember how to get to I-25 anymore, or what a cow would look like, even if it were in the next booth!"

They both laughed, and any nervousness that might have remained from their first meeting had now officially passed.

Aaron then told her about his pursuit of a degree in computer science and his latest grades, and the apple pie that led him into her restaurant.

"And today," he said, raising up his forkful of apple pie a la mode, "I'm halfway!"

With that they toasted mutual dreams with raised glasses of milk.

"To cows and education," Elizabeth said, laughing.

Their first date was that Friday night, and soon they were dating steadily. It was three short months later that they were married.

"You can thank the Beatles for this one," Dr. Allen said. Aaron felt the table move as he was slowly guided through the newest x-ray device scanning his abdomen.

"It's called a CT scanner." Dr. Allen hummed softly to the Beatles song as it did its job. "Before this, we had to do all sorts of tests, many of them invasive. This," he said, pointing to the scanner and obviously proud of the hospital's newest addition, "is a sweet deal."

The scanner bed went back to its starting position, and Aaron looked up at his doctor, curious. Was it done? Was it really that simple?

"Seems the Beatles' recording studio, EMI, did many things, including funding medical research," Dr. Allen continued. "This machine is state of the art and a fine addition to our hospital. Godfrey Hounsfield, the inventor, was just elected to The Royal Society of

Great Britain. Remarkable instrument, remarkable man, and it has saved many from unnecessary procedures."

Dr. Allen smiled at Aaron, reading his thoughts.

"That's it. That's all it takes. Now, I want you to take that pretty wife of yours home. Tell her to put on her nicest dress and then go out for dinner, maybe a bottle of wine. We won't have any results for more than a week, and the one thing I do know is that worrying won't help or change a single thing for the better. We just need one more thing, a blood sample to accompany this x-ray."

Dr. Allen, biting his lip, felt he knew the prognosis already, but didn't care to go there. Not with anyone, but especially not with Aaron and Elizabeth. They were wonderful people, and as much as he loved his work, he sometimes hated it. Pancreatic cancer, in all his experience, was incurable.

Aaron walked out of the x-ray area and down the hall. He had dealt with challenges all his life and, in his heart, knew Dr. Allen was right. Worrying wouldn't help, though he knew something was wrong. Something beyond the aches and the skin and eye discoloration. He pulled his hat down low to hide the yellowish tint to his face, thankful for the long-sleeved shirt. He waited for his name to be called for the blood sample.

"There we have it," Dr. Allen said, personally drawing the blood sample and applying gentle pressure over the newly placed Band-Aid. "Remember, these tests are extensive and will take a while. But this," he held up the vial, "as well as the CT scan, will end our guessing."

Two weeks later, the results came back positive for pancreatic cancer. It was then that Elizabeth made the decision to bring a baby into their lives.

"I can do it on my own" was her answer to Aaron's incredulity. "Many young mothers in circumstances less perfect than ours are going to school and raising children on their own. Besides, what finer gift can we give to a baby, our baby? To know that he or she"—though Elizabeth knew in her heart that her child would be a girl—"was loved so much?"

Eleven months later, Elizabeth reflected on their mutual decision. Her delivery date was growing near, and she knew Aaron's remaining days would be filled with the joy of their love and their child. Closing her eyes, Elizabeth prayed that her sweetheart's time would pass easily and that her unborn baby girl was healthy.

She had a very special gift, one that had been passed down from her mother and her mother's mother before her, as far back as the fourteenth century. It was almost religious in its passing, and she looked forward to the day when she would present it to her own daughter, sharing their history and from whom it had descended.

The gift was a small box that held a knife and a pair of earrings. The earrings were beautifully crafted, with a ruby on top, a braid of fine gold, a diamond in the middle, and a ruby on the bottom. Each was three inches in length. The earrings had unfortunately been separated from the complete set back in 1746. One hundred fifty years later, Elizabeth's great-great-grandmother traveled back to Scotland to find the missing piece, but it was no longer in its hiding place. Though sad at this turn of events, the family still rejoiced in owning and passing on the ancient box and the reminders of their proud heritage.

All had been appraised years ago and were considered priceless. "If you ever wish to sell these…" she was once told, but they were not for sale. They had never been for sale.

The next two weeks brought false labor and pain.

"We may have to induce, Elizabeth, and at worse, a C-section. Not to worry," her doctor said, as she held her hand. "These are just some of the challenges that happen when life tries to enter a brave new world."

Dr. Cady smiled, trying to alleviate the apprehension she knew Elizabeth felt. Elizabeth smiled back weakly. She so wanted everything to be perfect for Aaron in his remaining time.

That night, as Aaron and she lay in bed, she began crying. "Aaron, forgive me, but I'm scared. It's you who has endured so much. But somehow I feel my delivery won't be easy. That I will not see my child grow or," she paused to collect herself, "be able to pass my heirloom to our baby. Will you tell her?" Elizabeth caught herself, realizing the impossibility of what she just asked.

Aaron held up his hand. "Sweetheart, you'll be fine. Please stop worrying."

Elizabeth was quiet for a moment, then said, "Aaron, if my delivery ... will you tell my father I'm sorry and that I love him so very much?"

Aaron held his beloved and whispered to her, hoping her uneasiness would leave. "All mothers feel scared, sweetheart, right before they deliver. Everything will be fine, I promise!"

Aaron waited happily but impatiently in the waiting room, chatting occasionally with the other dads-to-be. One day, he hoped, the practice of allowing fathers to come into the delivery room would be more accepted, as it was in other countries. The U.S., he felt, for all its modern inventions, was still controlled by an almost religious backwardness. *Someday,* he thought ruefully, knowing this was his only chance. *Positives, Aaron,* he reminded himself. He leaned his head back, closed his eyes, and soon dozed off.

Aaron awoke an hour later and looked at his watch. Ten hours had passed since they'd admitted Elizabeth, and now he was very worried. He stood up at the same time his wife's doctor exited the delivery room.

"Aaron, could you come with me?" she asked quietly. Dr. Cady brought him into a private room and took his hand.

"You have a beautiful baby girl, born at 3:57 p.m.," she said, momentarily happy but obviously not finished.

She was holding back the grief that her profession sometimes brought. She knew of the challenges the couple already faced, so this was the hardest news she'd ever had to share.

"There were complications…" She faltered, and then tried to resume. "Her placenta tore, and she hemorrhaged. She's weak and has lost a lot of blood."

She took Aaron's hand and said softly, "I don't think she will make it."

Aaron stormed out toward the delivery room.

"Elizabeth!" he called out, bursting through the double doors to where she lay on the hospital table.

Aaron ran to his wife, his beautiful Elizabeth, who, in spite of her weakness, looked up at Aaron, glowing with happiness.

"It's a girl! Oh, Aaron, I am so happy! The doctor says she's healthy." Elizabeth looked up weakly and smiled. "I have an angel to remind me of our love."

Aaron's tears rolled down his face, as he looked at his beloved, knowing the sad reversal that fate had brought them. "With all your prayers, did you think there was a chance of her being a boy?" Aaron winked and tried to hide the anguish in his heart.

Dr. Cady pulled him aside.

"Aaron, she has only a few minutes at best."

Aaron was at a loss as he looked at the doctor. He pulled away and went back to Elizabeth and took her hand. It was already losing some of its warmth, and she had lost some of her glow.

"Oh, Aaron," Elizabeth said, trying to hold his hand with the little strength she had left. "I wanted our baby to be healthy. I had to have a girl, like my mother, and her…" Elizabeth stopped and sank deeper into her bed. "Aaron, tell my daddy. Please?"

Aaron squeezed her hand gently, and he nodded his head that he would. He felt her fingers relax as she heard his promise. Then she strained to tell him more.

"My heirloom. There is so much more I should have told you. You remember the combination to our safe?"

Aaron nodded, crying openly. "Yes, I do."

"Oh, *mo cridhe**, don't cry," Elizabeth said softly. "We will be together soon. The earrings. I so wanted to help her put them on for the first time, as…as my mother did for me."

Her breathing became labored. "Call our baby Marion, after my mother. She then must call her daughter Elizabeth to maintain our lineage."

She struggled for the strength to finish what she had to tell him. "She must pass the earrings to her daughter on her sixteenth birthday. They can never be sold. No matter how much… ever. Tell her," she squeezed his hand one last time, "that she is a Scot!"

Her voice trailed off as she slipped away into the ancient past; to the lineage that was created long ago, to the generations that now welcomed her home.

---

* *Mo cridhe* is Scot Gaelic for "my heart."

Elizabeth's services were held in Fort Collins. Her father was there, his anguish barely containable. Dr. Cady had closed her office for the day, and Aaron's brother, Hugh, and his wife, Sharon, were there as well. After the services were over, they drove south to the small town of Loveland, where U.S. 287 divided the cemetery.

"From dust thou art to dust thou shalt return," the preacher said as they lowered Elizabeth's casket into the ground, proclaiming in his words the circle of life.

Aaron knew that he, too, would soon be a part of that circle. Standing at the side of the grave, Sharon and Hugh each held onto Aaron, helping him feel the love they both had for him.

Minutes passed, and the wind blew gently through the trees. They all looked at baby Marian as she lay in Aaron's arms, cooing softly.

"Aaron," Hugh began awkwardly. "Sharon and I have been talking." Then he began to sob uncontrollably, knowing that he would be losing his best friend and brother in a short amount of time.

Sharon took over. "What we want to say, Aaron, is that we would be honored if you would let us adopt baby Marian. We will raise her as our own. We'll give her all the love in our hearts. She will go through life knowing of a dream for her future."

She held Aaron's arm as she said this; Hugh could only nod his assent as he listened to his wife tell Aaron what they had spoken of earlier.

Aaron nodded his head thankfully. It was all he could do. There were no two people more capable of providing for his daughter in the same manner as he and Elizabeth had planned.

A year slowly passed before Aaron began to fail from the disease that was consuming his body. Hugh and Sharon were in his life daily, helping him as he raised his daughter and helping Marian become used to them as her second parents.

It happened two weeks after Valentine's Day, and they were both by his side at the hospital.

"You know my wishes," Aaron said, his voice barely audible, "to be laid to rest next to Elizabeth. She has been waiting for me. Even after a year, I still dream of her nightly."

Aaron stretched his arm across his bed to the nightstand, where a small, ancient box rested next to an envelope, but gave up.

"I tried to remember everything Elizabeth said to me before she passed," he said, as Hugh tearfully picked up the box and envelope from the nightstand. "To Elizabeth, it meant everything. Promise me that you will give these to Marian on her sixteenth birthday."

Through her tears, Sharon promised. "We love her so much, Aaron! You know we will."

Aaron smiled up at them. He closed his eyes, feeling the welcome embrace of his Elizabeth, understanding finally the meaning of the circle in which she, and now he, played a part.

# TWO

## 1992 Elizabeth's Gift

It was Marian's sixteenth birthday, and she was ecstatic! Her mom and dad had surprised her with a party, and all her friends were there, even the doctor who had delivered her. She so wished her real parents were alive and with her, but knew they would be pleased. She would soon get her driver's license and be able to visit the cemetery on her own. Marian had heard the story many times of how they'd brought her into the world and the challenges they'd faced. She also knew she was about to be given an important letter. She could hardly wait!

Marian stood before her guests.

"You have no idea how very special this day is for me," Marian said, as she looked at each of them. "You have made this the most wonderful day in my life, and I will remember you forever!"

Dr. Cady came to her and gave her a hug.

"Your parents would be proud of you, Marian. I understand you are even taking college freshman courses now?"

"I am," Marian replied, "though I'm not sure at this point what degree I will pursue. But at least I can get the required 101 classes out of the way. And, Doctor," she added, "thank you for your kind words. All my life I have dreamed of the parents I never knew."

Dr. Cady smiled. "I'm sure your parents would be pleased to know what a wonderful young woman you have become."

Marian blushed and thanked her again.

It was after 8:00 p.m. when the last of their guests left. Hugh and Sharon sat by the fireplace and called Marian into the study. On the table was a sealed envelope, faded to a yellow patina from age.

"Marian," Hugh began, "we have told you for years of this letter. Maybe we shouldn't have and made it more of a surprise. What we didn't tell you about"—he lifted a small, aged box up to the table—"was this"

Hugh pushed the box toward her.

"You will need to read the letter from your father first, sweetheart," Sharon said. "I believe it should explain the box's contents."

Marian reverently touched the paper, and slowly ran her fingers over the word "Marian" on the envelope, loving that it was her father's handwriting.

Sharon saw the emotions in her daughter's face. "It was one of the last things he was able to do," she said. "We miss him so much."

Hugh's eyes filled as the memory of Aaron and how close they had been returned once more. They watched as Marian nervously opened the letter.

February 21, 1977
"Dear Marian,

I am writing to tell you how proud I am of you and how much we both loved you. Your mother and I knew I had only a short time to live, and she wanted me to have you in my life before I passed. It would have been her most precious joy to give you what you are about to receive from your parents. I know already you love them dearly, and I can't think of anyone who would know a greater happiness at raising you than they.

Things in life sometimes change, sweetheart. Your mother had a difficult delivery, and she passed almost immediately afterward. She would never know the joy of sharing the gifts that are before you, that should have been yours and hers together. The box, Marian, please take it now and open it. The earrings …they go from mother to daughter, and I know Sharon would be proud to put them on you now."

Marian put the letter aside and took the box, opening it slowly. Inside, nestled on aged, white velvet, was an old knife and two of the most beautiful earrings she had ever seen. Each earring had a strand of gold with a ruby on top, a diamond in the middle, and a ruby on the bottom. She pushed the box over to her parents.

"Oh, Momma," Marian cried softly, "look!" Hugh and Sharon both gasped as they looked at Elizabeth's present.

"These came from your mother?" Hugh said in astonishment. "I've never seen anything like these. How old do you think they are?"

Sharon grasped his hand, squeezed it, and motioned for him to let their daughter finish reading. "I think there's more to her letter," Sharon said.

Hugh nodded and waited for Marian. She read quietly a mo-

ALVIN KITZMANN

ment and said, "The letter says you are supposed to put them on me, Momma, and you are to say, 'You are a Scot!'"

Sharon reached into the box, then slowly put each earring on Marian. She stepped back next to Hugh, and they beheld their daughter, transfixed. Sharon, feeling incredibly inadequate for the occasion, said, "You are a Scot!"

"Would you look at that," Hugh whistled softly. "I had an idea of what a princess is supposed to look like from Princess Grace and Princess Diana. But, sweetheart, their light does not hold a candle to you."

Sharon nodded her head in agreement.

"Thank you, Daddy," Marian said, and she kissed them. "Thank you both so very much."

Marian looked down at the letter. "There's more that I need to read." She caressed the earrings gently as she silently continued reading.

> "The earrings come down from all the women in your family, sweetheart. They went from your mother to you, and from all the generations of women before her from which you are descended. I don't know how far back, but I know from your mother that they are at least five hundred years old. The knife I know nothing of, except that it is not as old as the earrings."

> Marian looked again at the knife, about seven inches in length, and touched the blade reverently. She continued reading.

> "Each mother would name her daughter Elizabeth, and that mother in turn would name her daughter Marian, as your mother asked I do for you. When you have a daughter, name her Eliza-

beth, and when she turns sixteen, you are to put the earrings on her. Tell her, like I am sharing with you, that they can never be sold, ever. They must be passed from mother to oldest daughter. From what I understand, there has always been a daughter in the lineage. I am certain, even after five hundred years, this chain will remain intact. One day, sweetheart, I know you will be as proud to give these to your daughter as Sharon and Hugh are today. Know in your heart that we both loved you so much, and our only sadness is that we aren't there to watch as you became a young lady.

Lastly, dear Marian, if your final resting place in life finds you in Colorado, the plots around your mother and I are already paid for. They are for you and your family, if you wish. For now, I know in my heart that you come to visit your mother and me often. We both rejoice in this, I promise.

Love you always and forever, Your Loving Father and Mother.

P.S. Please look up now, and tell Hugh and Sharon how much I love all they have done for you, and that I love them both so very much."

Marian fingered the earrings in awe as she read the loving words from her father. She smiled and looked up. "Daddy wants me to tell you that he loves the two of you so very much," she said, "and that he knows all of what you have done for me."

Hugh nodded, and then looked away, unable to reply. Sharon squeezed his hand. She picked up the box, admiring it, before handing it to Marian.

"If the earrings could only share their story," Sharon said, as Marian closed the box. "I wonder what they would say."

Hugh and Sharon stood and embraced their daughter.

"I ... Would you mind terribly if I went to my room?" Marian asked softly. "I hope you understand."

They all kissed goodnight, and Marian retreated to her room. She sat on her bed and took each earring off and placed them in the box. She looked out her window at the incredibly clear night. She wished there had been more her father's letter could have shared. She wished he could have written something about the knife, that maybe it had saved someone in her family at the last moment. She wished it had been her real mother who'd gently pulled back her hair as she put each earring on, her real mother who'd told her of her lineage, how the earrings been passed down from mother to daughter for hundreds of years, and said "You are a Scot." She had sensed Sharon's awkwardness when she put the earrings on, and felt sad for her. But her father's letter had brought the pain and realization that it wasn't her real mother who shared this special moment. Marian walked to her window and looking up to the North Star, lowered her head and began praying that one day she would learn their story.

Marian finished her prayers and fell into a troubled sleep, oblivious to the clouds that were being pulled inward, darkening the night sky of her mind, blotting out the stars one by one. She knew not the incredible will of her ancestry, her history that went back not five hundred, but seven hundred years. It went back to the Highlands of Scotland where the earrings had been crafted as a gift for the wife of a man who had been a guardian of his beloved Scotland. Now, seven hundred years later, the royal lineage was trying to make itself known, to reestablish its connection, and to gently pull her back to where it had all begun.

# THREE

## 2005 The Dreams

Marian sat at her vanity and took off the earrings, carefully placing them next to the knife in the ancient box that protected them. Her husband, Ian, watched each time she did this, always knowing the direction her thoughts went. It wasn't the passing of the earrings from mother to daughter that she questioned. Many mothers pass their jewelry on to their daughters. What she questioned was, why had it become so much more than that? Who started it? Who sat down all those centuries ago and began something that was to have such an impact on an entire lineage? Whose decision was it to have alternating names, and why?

Marian opened the safe and carefully placed the box alongside their most precious things. Closing the door, she tried futilely to shut her mind from these thoughts as soundly as she did the safe. She sighed and wondered if she would ever know. Hugh and Sharon were both as clueless as she was about the history of these gifts. It saddened her to think she might be the last link in the story.

"Where are these from, Mama?" Marian's future daughter would ask.

"I don't know, sweetheart, but they are very special and can never be sold," would be her only reply.

Without something more to share, how long would that small story keep the earrings from being sold if times ever got tough?

She felt familiar tears well up. Not knowing would never be enough. She would always try to find the answer. *Damn it*, Marian thought, as she once more pushed the thoughts out of her mind.

After graduating magna cum laude from Fort Collins High School, Marian had accepted a scholarship from the University of Missouri at Kansas City. Her college-level classes, taken while in high school, allowed her to begin as a sophomore. A doctorate in ancient archaeology, a choice made shortly after turning sixteen, was well on its way.

Now, Dr. Marian Dirks had finally moved home, with the man of her dreams, to take a job as archaeologist for CSU in Fort Collins.

Ian Dirks' family had originated in Aberdeen, Scotland, where, according to his grandmother, their family had changed their name to escape persecution. From there, they moved to Canada, and finally, more than eighty years ago, his great-grandparents moved to the little town of Marshall, California, just north of the Bay area.

Ian, too, had graduated high school with a 4.0, then began his studies at the University of Missouri before going on to med school. After finishing his third year of residency at St. Luke's Hospital in Kansas City, his best friend and fellow doctor, Michael, arranged a blind date.

"She's beautiful, Ian, and sharp as hell," Michael exclaimed. "You have got to meet this girl." Michael winked at his friend. "And you better do it quick, too, before Niall gets her."

"Who?" Ian asked, clueless.

"Niall. He's quite charming, according to Anna," Michael answered, recalling his wife's reaction. "He's in his late twenties and almost has his doctorate in archaeology from the University of Glasgow. From what Anna says, he was sent here to provide assistance with their pre-Clovis dig, and he seems to be quite the ladies' man."

Marian smiled at the memory of how she had met Ian through Michael and Anna. She still thought of Niall occasionally and heard of his work with the BBC, but that was it. She was truly happy for his success and enjoyed when their professional lives crossed paths on rare occasions.

It was four months after Ian and Michael graduated that she and Ian were married in Fort Collins, with Michael and Anna serving as their best man and matron of honor. Seeing the beautiful Rocky Mountains for the first time, Ian and Michael quickly decided to open a clinic on the southeast side of Fort Collins. The local newspaper noted it as one of the nicest clinics to be established in recent years.

Their homes, newly built as well, were on the edge of Lake Loveland, and each couple contemplated starting families. Marian loved her life, their friends, her work at CSU's archaeology department, being close to her parents, and above all, her husband.

All was perfect, Marian reflected.

Except these last few weeks, when Ian's nights began filling with dreams. He would awake suddenly and then be unable to return to sleep.

The clouds came past the western shoreline, dark and heavy with rain. They pushed east, over verdant forests of the ancient tribal lands of the Caledonii until they approached the castle. Beautifully constructed with the finest in ashlar stonework, the fortress stood magnificently, guarding the roads merging from the south. Ian watched as the clouds continued eastward to the edge of the island, before crossing the North Sea and finally into Norway.

*Norway?* Ian awoke suddenly. Marian had just dozed off as her own dream was slowly beginning to take hold, trying to piece together at night what her daytime research was unable to do. That is, until she heard his sudden awakening and knew something was again disrupting his sleep. She was thankful that his associate physician and neighbor, Michael, had prescribed a sleeping pill to help him sleep. He was always just a phone call away as well.

"Can't sleep again?" Marian asked.

Ian went to the window and stood there, looking out, wondering why another strange dream was interrupting his sleep. He watched as the night sky slowly filled with low-hanging clouds, echoing his dream. Northern California, where he had grown up, would have clouds of this type move in slowly from the ocean. Tonight, they refused to go any further east and simply blotted out the stars. Strange, he thought, as he turned from the window and smiled lovingly at his wife.

"No. Not tonight, either," Ian replied. Marian got up and offered him what Michael had prescribed.

"Thanks, sweetheart, but no," Ian answered. "I have to work at the clinic in four hours. That will make me groggy all day. Tomorrow night might be better. Would you remind me then?"

Marian gave him a loving "yes," as she got up and kissed him.

She went to the kitchen to get him a warm glass of milk. Ian never turned that down; hopefully, it would help him sleep. Marian heated it in a small pan, disparaging the new microwave above the stove. She hated its heating process and enjoyed passing the time looking out her window. She saw the clouds Ian had noticed earlier and watched as they engulfed the homes surrounding the lake.

"Here you are, sweetheart," Marian said, handing him the warm milk.

Ian smiled and thanked her.

"If this doesn't change soon," Marian added, "I'd like Michael to give you a thorough examination."

Ian did not share his dream with her. He could not understand where his dreams were taking him or why. He wished he could find an answer. *No,* Ian thought, *there is no answer. Dreams are dreams, and they will pass.*

Ian woke with a start later that morning. Looking at his watch, he figured he slept at best an hour and a half. Not enough, he knew, especially as the sleep deprivation was beginning to be cumulative. But it would be enough to help him through part of the day. No tough jobs, thankfully, mostly because his partner and friend knew what he was going through and agreed to help with his patients. Ian had no clue what he would do without him and loved him like the brother he never had.

He arrived at the clinic shortly before 7:30 a.m. His days as a resident had been tough, even demanding, but these last weeks, with almost no sleep, were turning into a personal grinder for which the emergency room schedule had barely prepared him.

*Why were these dreams happening now?* he thought, as he absent-mindedly watched his quart-size cup fill to the top with coffee, then spill over.

Michael, walking by, tapped his shoulder softly, and teased him.

"Looks like an addiction buddy!"

It was the usual harassment Ian received from Michael, who, along with the receptionists, always loaded his coffee card at Christmas. He grabbed a few paper towels to help Ian clean up, and then with concern, "You look like hell, buddy. I take it you're still having trouble sleeping?"

"Michael, I can sleep. The problem is that when I do, my mind is dreaming nonstop, and then I wake up in a cold sweat. Last night, I was soaring over an island and heading to Norway."

"Norway?" Michael asked. "What the hell? As in Denmark?"

Ian loved his friend's subtlety, and replied, "A little further north, but Michael, I was there! I could see mountains and how beautifully green it was. Then suddenly, I was awake." Ian added, "If Marian wasn't there with me, I'd think I was headed on the fast train to the loony bin."

"We won't let that happen," Michael said. "You're still on the easy shift. We'll keep you busy, but nothing too tough."

Ian smiled and thanked him.

It was now three thirty, and Ian handed a prescription to his six-teenth patient of the day, an older gentleman, in his mid-fifties, who was having trouble sleeping.

"You look like you could use the same prescription yourself, Doc."

Ian agreed and tried to smile. "Yeah. Some days are tough," he said.

Ian's mind went back to the first night he'd had insomnia, after Marian had surprised him with vacation plans to Scotland. She had walked out of their bedroom wearing the earrings that had been passed down from her mother. They were stunningly beautiful, and she wore them only on special occasions. They had talked of a vacation for months, not really confirming anything. Nova Scotia sounded good, they thought at first. According to his mother, it was where Ian's family had landed in 1719, after leaving Aberdeen.

"Your family descended from royalty," Marian said, recalling his grandmother's words. "She never knew your real family name herself, since it had been erased from the family's memory by the time she was born. But the royalty part? She said that was 'for certain.'"

Then she gently harassed him. "You know, I've never heard of the Dirks Clan. Connor MacLeod of the Clan MacLeod, I've heard of," she winked. "Even the MacDonald Clan and the Gordon Clan. But noo, I dinna think I've ever heard of the Dirks Clan. Are yoo an immortal?"

Ian threw his pillow at her, before pushing her onto their bed.

"We're ancient baby. Didn't I tell you I had just turned seven hundred?"

Then kissing her lovingly, he pulled her close, only to slap her rear. Marian turned quickly, a mock feeling of hurt on her face. Ian winked at her.

She had taken the day off and spent it with their travel agent, Rachael, making plans. "First, we'll land in Edinburgh," she said, smiling as she sat up on the bed.

"Baby, it's called Edin-bura," he chastised her playfully. "You will need to get that correct if you have any plans of staying anywhere besides the airport."

She tried again. "Edinboro," as only a native Coloradan can mangle.

He said it again, adding the lilt and brogue that she had become accustomed to as part of his family. "Edin-bura." It sounded beautiful. Marian grinned and continued laying out the plans she had made.

"First," she said, clearing the table for the travel brochures and map, "we'll land and rent a car. We'll go west through Glasgow and stay in bed-and-breakfasts throughout our trip. We can even take the scotch tours you've always talked of."

Ian smiled at the thought.

"Bruichladdich is still your favorite, yes?"

Ian watched Marian absentmindedly caress her earrings. Her voice became distant as he gazed, transfixed. The earrings were beautiful and pulled him into their depths. Ian could see the castle walls slowly materialize as he stared into the diamond's translucent beauty.

"Ian?" She had stopped talking and was staring at him. "Ian?" He shook his head and looked away from the earrings.

"I thought I lost you," she said.

"Sorry," Ian muttered. "They really are beautiful," he added, as though it were the first time he'd ever seen them.

"Thank you," Marian said, smiling, but with a moment's concern in her voice.

"Here's the brochure for the scotch distillery you like. Rachael said she met the Gaelic man who helped get it going about four years ago. She said he was delightful and told stories all the time. I think we should go there." She then handed him extra brochures for Islay's other distilleries. "Maybe you'll find another you like?"

"From Islay," she continued, tracing her finger north along the west coast of Scotland, "we'll go until we get to Ullapool, Armadale, past Thurso, and then down to Inverness and Aberdeen. Oh," she added excitedly, "here's a castle we can see that's west of Aberdeen, near the Cairngorms!"

She laid down the brochure.

"It looks amazing. We can visit it and then spend the night at the hotel nearby!" she exclaimed.

"It's called Kildrummy," Ian said.

"This says it's been abandoned since ..." Marian looked up. "What did you say?"

"It's been abandoned since 1716," Ian answered.

Marian looked puzzled. "You knew this?"

"I ... I guess so. I'm sure I must have heard it somewhere. Possibly from my grandmother when I was young, during her tales of the Jacobite revolution. She used to tell us stories of Scotland's past."

But Ian wasn't so sure. *Where in the hell did that come from?* he wondered. He continued looking at the castle in the brochure. It looked ... familiar. For some unknown reason, he felt a sense of recollection as he looked at the pictures. From here, one went through the Gatehouse, across the courtyard to the Great Hall, and the Snow Tower on the left. The recollection went away when he tried to pin it down. *No,* he thought, clearing his mind. *I'm sure I'm confusing this castle with pictures of ones my grandmother had.*

"From there," Marian continued, as she tried to get Ian back on track with her plans, "we'll go back to Edinburgh"—this time she proudly pronounced it correctly—"and come home. It would take a full two weeks! You could get away for that long, couldn't you?"

Ian smiled and looked at his beautiful wife, wondering how on earth he'd gotten her to marry him. He'd never know, but would always be grateful that Michael's wife, Anna, had introduced them.

Ian looked anew at the route and her plans. He envisioned the two of them together. Her excitement was palpable.

"I'd love to, Marian," as he reached over and kissed her.

She squealed with delight. "I gotta call Momma!"

That night, the dreams and fitful sleep began. Visions of a majestic castle rising against a beautiful blue sky were accented against billowy cotton clouds. The gates were open, and the towers flew bright banners. All the subjects of the castle were excited about the return of Lady Christian, in spite of the news of an attack that her husband's messenger had delivered.

*What in the world is going on?* Ian wondered, waking up. He quickly grabbed his glass of water. *Indigestion?* His mind went to the stuffed bell pepper he'd had for dinner and then the novel by Dickens he'd read: "an undigested bit of beef, a blot of mustard."

But the next few weeks would prove it surely wasn't.

Ian walked with his patient to the door, giving instructions for the sleeping pill.

"Let me know if this helps," he said. "I'll have my nurse call you on Monday to see if everything is okay. If you have an adverse reaction, which is very unlikely, give us a call."

Ian thanked him and turned to their receptionist.

"No patients for a half hour, right?" Ian asked.

"You have none for an hour," she replied. "Your 4:15 just called and canceled."

"Good," Ian replied, exhausted. "Call them back and thank them. No, don't. I'll be in Room B, trying to get a little sleep. I'm expecting Marian to stop by. If you don't see me in fifty minutes, will you knock on my door?"

"Yes, Doctor," she replied.

Ian lay back on the examining table, closed his eyes, and fell asleep immediately. Low, heavy rain clouds hung over the Grampian Mountains. The castle, beautiful and stately under the evening moon, flaunted its regal status and provided shelter from the impending weather for all within her walls.

*"Come to bed, my love," a woman said to her husband, in their native Gaelic. "Lady Christian will return soon, and I shall make you proud to have chosen me as your wife."*

*She put their baby into the thick woolen wraps next to their bed, and as he turned to her, she slowly vanished, along with the dark clouds and the castle.*

Ian woke up abruptly, sweating, to see Marian watching him, concerned. His eyes went from side to side in a panic, taking in the examining room, before slowly recognizing where he was. This time, he remembered more of his dream. The castle was Kildrummy. The slow-moving rain clouds had been floating over the hills of Scotland.

Ian had no idea why these dreams were happening. He had never been to Scotland. He only knew from his grandmother's stories that Kildrummy had been abandoned and quarried for its beautiful stones by the local people. He knew it did not look like what he had just dreamt it to be, with beautiful walls, splendid grass, and stately rooms. And he knew that even if he could answer any of the other questions, he could never answer a single question about why, in his dreams, he could understand the Gaelic language.

"Another dream?" Marian asked.

"Sweetheart," Ian replied, as he swung slowly from the hospital table, "I'm at a complete loss."

That night, Marian called Michael, asking for his help.

"Still the same? Is he getting any sleep?"

"Michael, for three weeks now, he's been going through this. At first, his dreams kept him from sleeping peacefully. He'd wake up and keep a vigil by the window. He may have gotten, at first, four hours a night. Now his dreams are becoming so intense and detailed, I think it's affecting him more than he's admitting. Have you noticed anything?"

Michael nodded. "We all have. He shared with me what he's

been going through, and we're both without an answer. He even asked me to take on his tougher patients. For Ian to do that..."

Marian closed her eyes, knowing what it must have taken Ian to ask Michael to do this, then looked toward their bedroom where Ian had just laid down. Her voice became quieter as she continued.

"You've known Ian since your sophomore year of college. Does he know any languages besides English that you're aware of?"

"What?" Michael asked. Both men were always trying to polish their Spanish for use in their clinic, but other than that, Michael knew of nothing. "If he did, it would have been before we met."

"The other night," Marian said, "Ian was talking, only briefly, in a language that I've never heard before. He had just fallen asleep, and if I didn't know any better, I'd swear it was Norwegian or something. Beautiful-sounding words, and it wasn't Latin-based."

Michael listened, disbelieving.

"I'm sure you must have heard him mumbling in his sleep. Had he been drinking?"

"Michael!" Marian's reply showed her frustration. "You know how little he drinks, and the answer is no! And if anyone should know if he talks in his sleep, it's me!"

Michael responded softly, an apology soothing his words. "It's my job to cover bases first and then prescribe after."

"I'm sorry, Michael. I know it's tough on him, but"—her tiredness clearly came through in her voice—"it's beginning to be tough on the two of us."

"When is your vacation to Scotland?" Michael asked.

"Less than three weeks," Marian responded.

Michael considered this briefly and then asked, "Can you move it up any? Ian is not helping much in the clinic at the moment, sleep-deprived as he is, and honestly, if he makes a mistake, he is a liability waiting to happen."

"I... I understand. I'll try on the vacation. We never considered moving it ahead to be an option."

"Make it one, Marian, please. We need Ian back in good health. His current condition is not helping anyone."

"I know. I'll call our travel agent first thing in the morning."

"Good, let me know the answer as soon as you get it."

After Marian arrived at her office the next morning, she called her travel agent.

"Rachael, I need a departure for tomorrow. Can you do it?" she asked. She paused, listening to Rachael's immediate questions. "I know, it's not as we planned, but things changed suddenly, and we need to go tomorrow, if possible. See what you can do for me and let me know."

Marian went back to her favorite "busywork": researching her past. She had been able to go back almost two hundred and fifty years on her father's side but rarely gained any progress on her mother's, which frustrated her. She gave up quickly and thought back to her conversation with Rachael, praying that she could arrange a miracle. Travel agents can do that, she had been told.

Within the hour, Rachael called back.

"I tried, Marian. The best I could get is a flight leaving from Denver this Monday the 22nd. You would arrive in Edinburgh on Tuesday, August 23. It's not the airlines that restricted anything," she said. "The bed-and-breakfast locations are all full, as well as the hotels. We couldn't get you a room until Tuesday night. From then on, it's no problem. You are traveling at the end of the tourist season, and on top of that, it's apparently the seven hundredth anniversary of the death of that Braveheart guy. It's limiting what I can do."

"We've no other options?" Marian asked.

"Marian, I promise, it's the best that can be done."

Marian thanked her. She knew Rachael had tried.

"I will keep checking with them, and if anyone cancels, we'll get you on the next flight," Rachael said.

"I know you will, Rachael. Thank you for everything."

Marian called Michael to inform him of the somewhat good news. He sounded relieved. "Okay, Marian. Tomorrow, keep him home. Tell him your trip was moved up, that he's on vacation, and that you are on a standby basis. Sounds good, and it's the truth, too."

That night, as Marian handed Ian a sleeping pill, she let him know they were on vacation and Michael would be handling everything at the clinic. She knew he had to get sleep, and she hoped the medication would be the beginning of a much-needed rest that would push all thoughts and anxieties out of his mind and help him recover.

Ian felt his eyes slowly close. The heavy clouds came in over the Rocky Mountains. He felt their weight pull him into a void, into a time and place from long ago, where a brazier warmed the chill and dampness in the air, and an Ian from a different time and place stood by his wife's side and awaited their royal guest.

# FOUR

## 1335 Battle of Culblean

It was a cool November morning. Sir Andrew Moray and his wife, the Lady Christian Moray, watched the steam rise from the haystacks as their children played on them, throwing straw at one another.

"Guardian of Scotland again," Lady Christian said to him, proud of his achievements.

"Aye," he replied. "It seems they felt my being in an English prison would give me a wee bit of incentive."

Lady Christian smiled and looked at her husband. Her junior by twenty-five years, he brought to their marriage three children.

"Do you think you will be gone long?" she asked.

Sir Andrew watched as his oldest son, Thomas, threw his brother, John, over the top amidst the squeals of laughter of their younger sister, Margaret. Sir Andrew knew his answer would not be what his wife wished to hear, but knew his obligations.

"The Earls of March and Ross await my return, my love. Though

King Edward III and I have declared a truce until Christmas, the earls and I feel it is but a short amount of time before David of Strathbogie strikes out on his own. He was not included in the truce and will likely take this opportunity to attack. He is arrogant and will continue his attempts to bring Scotland in line."

"Where do you think the battle will be? Have you any idea?" Lady Christian asked hopefully.

"Until the time he shows his hand, we do not," Sir Andrew replied, "but assuredly it will be soon. That is why I took this opportunity, now that our talks have concluded, to see you and the children."

Lady Christian smiled appreciatively, but her thoughts were saddened knowing it could be another year or more before she saw her husband again, if ever. They both watched as their children played, oblivious to the arrival of one of his guards.

"M'Lord," he said, walking up. "Forgive this intrusion, but I have been told to find you."

Sir Andrew felt the inevitable had happened. "No intrusion, Thomas. I am certain that if you were sent, it was for good reason."

"Aye, sir, it is. First, m'Lord, I am to convey that your supporters have arrived safely, and we await your return. More important, David of Strathbogie and the Comyns have assembled a large force and were seen in Perth. All believe they will be heading north to Aberdeenshire and possibly Kildrummy."

"They are certain of this?" Sir Andrew asked.

"Aye, sir," Thomas replied. "It was myself that saw them, and I reported it immediately. I stayed awhile longer to make sure."

"Damn," replied Sir Andrew. "How much time do we have?"

"Any day, sir," Thomas replied. "Their departure was imminent."

Sir Andrew placed his hand on Thomas's shoulder, and said, "You have done well. I need your help in just one more thing."

"Aye, sir, anything that you need," Thomas replied.

"I need you to go to Kildrummy. The warden in our absence is Walter Maule. Inform him of all you have told me. Tell him that Lady Christian will be returning immediately. You will be under his command until she returns. Our Lord in Heaven alone knows how little time we have before they arrive. You must leave quickly."

"Aye, m'Lord," Thomas replied.

Thomas stayed, an obvious question still in his heart.

"M'Lord?" he asked. "Is it as the men have talked? Is Strathbogie doing all he can so that King Balliol's son can retake the crown of Scotland?"

Sir Andrew looked at his guard and thought of the battles over the last few years since King Robert of Scotland's death, first Dupplin Moor, then Halidon Hill.

"Yes," he replied, "that is part of what they are trying to do. The Disinherited will do anything to regain the lands King Robert took from them, even if it means putting another puppet king on the Scottish throne and swearing allegiance to England."

Sir Andrew saw the fatigue on his guard's face, and softened. "We have food, Thomas. Eat first, and be sure to take plenty with you."

He placed his hand on Thomas's shoulder. "It is men like you who will do all they can to save our kingdom. Obtain a fresh horse from the livery, and may God bless your journey."

"Thank you, m'Lord!" Thomas replied.

Sir Andrew turned to Lady Christian. She knew he would be leaving soon to rejoin his men.

"The last few days you have spent with us have been wonderful," she said. "Thank you, my husband. Fear not, I shall return to Kildrummy ahead of David's forces and will defend her till you arrive."

Sir Andrew smiled, reminded of why he had married her. She was King Robert's dearest sister, she was quality, and she was Scotland. If anyone were to assume less, it would be at their own peril.

Lady Christian and Sir Andrew watched as Thomas rode off.

"It was almost forty years ago when King Balliol gave up the Scottish throne," Lady Christian reflected as they walked back inside their estate. "My father supported King Edward I during this period. We were young then, my brother Robert and I, but we knew the humiliation our father felt when Edward denied him the chance to assume the throne. This was the thanks our father got for supporting him. How convenient it was to forget our years of service, and that the Bruces were next in line to the throne. Our family vowed that we would remember this forever, but it was my brother Robert who did so, especially."

They were both quiet, lost in their respective thoughts, sad that it would be a while before they saw one another.

"Do you believe we will ever unite as one?" she asked, recalling her brother Nigel's wish for the prophecy of Merlin, in which Wales and Scotland would unite against England. Even twenty-nine years after Nigel's death, it still hadn't happened.

"Maybe," he replied, "if we win this battle, and we both live a few hundred years more."

She smiled and took his elbow. She loved her husband's humor, even in the face of adversity.

He shook his head. "I, too, am not as optimistic as I once was. We still fight, clan against clan, brother against brother, even fathers against sons. It took years of fighting before King Robert was able to win our independence. Even so, as the last few years have shown, the same battles continue."

He held his wife. "I promise, we will not let what he fought for go to waste."

Sir Andrew walked to his horse, stepped into the stirrup, and swung his leg over. Lady Christian handed him his sword and dirk.

"You are certain that you will be able to defend Kildrummy until I arrive?" he asked.

She did not hesitate. He watched as her entire demeanor changed before his eyes.

"My dearest brother Nigel was captured there and taken to Berwick to be drawn and quartered. My own son was captured and taken to England by King Edward II. Rest assured, husband, there is no man who could defend her better than I. I will give my life before I see David take Kildrummy. He will curse the day that he and his father turned their traitorous backs on Scotland and his grandfather's good name!"

Sir Andrew winked at her and leaned down to touch her face.

"These things I know, my love. Be strong, but as a personal favor to your husband and our children, let David of Strathbogie give his life, instead?"

She relaxed and smiled at her husband.

"Good," he said. "I will gather the men we have, plus any freeholders that await our cause. That should be close to eight hundred. By the time we arrive, I should have an additional three hundred more men. It shouldn't take long."

With that, he bent low to kiss his wife, waved once more to his children, and spurred his horse to a gallop.

By noon, all troops were rounded up and on their way to Kildrummy, with Lady Christian at the lead. Her mind, fueled with anger, filled with unanswerable questions. Why was all they had achieved with their independence continually whittled away, and the same battles refought? Had not her brother, King Robert, united Scotland? Had not England's King Edward III proclaimed to all in

1328 "that the kingdom of Scotland shall remain forever separate in all respects from the kingdom of England, in its entirety, free and in peace, without any kind of subjection, servitude, claim, or demand, with its rightful boundaries as they were held and preserved in the times of Alexander of good memory king of Scotland last deceased"? How conveniently short was their pathetic memory! Was not the ampule of oil given by Pope John XXII in recognition of Scotland's independence? Was this not poured over the head of her young nephew King David on his coronation day just four years past? Had not her entire family given their lives already? She would not only go to Kildrummy, she would defend her with her life and pass the saber to her husband with her last breath if needed.

"Go!" she cried to her men, and spurred her horse onward. "We shall not arrive only to see Kildrummy be a fortress for our enemies!"

They arrived late the next afternoon to see the gates opening, inviting her and her men inside. Raising her hand, she halted all.

"Where is my warden? Where is Walter?" she called out.

Ian de Airth, his wife, Marion, and their young daughter, Elizabeth, stepped out from the Gatehouse portal.

"Greetings, Lady Christian," Ian said, as he and Marion bowed low to the incoming matriarch. Marion looked at her daughter and encouraged her.

"Bow low, Elizabeth. Like mummy showed you."

Elizabeth grasped her dress clumsily and pulling it to the side, curtsied for the matriarch.

"Lady Christian," she said in a tiny voice, mimicking her father.

Lady Christian couldn't help but smile, her mood lightening as she watched the young maiden.

"Walter is away briefly at his estate in Panmure, Lady Christian. A serious matter arose that required his immediate attention. I am acting in his stead until he returns."

Lady Christian nodded her head. "And Thomas, my guard?"

"He arrived with the news of Strathbogie's impending attack, m'Lady. I dispatched him early this morning so Walter may be retrieved."

Lady Christian nodded once more. "Then may he arrive before Strathbogie does, or have the wisdom to find and join my husband if they have," she added.

Ian took her hand as she stepped down from her horse.

He bowed slightly, still holding her hand. "It is with great pleasure that I welcome you home, Aunt Christian."

Lady Christian looked closely at Ian, slowly recognizing her son-in-law's cousin.

"Ian!" she exclaimed and pulled him into her arms. "After all these years. It is so good to see you! I had no idea you would be assisting Walter. How long have you been here?"

"We arrived shortly after you departed, Aunt Christian, when Cousin John informed me that Walter needed assistance. We've been here about a fortnight."

Lady Christian nodded, and then turned to her garrison chief. "Get our men into position. Let me know when all is secure. We've nay time to waste."

She turned back to Ian. "Ah, yes," she smiled at him, "my son-in-law. Unlike others in our family, John's loyalties to Scotland are never in question. I am pleased he chose you. How is he?"

"Thank you, m'Lady," Ian answered. "He is fine and spends as much time as he can with Margaret, and your grandson, Alexander."

"Good," Lady Christian replied, sad that she had not seen either in years. "One of life's blessings as we get older is to see our lineage grow. My daughter, is she well? Alexander's birth was difficult on her from what I recall."

"Yes, she is well, but I believe Alexander will be the last she gives to her husband's lineage."

"Then I must make the time, after we win here, to visit them," said Lady Christian. Turning to Elizabeth, she asked, "And who might this be?"

Ian pulled his wife close.

"Allow me to introduce my wife, Marion," Ian replied. "Besides being the one who is currently providing order for your castle, she is also the mother of our young curtsier, Elizabeth."

Marion once more curtsied and beckoned Elizabeth to do the same.

"M'lady," they both said in unison.

Lady Christian looked carefully at Marion and then at Elizabeth, and for a moment, was speechless.

"Pray, child," she said, as she gently lifted Elizabeth's face and then looked quickly at Marion's. "Tell me, where did my nephew meet you?"

Marion looked at Ian, searching for a reason to explain this important lady's interest. Close scrutiny by nobility was most often not a good thing. Ian returned her gaze, uncertain himself.

"I was in the care of the sisters at Gilbertine nunnery until I reached maturation, m'Lady," Marion replied nervously. "After that, I assisted them for eleven more years. I have no parents, and they were the only ones I knew. They offered me work and a place to sleep if I stayed." She touched Ian's arm. "Then one day, I was sent to town to buy wool. That is where I met Ian."

Lady Christian's eyes opened wide, then filled with tears, and she hugged Marion to her.

"*Mo cridhe!*" she cried.

Ian was speechless. "Aunt Christian, you know my wife?"

"Yes," Lady Christian replied, as she wiped her eyes and released Marion from her embrace. "We were both here at Kildrummy so many years ago!" She took Marion's hand. "My child, we've so much to talk of. Can you give me the time I need?"

Marion again searched her husband's face for anything he could offer. Ian returned her look of bewilderment and shrugged his shoulders. Marion looked at Lady Christian, and nodded quickly.

Composing herself, Lady Christian immediately went back to her role as matriarch of Scotland.

"Ian, we need to prepare the castle. I see you have moved all items that can burn. Well done. I know they are close behind, and we will be vastly outnumbered until my husband arrives."

She looked at her nephew closely. "I believe this battle will be pivotal for Scotland. Whatever their forces, we must keep them at bay. I know I can trust in your help."

"Yes, m'Lady. If I may ask, when is Lord Moray to arrive?"

"It may take time to gather the help we need, after our losses at Dupplin Moor and Haildon Hill. But I'm certain he'll have an easier time than the English."

Ian saw her look become hard, her features forged from almost 40 years of war. "Unlike the English, we fight for what is ours to protect, not what they wish others to die for."

"Unlike the English, we fight for what is ours to protect, not what they wish others to die for."

Ian looked out at what Lady Christian had foretold. In just the last hour, the sun's rays silhouetted the shapes of men as they crested the hilltops, with many more coming into view as they watched.

"As you predicted, m'Lady," Ian stated.

"Garrison chief!" Lady Christian shouted. "I want your first line of defense to be our best archers along the top of the wall. Then, heat as much oil as you can. If they breach the portcullis, we will provide them a hot bath. Nothing stops the entrance of unwanted guests in quite the same manner. Finally, if they do breach our walls, I want short swords. If battling the English has taught us anything, our walls become our enemy with long swords or spears."

Lady Christian turned to Ian. "I must ask this. Since your arrival, have you or Walter had reason to question anyone's loyalty?"

Ian replied immediately. "Walter and I handpicked the last group from the men who fought at Halidon Hill. They are now our archers, Aunt Christian. Their only wish is to thank the English personally with the same longbows they used against us."

"Excellent," Lady Christian replied, smiling. "I hope you left enough men for my husband to choose from?" Then, seriously, she asked, "You know this for fact?"

"These men, m'Lady, will give their lives for Scotland."

Lady Christian softened. "I did not mean to question, Ian. I am sure each of them would. There was a time, many years ago, when one of our men in this very castle proved to be a traitor."

"I know," Ian replied sadly. "Walter said that it was a blacksmith who set fire to the corn in the Great Hall, and ..."

"Yes, that is all true." Lady Christian interrupted. "It was shortly before then that young Marion and I"—Lady Christian stopped and smiled at Marion—"were able to escape Kildrummy with the help of our current adversaries' grandfather, John of Strathbogie."

Marion asked, "You mean the man who is here, now, ready to attack us, his grandfather is the one who helped us escape thirty years ago?"

"The same, child," Lady Christian replied. "And I know he would put an arrow through his grandson's black heart if he were still alive. John led our escape. My brother Nigel stayed here to protect us and delay them."

Ian knew of Nigel and how he died allowing her to escape while he and his men defended Kildrummy. He could tell that her thoughts were never far from the memory of her brother. A harshness came into her tone, and Ian knew it was from losing one so dear.

"Nigel defended Kildrummy against Aymer de Valence and Longshanks's son. They even brought the king's master carpenter to build a War Wolf. You know what this is?"

Ian nodded. "Like a trebuchet, only larger. It's a type of catapult used to destroy castles."

"Who is Longshanks?" Marion quickly interjected.

"Ah, child. You were too long at Gilbertine," Lady Christian replied. "We've a few names for King Edward. 'Longshanks' is but one. And yes, Ian, you are correct on the trebuchet. In their haste to get here, and so close to winter, they felt they had no time to bring it. So, for weeks, they attacked, nonstop. My brother and his men proudly repelled all of their attacks. They were safe inside these walls, and they had plenty of food. Sadly, Osbourne set fire to the corn, which was stored in the Great Hall. I heard later that Osbourne got all the gold he was promised. I never saw my brother again. He endured the same terrible fate as Sir William Wallace and my brothers Alexander and Thomas."

Lady Christian cried softly at the memory and sat down. "Our independence has often been won by inches. And many times it is the same ground that must be fought for, over and over. We have fought these wars for almost forty years, and I've lost almost all my family."

Lady Christian was quiet for a moment.

"I heard my brother, King Robert, was brutal in his attacks against many of the cities up north, Nairn, especially," she continued. "I am certain for him to raise the dragon and kill all who got in his way, he must have felt there was no other choice. I'd like to think it was in retaliation for our losses at Methven and Strathfillan, and for the brothers we lost and loved so dearly."

Lady Christian looked at Ian and Marion.

"Please, I am tired. Our journey was long. We can continue our conversation on the morrow."

"Garrison chief, I will be in the Snow Tower. You know my chamber. Keep me posted if the English mount the offensive," she ordered. "Good night, children."

# FIVE

## 1335 A History Revealed

Through the night, the garrison chief watched as Strathbogie's men continued to arrive. In the morning, Lady Christian met with him in the courtyard.

"They have been adding reinforcements the night through, m'Lady," he said. "There are at least a thousand men, with more coming."

She listened carefully as he continued, "If Lord Moray arrives and has a grasp of the number of men here, I do not believe he will attack straight on."

Lady Christian was pensive and then agreed. "Yes, I am certain you are correct."

"Thank you, m'Lady. Sir Moray's tactics mirror his father's, as well as those of his partner, Sir Wallace. We have a much better chance against the English when we use the land to our advantage."

Lady Christian smiled at the memory of her husband's father and the victory they shared at Stirling Bridge. She smiled approvingly at her garrison chief, confident they were in capable hands.

"Yes, we are quite the bush thrashers, aren't we?" she commented.

She turned to see Ian and Marion walking up.

Bowing low, Marion said, "M'lady, I'm sorry, but my husband and I could barely sleep last night! All my life, I knew nothing of my life. And now, we find there is so much to learn! Could you …?"

"Oh child, it is I who should apologize!" Lady Christian interrupted. "You two have been so patient, only to be delayed by me. Chief, I will be alone with my family. Inform me of any changes immediately."

Marion felt a little overwhelmed. Finding that the matriarch of Scotland was related to her husband left her speechless. And now, learning she was here as a child at Kildrummy, with Lady Christian, left her awestruck. Her earliest memories were of the convent, but how she got there was unknown to her.

Lady Christian saw the look of incomprehension on the young woman's face. She gave an understanding smile.

"You were too young, weren't you?"

Marion nodded.

"You've grown up to be a beautiful woman. Your father would be proud."

Ian and Marion exchanged glances.

"M'Lady, you knew my father as well? Oh, please, forgive my persistence, but I must know!" Marion bowed her head slightly and then knelt before her.

Lady Christian patted the space next to her, urging Marion to rise and sit close. "Yes, *mo cridhe*. All of Scotland knew your father. What are your earliest memories, child?"

Marion replied slowly, "I only remember the Gilbertine nunnery. I was told I arrived in 1306 as a baby, and my name was Marion."

"Yes," Lady Christian said. "I don't believe they could have told you anything more. Not that they knew much, either."

Marion shook her head, not understanding what Lady Christian meant.

"I will tell you of our history, Marion. The good and the bad, but you must first promise to share this story with your daughter when she is sixteen. This is my request of you. Then I will tell you of your father. That is your mother's request. Do I have your word?"

Marion nodded her head, quickly promising.

"Excellent. Afterward, I have something I should have given you years ago, a gift."

Marion was bursting with excitement, pleased to learn anything about her father, as well as a gift.

"Good. Ian, this will concern you as well."

Lady Christian held Marion's hand and began. "Our battle for independence started in 1296 at Stirling Bridge. We won that day with the help my husband's father, Sir Andrew Moray. He and William Wallace were chosen as Guardians of Scotland. Did you know this?"

Marion shook her head.

"Then you shall have the whole story, from back when King Alexander III's wife died in 1275."

Lady Christian paused a moment, then continued. "When she died, she left him with two sons and a daughter. It wasn't long before his son, David, died. Soon thereafter, his daughter, Margaret, married the king of Norway and then died giving birth to a baby named Margaret as well."

"This only leaves the one son, yes?" replied Marion.

"Correct," Lady Christian replied. "Sadly, he, too, died, leaving only the baby girl."

Marion saw where this was going and said, "And as she was the last in King Alexander's line, with no sons to carry forth, he knew he had to remarry and have a male child."

"You are correct. He married the Countess of Montfort of France. This time, however, it was King Alexander who died before producing an heir, leaving only the young Margaret. Many noblemen contested her right as the next queen of Scotland, feeling she was barely more than a wee babe and they held a more legitimate right to the throne. Besides, a woman had never ruled Scotland in her own right, and most did not want this to happen. However, when these noblemen were threatened with excommunication, they each agreed to keep Scotland safe for young Margaret and accept her as the new queen. She was to marry King Edward's son, the Prince of Wales. They would rule Scotland and England together. Truth is, King Edward knew if his son married the young maid, she would be queen in name only and absolute property of the king of England. This became meaningless, however, because she died en route from Norway."

Marion asked, "If the entire lineage of King Alexander III had passed, who was left to rule?"

"Ah, child, exactly," Lady Christian said. "Two choices arose quickly: Robert the Bruce, who staked the first claim, and John Balliol."

"Robert the Bruce?" Marion asked. "This was not your brother, King Robert?"

"No, child, he was my grandfather, the Fifth Lord of Annandale. Then came my father, Robert the Bruce, the Sixth Lord. My brother was the Seventh. What happened next is where many Scots believe our problems started. Instead of fighting amongst themselves, they decided to ask a man clearly versed in law which of the two men would have the most legitimate claim to the throne. Unfortunately, they asked King Edward. He was cunning. He wanted Scotland and saw the perfect opportunity. He would be glad to assist but needed us to meet across the River Tweed, at Norham Castle. This was in England! We Scots immediately began to smell a rat, especially our fiery Bishop Wishart. He said as much to King Edward, "That the kingdom of Scotland would not be held in tribute or homage to anyone except God alone! No issues of Scotland could be decided outside of Scotland."

Ian added, "That was part of the Treaty of Birgham. King Edward was trying to ignore a law that we Scots felt valid, even though our Maid of Norway had perished. Edward vowed to remember the bishop's treason for a later date. Then he added final demands: he wanted his position as high overlord over Scotland acknowledged by all. Once he got this, he added eleven more claimants to the throne."

"Why would he do this?" Marion asked.

"He wanted Scotland." Lady Christian responded. "He would use the claimants to the throne against one another and with their vows of fealty would guarantee himself as king over all. Our grandfather hoped he would be chosen, so he was the first to swear fealty. The last was Balliol. This allowed King Edward to do what he'd wanted all along, which was to make Balliol king. King Edward stated the law of primogeniture, but in reality, he got what he wanted: a king he could control. My grandfather felt this was unjust and argued for more than a year that primogeniture was not the rule of the land. Edward ignored my grandfather and began the steps needed to control Scotland. He undermined all of Balliol's decisions. Balliol tried to hold strong, knowing if he didn't, all of Scotland would soon be under English rule. King Edward, however, never stopped planning. He had already "acquired" nine men to appeal Balliol's decisions to a higher court …his court."

Ian shook his head sadly. "I've even heard tell that Edward had King Alexander killed that stormy night so he could gain Scotland."

"We will never know," Lady Christian replied. "We later found out that three of the nine appellants were English. After refusing the first order to appear before the king, Balliol was finally forced to appear. He was humiliated, found in contempt of court, and three of our castles were confiscated. Balliol finally submitted all of Scotland to Edward's authority. From then on, any decision he made had to have Edward's final approval. Edward then began taxing us for England's battles. The final straw for Scotland was when he issued a writ to Balliol, ordering him to send two Scottish earls and sixteen barons to Portsmouth. There, they would lead Scottish troops to fight England's battles against the French at Gascony. The French, however, were our friends and trading partners! That was enough for Scotland.

"Not surprisingly, the Welsh, too, had had enough of Edward's brutality. They took the weapons he had given them to fight the French and used them against him. He was forced to send his troops to Wales to squelch their uprising, and we used this time to form our own Parliament in Sterling. Twelve men were quickly appointed to form a council. It was made up of earls, barons, and bishops, though controlled by its strongest members, the Comyns. These men began making the decisions regarding Scotland, taking control away from Balliol, though keeping him as their king."

"So how did the Bruces become involved in all this?" Marion asked.

"Balliol summoned my father and brother to support him, but we refused. We held lands in England that paid our family substantial rent, and besides, our father had already sworn fealty to Edward and was made the constable of Carlisle Castle. Balliol retaliated by seizing our lands in Annandale and giving them to Balliol's father-in-law, John Comyn. This did nothing but add more hatred between our family and the Comyns."

"Sides were switched often, weren't they, Aunt Christian?" Ian asked.

"Too often, Ian. Land and power divided us. I have often wondered where we would be if we Scots and the Welsh had chosen to unite against the English as my brother Nigel had dreamt. It's too often brother against brother, or even father against son, that we can nay see the advantage of uniting against a common enemy."

Lady Christian continued, "In the meantime, the council decided to meet with the French. Four months later, a treaty was established, in which each country would assist and defend the other against all others. The timing was perfect, the council thought, as King Edward had just finished with the uprising in Wales and would now be concerned with France. With this in mind, the council sent John Comyn to attack the English at Carlisle."

"Isn't this where your father and King Robert were?" Marion asked. "Would they now be fighting against Scotland?"

Lady Christian nodded her head. "Aye, child, they were. King Edward, however, learned that Scotland had been in negotiations with the French. Scotland, the country he nay had to raise a sword to get, was now conspiring with his sworn enemies and attacking English soil. He stayed his attack on France and decided to personally lead his forces against Berwick. So fierce was this attack that blood flowed for two days in the river. Thousands were killed, mostly men, but there were women and children killed as well. Some say as many as eight thousand Scots died that day, though many believe there were more."

Ian and Marion looked at each other, aghast.

"Wasn't France supposed to help Scotland now?" Marion asked.

"It did not happen, *mo cridhe*," Lady Christian responded. "If there ever was a chance for King John Balliol to unite us as one, this would have been it. But again, he did not. King Edward continued his drive into Scotland, killing more at Dunbar. Finally, King Balliol sent a letter to King Edward, begging his forgiveness. He declared the treaty that Scotland made with Paris false, citing evil and false council, and turned himself over to King Edward for him to do as he wished. He was made a spectacle before Scotland and England. He was removed as our king, and his tabard was publicly stripped of its royal insignia. He was thereafter called *toom tabard*."

Ian whispered quickly into Marion's ear, "It means 'empty coat' or 'a disgrace.'"

"He was sent first to the Tower of London and later to France," Lady Christian continued. "This was in 1296. My father, seeing the Scot throne was empty and knowing our family was next in line, asked if he could assume the throne. Edward's reply was, 'Have we nothing to do but win kingdoms for you?' My father knew then that the legal course our family had pursued was no longer an option. Edward never had any intention of giving it to a Bruce. From that day forward, my brother knew that if a Bruce were to ever gain the crown, it would have to be taken. That's when Robert went against our father and sided with Scotland. He did this for four years, until he realized that his attempts to win the crown were poorly timed. With the pope's continual pressure on King Edward to allow Balliol's return to the Scot throne, my brother decided to return his fealty to Longshanks once more and bide his time."

"He did not have to wait long. In 1304, Balliol was given the right to return to Scotland, but he refused. He no longer wanted the Scottish crown or the fight that went with it, so he stayed in France until he died. It was this vacancy of the Scottish crown during Balliol's imprisonment that led to Sir Wallace's fighting for Scotland, and then, finally, my brother's secret agreement with Bishop Lamberton to become our next king."

Marion nodded and reached for Ian's hand. "I learned some of this from my husband. They taught us many things at the nunnery, but politics was not one of them."

Lady Christian smiled. "I'm sure, especially when it concerned Scotland. I was with you at Gilbertine until 1314, when my brother, King Robert, won at Bannock Burn, and I was finally given my freedom through a prisoner exchange."

"I wonder why I never saw you there," Marion said, curiously.

"I was there, child," Lady Christian replied, "but they kept us separate so I was never able to see or visit you."

A knock interrupted their conversation, and her garrison chief entered the room.

"M'Lady, they are beginning their assault."

Her tone quickly changed. "We'll continue this later."

Lady Christian watched the battle through the arrow slits in the castle wall. Many arrows, some lit with fire, fell into the courtyard, useless.

"Garrison chief," Lady Christian called out. "Position your men at these portals, and keep the fire going on the oil. Let them waste their arrows all they want. Above all, do not let them scale our walls."

She took her chief aside and asked, "They have laid siege for weeks to no avail. Do you think they will bring a trebuchet?"

He thought carefully and responded, "M'Lady, you said Sir Andrew felt this was a quick attack, and he barely got word of it before sending you here. Yes?"

"Yes," said Lady Christian. "You were sent word immediately thereafter."

"Then," her chief said, thoughtfully, "I do not believe they will have this type of armament. Their goal would have been to mount a quick and decisive battle. If they were to bring a trebuchet, we would have known weeks ahead."

Lady Christian thought of this carefully. "Do you think we can continue to hold them off?"

Her chief smiled. "Twenty-nine years ago was tough on our castle. Now, with the fortifications made since then, they have no chance. Unless they can scale our walls, m'Lady, which we will make certain does not happen."

Lady Christian smiled. "I was hoping you would say that. Keep the necessary men at the walls."

She heard his orders as he shouted to his men. "We will defend her till Sir Moray arrives. We will not let her fall. Do you hear?"

A cheer went up.

"Lay on! Lay on! Til' they fail!"

The men's chant echoed inside the castle walls a chant her men had chosen in her honor, as it recalled her brother's glorious victory at Bannock Burn over the English. Their combined voices meant so much to her; its uplifting effect was contagious. Ian and Marion watched as Lady Christian's demeanor changed. She seemed to be lighter in spirits, almost happy, in spite of Strathbogie's attack outside their gate.

Three days later, the garrison chief came to her with good news. "M'Lady, their attack has ceased, and they are departing."

"To where?" Lady Christian inquired, pleased.

"I know not," he replied, "but I doubt they would have just given up. It is possible Sir Moray may have arrived to do battle."

They turned, followed by Ian and Marion, and climbed the stairs to the Interval tower. Peering out at the troops marching south, she watched them disappear over the ridge toward the woods of Kilblane.

"If your grandfather were alive," she said softly, "he'd put an arrow through you himself, David of Strathbogie. May my husband do it in his stead."

Leaving the garrison chief, the three of them walked down the narrow steps, and across the courtyard, toward a servant. Speaking quickly, she dispatched the young girl with orders for food.

"Ian, Marion, I've ordered food to be brought to us in the Snow Tower. I too have been anxious for this day, so we can resume our talk. Now," she said as she settled into a comfortable chair, "where were we?"

Marion began, "You left off saying you and I were at Gilbertine. And that you have a gift for me!"

"Yes, *mo cridhe*," said Lady Christian, smiling briefly at her excitement. Her tone immediately became serious. "It was shortly before we found you. Robert was now our king, and finding Aymer de Valence at Perth, challenged him to do battle. Aymer refused Robert until the next day. We headed west, and camped that night in Methven woods. Robert, not knowing that Edward had '*Raised the Dragon*,' posted no guards, and sent almost a third of us to gather food. It was then that de Valence attacked. We lost so many," Lady Christian said. "Our men were trampled by horses or killed outright by English swords as they tried to get up from their beds. Twice they attempted to unhorse King Robert, and each time Sir Fraser and my second husband, Christopher Seton, came to his rescue. I never saw my husband after that night. I later learned that he and his brothers, John and Humphrey, sought refuge at Loch Doon Castle, where MacNab betrayed them. For my husband's disloyalty to King Edward, and taking part in the slaying of Comyn, he was taken to Dumfries and executed. His brothers were taken to different places, and each met the same fate."

Ian and Marion stared as they listened to her story, both shocked at what this lady of nobility had endured in her life. Both knew what '*Raising the Dragon*' meant: that no one would be spared. Not women, not children. No one.

"Once I was set free," she continued, "I had a chapel built at Dumfries to commemorate Christopher's life."

"I saw it once, Aunt Christian," Ian added. "It has Oriole windows and it's beautiful."

Lady Christian smiled, softening at his words and the memory of her husband from almost thirty years ago.

"It was after our battle at Strathfillan that Robert felt it best to split up. He sent us back to Kildrummy with instructions to John of Strathbogie to take us to the Orkney Islands if it looked like we were in danger. From there, we would go to our sister, Isabel, in Norway. Robert was correct in believing the English would pursue, but it was not him alone they wanted. It was all of us Edward wanted, either to be killed or used as political pawns. After three days, we fled, leaving my brother, Nigel, at Kildrummy. His fighting gave us the extra time we needed to escape."

"Aunt Christian, who was with you?" Ian asked.

"Sir John of Strathbogie; your wife, Marion; my sister, Mary; Isabella MacDuff, the Countess of Buchan; King Robert's wife, Elizabeth; and his daughter, Marjorie; and a few others, plus our guards. Sadly, when we arrived at the St. Duthac sanctuary in Tain, they were waiting for us. Uilleam II of Ross turned us over to the English as traitors. You and I, Marion, were sent to the Gilbertine nunnery. Mary and the countess were imprisoned for years in wooden cages and hung outside different castles. John of Strathbogie, my dear brother-in-law, was hanged. When King Edward was reminded that

John was related to him, he had his gallows raised an extra thirty feet. He then burned John's body and fixed his head on London Bridge. Poor Princess Marjorie, she was just ten when she was imprisoned and kept in solitary confinement until she was eighteen. She was another angel who died too soon, having spent almost half her life in prison."

Marion was horrified, unable to grasp what her companions had endured and what she had been spared. Ian, equally shocked, held his wife's hand and silently prayed that their daughter would never have this in her future.

# SIX

## 2005: The Trip to Scotland

Marian felt Ian thrashing. She slid over to his side of the bed and leaned over him. His eyes opened wide, taking in his surroundings.

"Where are we?" he asked, confused.

"We're here, sweetheart, in our bed."

Ian blinked his eyes rapidly, trying to take in the room and his place in time. Recognition flashed across his face, and he relaxed slowly before closing his eyes, determining all was safe. Marian snuggled close and held him, listening to his breathing as it returned to normal, and he once again fell into a troubled sleep. She softly caressed his face and prayed that he would sleep without dreams.

Ian awoke in the morning to Marian wiping his forehead with a damp cloth, soaking up the sweat that seemed to accompany his sleep these days.

"I don't know," he said, answering Marian's questioning look. "It is so strong, this pull I feel as I enter my dream. I went to the castle in your brochure, Kildrummy, but this time there was a Lady Christian. Also, there was an Ian de Airth and his wife. Kind of like you and I, sweetheart, but long, long ago. We were, I mean, they were defending the castle against the British. Damn it," Ian said, looking confused. "They were defending against the English, who were led by a David of Strathbogie. Suddenly, Strathbogie's men leave, and all the while, Lady Christian is telling Marion of a past that they both share. That's when my dream ends and I wake up."

Marian nodded, consoling her husband, silently praying for an earlier flight but knowing this would be nearly impossible. She was sure the next two days would pass slowly, especially for him.

Ian, however, got an unexpected reprieve. Marian had been asked to fill in for a lecturer at Denver University and would be gone for the next two nights. While the thought of being away filled her with worry, Ian assured her he would be fine.

"I might take two of these"—he pointed to the sleeping pills Michael had prescribed—"just in case. At least you'll know I won't move an inch!"

Marian tried to be comforted by his attempt at lightheartedness, but that night was her most sleepless ever. She hated not knowing how he was doing and was equally frustrated that if she called him, she might awaken him. The next morning, she was astonished to hear he'd had a very different night.

"No dreams? Seriously?" she asked.

Ian was just as surprised. "None," he answered. "It was ten thirty, and I was lying in bed. I had just finished watching Channel 4. You know I can't go to sleep without my favorite newswoman."

Marian yawned. "You brat! I can tell you got a good night's sleep!"

"I was lying in bed and wondered if I should take the sleeping pills," he continued. "Sweetheart, I don't think I even reached for the prescription! I fell asleep immediately and got the best sleep in weeks."

The next night was the same. Ian had a dreamless night and slept well. Once Marian was home, however, Ian returned to dreaming fitfully throughout the night.

"We need to hurry, Ian," Marian said, as they rushed for the shuttle that left at 8:00 a.m. "Once we're on the plane, you can try to get more sleep."

Ian was still a little groggy, and she was glad their bags had been packed for the last two days. She was also thankful when they could finally board the plane and start their vacation. The first leg of the trip was to New Jersey where they connected to the six-hour flight to Scotland. They were traveling in first class and told the flight attendant, Angie, they were going for a long-overdue vacation.

"You will so love it!" said Angie enthusiastically, telling them she had returned from there recently with her husband. "We've been there twice now. May I recommend that you see some of the castles? We've seen Cawdor and Urquhart castles and Elgin Cathedral, and we recently spent time at the ruins of Turnberry. To us, it's almost like hallowed grounds. We plan to see more on our next vacation."

Marian and Ian both thanked her. "We've no idea what additional places we'll see. But so far, it's scotch, renting a car for a trip around the countryside and B&Bs, plus some well-needed rest," Marian said, leaving out Kildrummy Castle and the reason for their visit.

Angie smiled at them. "If you have any more questions, please ask for me."

They assured her they would. Marian turned to Ian and said, "And now," mimicking his newscaster in a sexy voice and pulling back her brown hair, "for the local news at ten and, for you sir, to get some sleep!"

Ian did not need any encouragement, and pushed his seat back as far as it would go. The time change from Colorado to Scotland would be huge, and both would feel the effects in the morning.

"Absolutely," he responded, giving Marian a quick kiss.

Ian closed his eyes and was pulled swiftly into sleep's welcome embrace and then, slowly, to a different time and place.

# SEVEN

## 1306: New King/
## Bad Decision

The sun sank below the horizon and allowed the night to stretch its shadowy fingers across the land until darkness slowly covered their faces. Their cart creaked wearily under its heavy load of food. Lady Christian de Seton was pleased. It had not been easy to find enough to feed so many men, women, and children in an area known for its support of the Comyn clan. And yet, they had found an elderly couple who had given them a cart and all that was left from their garden.

"I never liked the Comyns," the old man had told her. "In the end, they were like Balliol: couldn't wipe their arses without Edward's blessing. Not an ounce of Scot spine in the lot of them. I only wish your grandfather was still alive to see this day. I'm sure it'd make him proud."

His wife took Lady Christian aside, and said, "Please forgive my husband's anger. We lost our two sons, though we're not sure in what war. They'd of come home if alive, but they never did. We have more than we can eat these days, and it will soon go to spoil. Take it, please …the cart, too. We've no need for it."

Lady Christian thanked them both repeatedly for their gifts.

"You take care," the old man said. "To many in these parts, our King Robert is nothing more than a usurper and a murderer, and that don't count the English."

Lady Christian hid the trepidation that his comment caused her and hugged them both, assuring them their new king would remember them. She tried to turn her thoughts to the warm fire and her husband, who awaited her return. But as she walked alongside the cart, she wondered about his comment. Was it like he said, that many felt her brother was nothing more than a murderer and usurper to the throne? What throne? Certainly not Scotland's! King Balliol had refused to come home to Scotland to resume his kingship, even though the pope had gotten Edward to reconsider.

A smile pulled at the corners of her mouth. Even after the death of the Comyns at Greyfriars Abbey, her brother, Robert, had not only been forgiven by Bishop Wishart, but the good bishop was now heading to Cupar Castle and proclaiming Robert as the new king at every church where he spoke. Even the Countess of Buchan had gone to Scone to inaugurate him king, as was her ancient right and privilege. *Was it as easy as this?* she wondered.

Lady Christian shook her head, uncertain. She reflected over the recent turn of events. Aymer de Valence could have agreed to fight this very night at Perth; yet he did not. Maybe on the morrow, they could meet on a field of honor, go back to their respective lands, and become mutual allies, as in the days of good King Alexander. Maybe. It was still hard to believe their lives could be changing for the better. Lady Christian was happy, and she exchanged quiet conversation with a few of the men walking back with her.

Then softly, almost imperceptibly, the sounds of the night changed. It was almost indistinguishable from the wind as it moaned through the trees. Each of them could hear it. Then, it caught another note, and pain was added to the sound, unnatural in its origin. Quickly rising in pitch and then amplified, the whole of the woods came alive. The cry of horses combined with the sounds of men dying from the slash or thrust of a sword. Lady Christian shuddered. One never made a mistake with those sounds. Dropping the food still in her hands, she ran toward Methven, leaving everything behind.

"Christopher!" she screamed and then clamped her mouth tight to silence any more words of anguish. She ran toward their camp, quickly outpaced by the men, each in a desperate attempt to get back to camp and help their comrades. She tried to keep up in the dark, but her foot struck a rock and sent her headlong into a stream. She lay motionless for a moment, before lifting her face and arms out of the mud, and saw a young man standing before her.

"M'Lady," he said, offering his hand. He pulled her up, and she faced him.

"What has happened?" she asked desperately.

"I ... I," the soldier, barely seventeen, stammered. "Longshanks has raised the dragon, and Aymer de Valence has attacked. King Robert may have been lost. We must leave!"

Lady Christian wiped the mud from her face and eyes, and the young soldier quickly recognized the king's sister.

"M'Lady," he said again, quickly bowing.

Lady Christian grabbed his blood-soaked surcoat and pulled him to her.

"What? What do you mean our king may have been lost?" she screamed.

"I ... I mean, I am not sure he survived," he replied. "He was unhorsed twice. Sir Fraser helped him, but it was toward the end. When the king called retreat, I ran. It was terrible, m'Lady! Most of us were eating supper, and others were getting ready to sleep. Then suddenly, on horseback, they charged into camp, trampling those who were still in their beds, and pulling their swords on the others, until so many of us were cut down."

The young man's eyes never faltered as he stood before her, proud, his sweat running small streaks of dirt down his face. "I got three, m'Lady. I swear our king had called retreat. This is why I ran."

Lady Christian was compassionate, but looked sternly at the young man. "Look around you now. The men who were with me have gone to join the battle, and your king may need you. In what direction do you see your fellow Scots running? Your help and theirs may be all it takes to win!"

The last of her group were now out of sight, though their war cries echoed throughout the hills. His gaze returned to his matriarch, a new sense of hope and pride restored. Unsheathing his sword, he bowed and said, "I am Reginald, m'Lady, and I shall see you at Inchaffray Abbey!" He turned to rejoin his fellow soldiers, whose voices were fading into the melee of Methven, a quarter mile away.

*Please get there in time,* Lady Christian prayed silently. She knew well what "*raise the dragon*" meant. She walked to the hill where the young man had just disappeared and watched for her husband. The sounds of battle were dying down, although the occasional clash of steel upon steel still could be heard. Lady Christian slumped against a large granite boulder and sank slowly to the ground. She could hear the anguish of men and prayed silently for their lives. Then another voice rose above the din, much closer to her: a man's cry, barely audible. She rose to her feet and went around to the other side of the boulder. A young man was pulling his friend's body to him, cradling his head in his lap.

"We'll get them," the young man said, as he rocked back and forth, tears running down his face. "We'll get them. Don't you worry about that." He continued rocking, back and forth, his actions reminiscent of a mother with an inconsolable babe. "Don't you worry."

Lady Christian could see his friend's mortal wound, his side pierced from a sword. She recognized both men as young recruits Robert had enlisted in Glasgow and Rutherglen. The dying lad shuddered and, looking at his friend, said at last, "William, I'm so cold. Can ... can you cover me with something?"

"Oh, James, yes. Yes!"

William rose slowly, ready to find something for his friend, when his companion let out his last breath, and his face turned slowly to the right. The young man sat back down and wailed, devastated at the loss of his friend.

Lady Christian gently touched his shoulder and said softly, "Please ... come. Your friend's pain is over, and our lives may be in danger if we do not move."

The young man looked up, lost. Taking him by the arm, she helped him to his feet. "We will come back and give him a Christian burial, if we have the chance. Would you like that?"

William slowly nodded his head.

"Good," she said. "Now, tell me what happened."

The young man, still in shock, pointed in the direction of Methven.

"King Robert was unhorsed, m'Lady. My friend and I slew as many as we could to save him. He had fallen, and James ..." William began sobbing once more. Finally, he was able to say, "My friend was struck as we were defending Sir Seton." He looked down at the quiet body of his friend. "We've known each other since we were lads," and he said no more.

Lady Christian turned quickly at a sudden noise, drawing her sword. Branches gave way to the sudden appearance of a group of men. Then Robert's horse broke through as well, leading another horse and rider. On it was the young soldier, Reginald, whom she had sent back earlier.

"Robert!" she called out, as she ran to him, happy and relieved to know he was alive.

She had never seen him after a battle. His surcoat, no longer white, was covered in blood. "You are unharmed?" she asked.

Robert nodded wearily. She touched his leg. Words were not needed to convey her happiness. Her thoughts went immediately to Christopher.

"My husband. Have you seen him?" she asked.

Robert dismounted and said, "He was with his brothers, John and Humphrey. They are likely heading to Inchaffray Abbey."

"Inchaffray Abbey? Why there?" she asked, recalling the young man's words.

"It was decided after you left for food. I must talk with Abbot Maurice."

Lady Christian looked around at the men who were now wandering into the clearing. "How many are we now?" she asked, knowing there would not be many.

"I'm not sure," Robert replied. "Even counting the men you brought back, a thousand at most."

She gasped, "From three thousand?" The sudden realization of the number hit her, and she screamed. "Christopher!" and started for the battlefield.

"Christian!" Robert ran after her and grabbed her arm. "Please, listen!" He is not there. I know he was with his brothers and should be safe. For a fact, if you go, you will be killed as quickly as any man. Believe me, he is not there."

Robert paused and, taking her hand, added gently, "Kerstie, we must leave, but know this. If not for his help, and that of these young men as well, I would be dead. They truly saved my life."

She nodded, an overwhelming numbness coming over her. Robert continued, "I was unhorsed twice. Each time, Sir Fraser helped me regain my horse, while your husband defended us, and these two young men guarded his back."

"Kerstie, your husband and his brothers must be together, and I'm sure we will see them at Inchaffray Abbey. But we must leave immediately. De Valence, I am certain, will pursue us. Give me your hand. Mount up."

She refused. "I will help your young warrior first," she said, pointing to William. "His deed and sacrifice have been great this day."

Robert nodded and watched his sister help the grieving young man to his feet.

"You two will ride together," she said, pointing to Reginald.

Robert reached for his sister's hand and pulled her onto his horse. The four quickly rode off to rejoin the remaining soldiers who had already found their abandoned wagon.

"Bring everything," Robert called out, "and meet us at Inchaffray Abbey!"

# EIGHT

## 1306: To Strathfillan

They rode quietly through the night, stopping only when they heard voices or the occasional footsteps. Lady Christian hoped it was her husband; Robert knew it could easily be de Valence or his men. By early morning, they reached Inchaffray Abbey. Robert set up two men as sentries, then fell exhausted onto a small grassy hill where he could look out when he awoke.

Lady Christian woke awhile later, still tired but anxious to see if Christopher had arrived during the night. Walking quietly through what remained of their scattered group, she called out his name repeatedly. Was this all there was left of them? She couldn't see how many there were, but it was far fewer than the thousand Robert had guessed ... far fewer.

"Christopher!" she called, tears welling up as she did. "Christopher!"

With anguish in her every step, she went to where her brother had been sleeping. Maybe, just maybe, her husband was there. She found her brother awake and alone, beginning his prayers. She wiped at her eyes and waited patiently as he prayed, unaware of the quiet approach of the Abbot of Inchaffray.

"Has he been in prayer long, my child?" Maurice asked.

She turned quickly, taking in the presence of the man. He was older, gray of beard and bald, with a fierce countenance that waxed soft as he reached out to touch her arm. The brown tunic he wore was tied with a simple rope around his waist. He noticed the surprise in Lady Christian's eyes.

"Forgive my intrusion," he said. "I am Abbot Maurice. I just left your brother, Edward, and his men. He told me of Aymer de Valence's attack and of the men you have lost."

Lady Christian turned back to Robert and nodded absently.

"Yes," she replied, thinking of her husband. "Too many. Robert thinks as many as two thousand may have perished, but prays they are but scattered."

Abbot Maurice crossed himself and said a silent prayer.

Robert rose from his prayers. "I see you have met my sister," he said.

"Aye, I have," Maurice replied, "but I recall seeing her and your young ward, Donald of Mar, at your coronation in Scone."

Robert nodded.

"She and your brother have shared your losses at Methven," Maurice continued. He laid his hand on Robert's shoulder. "The Lord grieves over the loss of all lives but especially those of his favored children."

"Even one was too many, Father," Robert snapped, "for my lack of foresight. It should never have happened."

Maurice nodded his head. "As our new king, you will endure many more sad times before good ones return. Will you walk with me?"

The land sloped down from the abbey toward a small loch, its black waters filled with rushes and dark-green algae from long ago being cut off from any current. Incredibly still, the loch was known for its many eels and fish.

"I have two very dear friends of God," Maurice began. He guided Robert to a stand of tree stumps that had been cut down years before and were now used by the priests and lay brothers to reflect. "Won't you sit, please?

"One of them," he continued, "is heading to Cupar Castle to do battle at this very moment, proclaiming at every church that you are their new king. The other, our dear friend Bishop Lamberton, has once again put his life in danger by openly supporting Scotland's independence."

Robert looked at him but said nothing.

Maurice continued, "Bishop Lamberton was first noticed by Edward when he began openly supporting Wallace and his fight for our independence. Now, as well, he openly supports you."

Then, lowering his voice, "I understand he has made a pact with you, to prudently resist all attacks by rivals and to be one another's council in all business and affairs, without deceit. Did I understand this correctly?"

Robert looked at his dear friend and mentor closely, wondering how he knew this, but again said nothing. He had made this pact with Lamberton two years ago, after Robert's father had passed and Robert was still in Edward's servitude.

"Do not worry," Maurice said. "All things of God's purpose are kept unto him and those whom he trusts. Yours and Lamberton's secret is safe. Each of us will die before uttering a word. However, Robert, these holy men's lives are in peril. Only Longshanks's fear for his immortal soul will stay his hand from killing these men of God.

You will not be so fortunate. At every turn you make, as at Methven last night, you must be prepared."

Robert began to speak, only to be quieted by the abbot.

"When I was with your men earlier, I had the chance to speak to Archie Forbes. He mentioned the fighting tactics of Wallace and how well they worked. You recall the conversation, do you not?"

Robert nodded his head. "Aye, he mentioned them the day before, when we were in Perth. That we should not wait to fight de Valence, but even more, that we should never fight Edward's men straight on …that we must do it from behind every tree, every rock. I did not listen."

"You will make a good king, Robert," Maurice responded. "This is a hard lesson, but you have learned. You must listen to the council of your men, and you must learn to fight as Wallace if you wish to stay alive."

Maurice looked out across the stillness of the loch, then continued. "This loch is like Scotland, overrun by eels. Our eels, however, are English. They have come to our land and taken it without ever drawing a sword. They are like spoiled children who do not want to return what is not theirs. Many in Scotland have become accustomed to these eels and believe they are beneficial, though I'm not sure why. Fish taste better by far. So, too, does the sweetness of our land when it has not been desecrated.

Robert, to keep Scotland free, it can be accomplished only through a leader with vision. King Balliol, though his intentions were good, had no stomach for a fight. When given the chance to come back to resume his kingship, he said nay, and to this day he lives in France. Now, the only way for Scotland to be free, as in the days of good King Alexander, is to stand behind a strong leader. We need you as our king, Robert, no matter the pitfalls."

Maurice stopped, then asked, "Have you heard the prophesies of Thomas of Erceldoune? That you were to be our next king?"

Robert nodded his head. "Aye, I have. I even met him once, when a wee lad at my father's castle. My father revered his prophecies greatly, though I nay put much faith in them. These people can predict anything. Sometimes they are right, and sometimes not."

"Nor did I believe," Maurice continued, "until the day after King Alexander died. It was just hours before it happened, when naysayers came to Thomas's door and mocked him. To a man, they said, "You predicted King Alexander would die this night through a fierce wind. Yet he lives! Thomas replied that the day was not yet over. The next day, King Alexander's body was discovered. He had fallen off a cliff during a terrible storm, as he was trying to go home for his new wife's birthday. Besides predicting you as our king, he also predicted your victory eight years hence at Bannock Burn and other things in Scotland's future, though many will not be alive to know the truth of them."

Maurice placed his hand on Robert's and asked, "Though you are in doubt of Thomas's predictions, as a Christian man, do you believe in God with all your heart?"

Robert agreed, "Aye, Father, always. You know I do."

"Then, as I believe in your destiny, as do Bishops Lamberton and Wishart, you must also. Robert, would you trust in the blessings of St. Fillan's Holy Arm if I were to come with you?"

Robert, as well as the whole of Scotland, knew of St. Fillan. Born in the late seventh century, he was well known for his ability to heal the sick and the mentally ill. His left arm, it is said, gave off a glow that allowed him to write Holy Scriptures at night.

"For your belief in me, Father, and the blessing you will provide, aye!"

"Then trust as well the men who surround you now. They know you failed to post a sentry; yet they hold you no malice. As their king, you must now decide your next course of action. Scotland is nay safe for you any longer. Especially for your family."

"This I know," Robert replied. "I have thought of nothing less these last few hours. Though Ireland is under Longshanks's control, I believe it to be our safest option. And the sooner we get under way, the better."

Robert and the abbot stood and walked back to where Lady Christian was still waiting.

"Christian, I want everyone to meet with me," Robert said. "This means men, women, and children. Everyone," he said, leaving no doubt.

Within moments, everyone had gathered: Robert's brothers Edward, Thomas, Nigel, and Alexander talking amongst themselves and sharpening their swords; his sisters Mary and Lady Christian, both quiet, waiting for their brother to speak; his wife, Elizabeth, comforting his daughter, Marjorie; Isabella, the Countess of Buchan; and John of Strathbogie. The rest of Robert's men surrounded them in a huge half circle, with Inchaffray Abbey in the background, its peaceful presence bearing silent witness to all that would be discussed this morning.

Robert looked at each of his lieutenants. Most had survived, but it was easy to see who was missing. In their honor, the men had kept open the spots where those who were missing normally sat. Those spots included places for Lady Christian's husband, Christopher, and his two brothers. If there were even a thousand alive after last night's battle, Robert would be surprised.

Standing before them, he began to speak, then stopped to weep openly. After a minute, he began anew.

"Men, you have stood noble before our enemies in our fight for independence. I however, have failed you. By lack of foresight, by not listening to wise council, I have allowed many of our family, our friends, and companions to be killed or taken prisoner. As you are all aware, Edward has raised the dragon, and our path, wherever we go, will be fraught with enemies. We have lost many, and our forces are too small to fight and too large to travel unnoticed. I must now ask your lieutenants to dismiss many of you, and if you are chosen to return to your families, then please take the time to give the ones we lost at Methven a Christian burial. May God bless your return with safe travel."

Robert went to his lieutenants and bid them to choose which of their men would be dismissed. This done, he gathered the rest of his soldiers and shared the last of his plan.

"We will head west to Loch Etive and, from there, by land and boat, go to Ireland."

A collective murmur went through their ranks. Robert raised his hand, and all fell silent.

"As the Earl of Carrick through my mother's lineage, they will shelter us. We are between the Comyns in the north and the English to the south. Unless there is a better option, we will leave within the hour."

Gilbert de la Haye, whose brother, Hugh, was among the missing, spoke up.

"Sire, what you say is true. But surely you know that Alexander MacDougall and his clan are to the west of us. His wife is the daughter to the man you slew and about as English of a Scot as they come. Will we fare any better by traveling through their lands to Ireland?"

The discussions became louder and heated. Robert let them continue for a minute; then, raising his hand again, waited until all fell silent. "Aye, but it is the shortest path to safety. This time, however, we will travel with Abbot Maurice. He assures me we will be under the benediction of St. Fillan and our passage will be blessed. We have stayed here long enough."

Their band, now diminished to five hundred, departed within the hour. Young James Douglas and Abbot Maurice led, with Robert and his family bringing up the rear.

"The small amount of food we have left," Maurice said to James, "won't last much longer. Our king says you are quite the hunter. Is this true?"

James smiled. "Aye, Father, I do well. I used to hunt in the outskirts of Paris with Bishop Lamberton." James was about twenty, of slight build with broad shoulders, pale skin and almost black hair. His voice was accented from living in France since he was a child, and he had a slight lisp.

He had been sent to France to escape the wrath King Edward had bestowed upon his father, but not before witnessing his family's lands forfeited to Robert de Clifford. James had met Bishop Lamberton in Paris and became his knife bearer until he learned of his father's death at the hands of the king. Returning to Scotland with the bishop, he had hoped to regain his family's lands, but Edward had no intention of returning them to the family of a man who had helped William Wallace. Since the time he had met Robert, James had become one of his youngest allies and supporters, always hoping one day to regain those lands.

"Our journey will take us through some rough country," Maurice said. "Before we can go much farther, the little food we have left must be consumed and the wagon discarded. Do you think you can hunt to feed this group?"

"Aye!" James replied quickly, filling with an immense sense of pride.

Maurice smiled at his youthful exuberance, as James pulled his horse's reins to turn around.

"By your leave, Father, I'll get King Robert's permission to bring Archie with me. Archie knows Scotland like I know hunting!"

He rode quickly to the rear and found Archie in an animated conversation with Robert about fighting with Wallace.

"Absolutely, Sire," Archie was saying, pleased that his king was listening intently. "From behind any place we could find. A rock even, if it was big enough! He knew he could never win head-on against the English. Wallace called it a secret war."

"Your Highness," James began, interrupting. "I ..."

Robert interrupted, "James, out here, we are fellow soldiers. For now, call me Robert."

James nodded his head, "Sire, I ..." He tried again. "Robert, Abbot Maurice was talking about our food, and he feels that soon we will need more. The wagon from Methven can't make the trip, and Archie and I could scout ahead. He knows this area much better than I, Sire."

Robert smiled at James's attempts to be more familiar, and nodded his head in agreement. "Excellent idea, but do keep your eyes open. And, above all, watch for MacDougall's men."

"Aye, Sire, we shall," James replied.

Archie and James rode quickly toward the River Dochart and, staying to the south, pushed into the glen. Heavily forested, it would easily conceal them from deer and other small game they came to hunt. Both knew it could also conceal MacDougall's men as well.

"We need to stay downwind," James said, "and above all, be quiet."

Archie nodded his head and added, "There are better areas we can go to later, where there should be more deer. But we'll do well enough here for a start. There should be plenty of smaller game as well. There are also salmon we can catch."

By early the next morning, James's hunting skills and Archie's knowledge of the land had paid off, and they headed back to find their group a few miles north of Lochearnhead.

"All this?" Robert asked, very pleased. Over the backs of James and Archie's horses were four red deer they had caught and cleaned, a small bag containing eight squirrels, and a string of salmon James proudly held up. "This ought to help break our fast!"

Pleased by Robert's comment, Archie added, "We'll go deeper into the glen after lunch. There's a large group of deer I often see in a hidden meadow."

They left by early afternoon, pushing deep into Glen Dochart, toward the meadow Archie knew of.

"It's best if we tie off our horses and walk in," James suggested. "We'll be able to approach them from downwind. We should be able to get a few."

Crawling on hands and knees toward the largest outcrop of rocks, James motioned for them to stop. In the center of the meadow were several stags surrounded by a few hinds and many calves. Rising up slowly, both pulled out arrows and quietly notched them to their bows. James motioned to the young stag on his left and pointed to a hind for Archie. Both pulled back slowly, taking aim, ready to release. Then suddenly, the deer burst forward and past where the two of them were hiding. They looked at each other, uncertain as to what had caused this.

Then they saw it: two shadowy forms obscured by the trees until they entered the meadow. Talking softly, they were unaware of the deer they had scattered, or of the hidden men.

James and Archie whispered, almost in unison, "MacDougall's

men!" They knelt low and waited for them to pass, overhearing a portion of their conversation.

"...says they were spotted south of the river and should be coming through here any day." The other man added, "Remember, we do nothing and are to remain unnoticed. His Lordship and the barons want to know their numbers only."

They waited patiently for the men to leave, thankful neither of them were seen, and prayed their horses would remain quiet and tethered. Minutes passed, and all safe, they gathered their waiting horses and rode off to find Robert and their group.

"Sire, there were two scouts who were watching for our travel, and we believe them to be MacDougall's men. They did not see us," Archie reported.

Robert thought about this and was quiet. His men had gathered around him and awaited his decision.

"There were only two?" Robert asked.

"They were the only ones we saw," Archie replied. "We heard a small portion of their conversation. They were curious as to our numbers."

"I thought they might be waiting," Robert said. Then raising his voice, he announced to the group, "Other than protecting our women and children, there's nothing we can do except be prepared and keep going. It is now up to them to make the first move."

This time, James and Archie stayed closer to the main group, though they still set an occasional trap for salmon, as well as eels, fish, and squirrels, to feed their hungry numbers. Anything that wandered into their path would be used for food.

For the rest of the day, they rode along the river and deeper into the glen, wending through the woods and around the many rocks. In areas where the woods opened up to moors and became woody thickets, they coaxed their horses into the river until they could once more get back onto dry land and away from the ocean-bound current. By nightfall, weary and hungry from their journey, they bedded outside Crianlarich.

"Robert, is it still Ireland that we be heading to?" James asked.

"Aye, it is. We should be safe there. My mother's people are none too fond of Longshanks, either."

Throughout the evening, until their fires slowly burned down, Robert regaled them with stories, lifting their spirits.

"I swear it to be true," he said, when asked about the holy arm of St. Fillan. "Is it not, Father,"—Robert turned to Abbot Maurice—"that his holy arm would glow at night, and from the light he was able to write down scriptures? We are traveling now under his blessing! Abbot, tell them about how Scotland will win eight years hence and of our future."

Abbot Maurice smiled. "Your king knows as much as I, but aye, it was predicted by Thomas of Erceldoune. Even the prophecies of Merlin foretell of Scotland and Wales uniting against England. We are now at the very beginning of these days."

Most had heard of Thomas and his prophecies or of St. Fillan, or both. Robert and Maurice added more stories of Scotland's future, doing their best to keep everyone's spirits high. All knew that the morrow could bring battle.

It was that night, after everyone had retired, that the two young men who had helped save Robert's life at Methven came forth.

"Sire," said young William, the youth from Glasgow, "Reginald and I have been talking." Since the night at Methven, the two had become close friends. "I believe my friend, James, would be proud to know I have stayed with you and will help you fight for Scotland … that his life was not lost for naught. But more so, Sire, Reginald and

I have come to know the men who count you as their king. Some are earls, some are knights, and all, Sire, are men and women of honor and title. We know if it were not for serving you and fighting at Methven, we would never have the honor of being in their company. Sire, if you count our support as worthy, we would like to stay with you until the day you have united Scotland or until the day we die in its attempt. Would you allow this, Sire?"

Robert smiled in gratitude, and replied, "On the morrow, I shall let you know." Later that night he knelt and looked up to the star that all the heavens spun around, and prayed. He thanked the Lord for the quality of men he was fortunate to serve with, specifically the two young men who had asked to fight at his side, until Scotland was free.

Freedom! How elusive this word was proving to be. Yet it had been foretold that one day they would be as free as in the days of good King Alexander. Even after his disastrous decision at Methven, his loyal supporters and friends were still here to fight with the man they considered their king.

Robert rose slowly from his prayers. On the morrow, they would go north and then west to Loch Etive, where Alexander MacDougall, the son-in-law of the man Robert slew just a few months earlier, would likely be waiting.

There were no stories that would make that reality disappear. Robert's mind went to a passage from Luke 12:48. "To those who are given much, much is expected." The passage pushed into his thoughts until sleep finally accepted his tortured embrace. His dreams, however, would not release him from fears of a battle he might lose and the decision he would have to make if he did.

# NINE

## 1306: A Doughty Deed

John, the Lord of Lorne and eldest son of Alexander MacDougall, waited patiently. The murdering usurper Carrick, or King Robert as he was wont to be called, had been spotted the day prior in Glen Dochart. Though there were other ways out of the glen, this was the easiest path and would be the one he used. Robert's wife, Lady Elizabeth de Burgh, of English heritage and title, was with him. She had been given by King Edward to Robert the Bruce when he once again swore fealty. John shook his head, and wondered how this vacillating man, this 'king' of no loyalties had ever got King Edward to accept him back. And now, Robert was wandering through Scotland like a damned highlander, endangering his English wife by taking her to God only knows where.

John swatted at another midge, grinding its miniscule body into his skin. It would be a pleasure to make short work of this king, one who could claim neither land nor people, and get back to the comfort of his castle. He would then tell his mother that the man who had murdered her father was now dead. Then, before King Edward passed, John would inform him personally of Robert's death, and that he had personally returned Lady de Burgh to England. Pleased, Edward would readily grant more lands to his and his father's clan for this act of loyalty.

Walking back down from his vantage point, he looked at the men of Argyll and MacNaughton who were mustered before him. Numbering more than a thousand, half-naked and fierce, they were ready to fight at a moment's notice.

"Bring me the men of MacIndrosser," John ordered. He knew they also bore hate for the Bruce family. In line for the throne as well, their chance had been stolen when Robert killed John Comyn and got that disloyal countess to coronate him. *Yes*, John thought, *King Edward would be pleased to hear of her death as well. So too*, he thought, *would her husband.*

Out of the crowd walked three men. One, fierce of countenance, was the father. The other two were his sons.

"Today," John began, "you have the chance to make all wrongs right. Today, here in Strathfillan, you can take back the crown of Scotland from the man who most cruelly and calculatingly stole your family's chance to have it! Remember this as you do battle: You fight for Scotland and your God-given right under King Edward to be a contender for the Scottish crown!"

Yes, it would be a decisive battle. John's men were almost double the number of Robert's. King Edward would indeed be pleased with this news, exceedingly pleased at the rescue of Elizabeth, and would most assuredly provide him with additional lands and money. John, the Lord of Lorne, waited patiently.

Fog, thick and deep, hung like a gray blanket, covering the lowest parts of the glen and hiding the feet of Robert's men and horses as they headed north. They were entering MacDougall lands, and if MacDougall's sentries had watched their course through the glen, then this area, flat after it cleared the steep bank of Ben More and the loch, would be the area where they would attack.

"Keep your eyes open," Robert had cautioned before they moved out. "If they attack anywhere, it will be there."

All five hundred were quiet—ominously so—as they left the comparative safety of the glen, and entered Strathfillan. Most had cleared the pass when a cry of pain came from one of the men at the front, and then another, and another, as arrow after arrow hit their marks. Then a battle cry went out, as half-naked Highlanders, their forms like wraiths in the fog, let more arrows fly as they ran toward them with swords and axes held high.

Edward Bruce, a third of the way to the front, turned to the men at the rear and shouted, "To arms! They are here!" Another group of men fell from arrows shot from hidden areas.

Leading the attack was John of Lorne, his huge sword pulled as he rode toward the royal party. His scream of anger filled the area, as he guided his men. "I want the Lady de Burgh! Do not let them retreat! Cut them off!"

Archie had been riding next to James Douglas, the queen, and Robert's sisters when they heard Edward's warning. "Get down!" he said, shoving the queen and Mary from their horses and onto the ground before an arrow went whizzing by.

"Get the others to the ground, now, and make sure our queen is protected!" he shouted. Nine men drew in quickly to surround the women, wielding swords in a desperate attempt to protect them against Lorne's men as they guided them back toward the shelter of the glen.

"The women are safe!" Archie hollered to Robert as they cleared the steep bank of Ben More. All heard but did not respond, nor did they stop. Valiantly each slashed down from their horses, catching many with their blades, protecting the lives they cherished. James rode up quickly to Robert's side, as did Gilbert de la Haye.

"Kill their horses," John screamed to his men, who with long pole axes and swords, charged into the desperate mix of Robert's horses, cutting flesh and bone. Crying out in pain, their dying horses added to the carnage of the morning.

"Pull back!" Robert cried out, and then drove his sword down, cutting in half a poleaxe. "Do not let them kill our horses!"

"Keep moving," James shouted, encouraging their men as they neared the pass to push through.

Then, suddenly, a slashing blow came down from one of Lorne's men, cutting into James's leg. William saw this and rushed forward from where he had been fighting alongside Reginald. Wielding his sword high, he dealt a mortal blow to the man who had attacked James.

James smiled weakly in appreciation, the pain in his leg fierce. He never stopped, and defended the rear, continually urging their group back into the glen. Then Gilbert de la Haye caught a sword as it glanced off his shield and into his shoulder. Thomas, raising his sword, cut into Gilbert's assailant, killing him instantly.

"For my sister's husband!" he shouted, and turned his horse to join his brother Edward's fight at the rear. Each hoped to gain time so others could go through the narrow pass, barely wide enough for a horse to get through, and spread out. Robert now held the rear, urging his men and family to go ahead, as he defended their retreat.

"Keep moving!" he hollered, urging them beyond the pass.

When everyone had cleared, it was his turn. It was then that the three MacIndrossers attacked.

"Today you die, Earl of Carrick!" one brother screamed, as he grabbed the bridle of Robert's horse. The other brother reached between Robert's leg and saddle, wrapping his arm tightly into Robert's cloak, and held his leg. Robert stood up in the stirrups and with all his might, drove downward with his sword at the man who held his horse's bridle, cleaving his arm and shoulder from his body. Robert spurred his horse forward and dragged the other man, his arm trapped under Robert's leg, through the banks of the river. Their father, who had climbed up the side of the hill, jumped onto the back of Robert's horse, directly behind him, and attempted to grasp his arms. Robert, pulling him mightily over his shoulder, drove his sword, and killed him instantly. The only man left, his arm still caught in Robert's cloak, was dispatched as quickly as the other two, and fell into the banks of the loch.

Baron MacNaughton and John, the Lord of Lorne, watched as Robert ended the life of the last MacIndrosser. Then, guiding his horse between the waters of Loch Dochart and the steep bank of Ben More, he escaped with his men and family.

The baron, in secret admiration, said, "Surely now, before you, is the bravest man you have ever seen in your life. By his doughty deed, and through his courageous manhood, has he quickly slain three men of great strength and pride. So quickly has he done so that no man dare go after him, and if I may say, it seems he has no fear of us."

John turned to him, "It seems you find pleasure in his slaying our men."

"Sir," replied MacNaughton, "God knows that by your presence, this is not true. But whether he is friend or foe, when one wins the praise of chivalry, men will speak loyally hereafter. Surely, in all my time, I have never heard in song nor rhyme of one who so quickly achieved such great chivalry."

And so the surviving men of Argyll and MacNaughton, whom John had beseeched to kill Robert the Bruce, went home, despairing of the pain they had suffered at the hands of Robert and his men.

# TEN
## 1306: A Decision to Separate

Robert led his people to a large cave near Balquhidder. It was there that his family, bound by love and loyalty but exceedingly tired, talked of what lay next. Robert searched the faces of his family. Marjorie, his daughter, suffering as she did to be with him, lay exhausted on his wife's lap. What was he to do? Was he to continually expose his young princess to his battles, each with the potential to end her life? His wife, Elizabeth, raised as a lady of title, must surely be praying for this to end, but said nothing. He knew of her love, and knew she would stay with him, if he asked.

Robert, too, was tired. But more, he hurt for the men who had fought for him and for those who had been lost. Even John of Strathbogie, his loyal brother-in-law, was weary and desired to go home. And Christian, his dear sister whose husband was still missing, was now almost expressionless.

Throughout the evening, Robert did his best to lift their spirits, always with hope in his heart for their, and Scotland's, future. Even

Abbot Maurice tried to help lift spirits, telling them, "All this will pass, my children. Nothing great has ever been earned without struggle." They talked of Alexander the Great, and Hannibal, and how God had shone his light upon Scipio and saved the people of Rome.

"Who knows how short the grace of God is," Robert added. "We are truly blessed among those who fight in his name!"

That night, however, as they broke up and searched out places to rest their worn-out bodies and spirits, Robert thought, *I shall make a decision by the morrow.*

He awoke early and, searching for a quiet place, knelt and began his prayers. "Give me strength, O Lord! Your way divine. Show me the light I need at this troubling time. Guide my decisions so I may best follow your plan, and give me the wisdom to lead."

His thoughts were muddled from exhaustion. What was he to do? At every attempt, he had failed. At Methven, many had died solely because of his not posting a guard. His fist tightened, the memory never far. King Edward, he knew, would put a stop to any attempt he made to maintain his hold on the Scottish crown and his country's independence.

Lady Christian knew her brother would be in prayer and found him near where he slept, facing the rising sun. Robert, hearing footsteps, crossed himself and stood to embrace his sister. He knew what she hoped to hear, but he could tell her nothing new. The challenges of the last few weeks wore visibly on her.

"Kerstie, we have yet to see your husband. To a man, I went to each to see if any had seen him or his brothers."

She held onto Robert and cried; knowing in her heart the embrace she shared with her husband at Methven was likely their last. Robert held her. "You can't give up hope," he said. "He may still be in hiding or trying at this very moment to get back to us."

"I hope you are right," she said. "Oh, Robert, what do we do now? Do we still go to Ireland? Is that our safest option?"

"I am no longer sure," he replied wearily. He relaxed his arms from around his sister and said softly, "I'd like a few more minutes alone."

Robert knelt and, crossing himself, guided his thoughts back to his prayers. Was God's plan so elusive, or was it man's thoughts that were so self-centered? He wished he knew. He had secretly entered into the agreement with Bishop Lamberton to pursue the crown, now that Balliol had refused to retake it. Scotland wanted, as a country in its own right, direct contact with the pope. If Robert did not succeed, Scotland's bishops would be forced to go through King Edward, and he would translate all their requests to the pope through his own personal agenda.

"It must be pursued correctly," was one of the last cautions given to Robert by Bishop Lamberton. They were to wait until King Edward breathed his last. But it was Robert slaying Comyn that had advanced their cause. Now, both bishops were doing all they could to pick up the pieces that Robert's actions had caused. And as Abbot Maurice had shared, Bishop Wishart had gone to Cupar Castle to destroy it. Had he succeeded? His life, too, was in peril for absolving Robert and allowing him to be crowned king.

Robert stood, knowing what needed to be done. He must show his men, in faith and deed, that they could win. Never again would he fight the English with honor. If the dragon could be raised against him, then he could raise it against the English. Robert crossed himself, and said quietly, "Thank you, Lord, for understanding the weakness of your new king. May Your will be done, forever. Amen!"

Robert felt a new sense of purpose as he walked to where his men and family awaited his return. He stood before them and began, "We must split up." Gasps could be heard throughout the group. "I have been in prayer. As you know, I thought our best option was Ireland. Longshanks, however, will likely have all coasts watched. No matter where we go, he will have alerted everyone that usurpers to the throne are about. I believe once we split up, they will have a harder time trying to find smaller groups. I also believe he will search for the group I am in before he chooses anyone else's. He is in his final days, and nothing would make him happier than to know my head is on a pike on London Bridge."

"Anyone who is loyal to the Comyns would like to see your head there as well, brother," Edward added. "John of Lorne is one who is still sharpening his blade, to be sure. Did you hear how he wanted the queen?

Words of confirmation echoed throughout their group, many having heard this as well. "It's not just those loyal to the Comyns we need to worry about," Edward continued. "Everyone should be treated with caution. Our first loyalties should be to the queen, the princess, our sisters, and our countess. She made a statement by crowning you King of Scotland, and that will secure Longshanks's enmity toward her forever."

Robert nodded his head in agreement. "I thought the same."

Thomas stood, interjecting, "I agree with Edward, but as Robert said, we should split up and do so immediately. If I may suggest, our women and children should go to Kildrummy. I believe John would provide them the best protection, and there's no one who knows the Highlands like he. Robert, if you've no objections?"

John of Strathbogie stood. "Thank you, but I believe my help would be better directed if I stayed and helped fight Edward's men."

Edward laughed and reached up to slap John's back. "I'll whack two of them for you! And if I miss, there's always our young James

Douglas who'll help!"

James stood, his leg now swollen, and bowed stiffly. His skills with a sword and his ruthlessness had been noticed at every battle. "You can count on that. Well, soon that is! I've yet to cleave the head of England that I really want."

"And if Kildrummy is compromised?" Alexander interrupted, amidst the laughter James's comment brought. "Where then? Do we have other options if it fails?"

Thomas stood, and asked, "Kildrummy fail? How?"

"We all know her strengths," Alexander replied. "But as history has shown, nothing is impenetrable. We'll let John decide their safety when they get there. As our last two battles have shown, being with us is the last place they should be."

He looked at his family and friends surrounding him. "No one knew what was in store for us before Methven. I am sure Robert agrees that what we have put our queen and princess through in recent days is inexcusable. They could have been killed. I'm with Thomas. Kildrummy is our safest option."

Robert valued his men's wisdom and knew the decision he was about to make was correct. "I will send them to Kildrummy," he said. "John and Nigel, you will take them. You will leave on the morrow. We will talk more on this tonight."

That evening, his men stood in a small circle, their small fire crackling and sending sparks skyward. Robert joined them, his gaze drawing them in to the truest of bonds.

"You are not only my family but my most loyal advisers, and I could not have been given better support by anyone. Other than the few that I will keep with me, I will send most to Kildrummy with John and Nigel."

This time, there were no murmurs, no argument. All were tired and awaited Robert's direction. "John, you and Nigel will take our horses, my queen, the countess, my daughter, our sisters, and our soldiers to Kildrummy. Once we separate, Longshanks will concentrate on me. They smell blood ... my blood ...and believe once I am defeated, their issues with Scotland will be over. By sending our women with you, I believe they will be safe."

"Where will you go?" Nigel asked.

"I don't know," Robert replied, staring into the fire. "Not yet at least. Even if I did, I would not tell you. If you are caught, they would torture you until you spoke."

Nigel nodded his head, knowing what his brother said was true.

Robert continued, "Nigel, come with me." They walked to the loch, where Robert could share his thoughts with his brother.

"There is no one I trust more than you to take care of my wife and family. But if their lives become a concern, if it looks like they may be in jeopardy, then it is John who I want leading them to safety, and you at Kildrummy."

Nigel understood what Robert wished and what his purpose would be, if it came about: to give the family the time needed to escape, letting the English think the royal family was within Kildrummy's walls.

"Finally," Robert continued, "keep your eyes on Christian. She has been through a lot, but especially these last few weeks. Her first husband's death, and now Christopher is missing. Hopefully, they will find their way to safety or to Kildrummy."

Nigel nodded his head. "I'll watch for him. And if we haven't seen him by the time we reach Kildrummy, I'll send out our messenger. You need not worry about Christian, though. She's tougher than all of us. But I will help her. We've always been close."

"Thank you," Robert replied. "Whether she says it or not, we both know she feels we are doing the right thing."

Nigel nodded in agreement. He stared intently at his older brother and asked, "How are you doing?"

Robert looked steadily at Nigel, then looked away. "I pray daily for the lives lost at Methven. Even now, I pray I am doing the right thing by splitting us up. If it were just battle, I could endure. But when it may harm all whom I love, that's the toughest. Nigel, the one thing I know for certain is I can't keep them with me. Sending them away to safety seems to be my only option."

"If it looks like their safety is jeopardized," Nigel said, "I'll give John the diversion he needs. You chose wisely with him."

Robert smiled. "Thank you. Of our friends, there is no one more loyal. He knows we will get through this."

Nigel nodded. Then, waiting a moment, he asked, "Robert, I overheard James earlier. I know he's young, in pain, and I'm sure that's the most of it. But what he said has a truth to it. Should we have waited until Longshanks died? Most feel his son eventually would surrender to us what we fight his father for daily."

"Aye, he's young, but he's no fool." Robert replied. "I should have waited until Longshanks died, as Bishop Lamberton wanted. But it was my meeting with Comyn where I lost control. I've never hated another so." Robert was quiet a moment, then asked, "If I had waited, and not slain Comyn, do you think it would have made a difference?"

Nigel responded slowly. "What I believe is not important. What I know is we have filled Longshanks with a resolve to eliminate the Bruces and all who support us."

"Aye," Robert replied, thoughtfully, "I'm sure you are right. But I hope, nay, I pray that one day we will look back at the sacrifices we have made, and say, 'it was the right time.' We may lose many a battle, but we will not lose this war. Longshanks will die, and we will win against his son. It may not be tomorrow or the next year. But the men we have now are our beginning. As we learn Wallace's fighting tactics and win, many more will join us."

Robert was silent for a moment and then, chuckling, looked back to see if James was within earshot.

"Have you seen him fight?" Robert asked. "One would never guess just by looking at him. Slight of frame and barely out of his teens. But he fights like a madman! I'm glad he's with us, and not against us. Single of mind, he nay stops until the battle is over!"

"Aye," Nigel said, smiling. "I, too, am glad he fights with us. Many of the English are now calling him The Black Douglas."

Both were again silent in their thoughts. Nigel looked at his brother, noticeably older in these last few weeks. He put his hand on Robert's shoulder, and asked, "Are you sure you are okay?"

Robert slumped, almost imperceptibly, then replied, "Nigel, to you I'll admit, even with my prayers, I've been at my lowest these last few days."

Nigel looked at his brother with pride. "Yet you are the one who encourages us daily?"

"Aye," Robert replied. "To stay strong. We've too much to lose if we quit. I tell myself that eight years is not long, that I can endure. I must believe in Thomas's predictions and our abbot's faith, else it will be me who goes to St. Fillan's pool for the sick in the head!" Both men laughed.

"Robert," said Nigel, becoming serious, "we'll take care of the queen and our family. Be our king, and stay strong. Above all, do not worry."

The brothers embraced. "I love you, brother," Robert said.

"I love you," Nigel replied.

"Would you let John know I'd like to speak with him?" Robert asked.

Robert was wiping his eyes as John approached and handed him a piece of venison. "I thought you might be hungry," he said. "There wasn't much left, with so many mouths."

Robert took the venison and ate hungrily. John sat and waited for him to begin.

Robert wiped his mouth with the back of his hand. "John, you and I are like brothers and go back from before I married my first wife ..."

John raised his hand, stopping him. Nothing else need be said between them. They had been friends for years, even before the days when they had married the Earl of Mar's daughters. Since then, and especially since the time Robert began making plans for the Scottish crown, John had supported him, though he knew this treason would forever secure his enmity with King Edward.

"My family, John. There is no one I trust more. If Kildrummy ..."

"To Orkney, aye," John interrupted. "I knew your thoughts this morning. From there, I will contact your queen sister in Norway."

Robert smiled. "Aye, you truly are my brother. If you feel you must leave Kildrummy, take the men you need and leave Nigel with the rest. Though he may guess where you are going, do not tell him. If he knows and is tortured ..."

John nodded his head. Words were not needed.

"John, I know you are tired. We all are. Enjoy the time you have with your wife," Robert said, trying to hide his deep sadness. "Tell her I named my daughter after her."

John gave a faint smile. "I thought you named her after your mother?"

Robert smiled, "Not her alone, I promise."

"Thank you," John said, as they bid one another, dearest of friends, good-bye.

"To Scotland," they said, trying to smile, knowing it may be the last they shared.

Alexander walked up as Robert and John said their parting words. "Robert, the two young men who were with us at Methven are hoping to stay with us. They mentioned talking to you about this but will go where you decide."

"Those men I will keep with us," Robert replied. "They have earned the right to fight, if that is all I can give them."

The two men walked back to where the others were. James Douglas was lying by the fire, hoping Robert would speak with him as well. His family's lands were always at the top of his mind, and Robert's winning Scotland would help him regain them.

Robert knelt next to his young friend. "Pretty sore?" James only nodded, the pain in his leg terrible. "You know that I support you, don't you?" Robert asked.

James smiled, "Aye."

"Then stay with me, my young friend. One day, when we have won Scotland, your lands will be returned to you. When your leg has healed, I will have you lead our men to the south. I know how you fight. All of us do. Edward's old age is to our favor, and he will not live much longer. Thankfully, his son will never be the adversary his father is, and he will one day return to us willingly what his father took by force."

James murmured his assent as Robert stood. "And take care of that leg!"

James smiled up at Robert. "For Scotland!" each said as they parted.

Robert went to his wife, who was standing next to their fire. He could tell she was still upset from the decision he had made to split them up. Robert pulled her into his arms, his head next to hers.

"My wife, my queen," he whispered, "I know no other way. To you alone I am vulnerable and would gladly give my life to make sure you are safe, as well as my daughter, Marjorie." He stopped to correct himself; though Marjorie's mother was his first wife, Elizabeth loved the little girl as if she were her own. "Our daughter," he said. "Take her, the Countess Isabella, and my sisters, Mary and Christian, to Kildrummy. You should be safe there. You will have my best guards and most of our men." Robert paused, adding, "Elizabeth, if Kildrummy is compromised and John fears for your safety, he will lead you north. He will tell you of your destination once you are safely en route, not before."

"My husband, when will I see you again?"

"The most important thing is for you and our daughter to stay safe. I can handle all as long as I know this is so. Do this for me, please? One day, my queen, I promise, we will not be king and queen for a day. Now, my love"—he kissed his wife tenderly—"I must say good-bye to our daughter, and in the morrow, before you have awakened, we will be gone."

Robert knelt by his daughter, who lay sleeping close to their fire. Picking her up, he pushed the strand of hair that had dropped into her sleepy eyes.

"Look at you," he said softly, trying to wake her. "I have never met a more courageous young lady in my life. Do you know this?"

Marjorie shook her head as she laid it on her father's shoulder.

"Oh, my daughter, even John has said this many times. I've heard him say it."

Marjorie's eyes opened up slightly. She looked into her father's face and saw he was telling her the truth.

"He did?"

"You'll have to ask him yourself," Robert replied. "I've never been more proud of you and thankful that God gave you to me to be my daughter, my princess. You know this, don't you?"

Marjorie nodded her head.

"You know I must leave."

Marjorie nodded again. "I heard you telling your men. Will you be back soon?" she asked.

"You know I will always tell you the truth."

"Yes," Marjorie replied, softly. "I won't see you for a long time, will I?"

Robert knew his answer was not what either wanted to say or hear. He looked up to the heavens and pointed to the North Star.

"Each night, I want you to look up at that star, the one that the heavens spin around. Do you see it?" She nodded. "That's my girl. Each night that you do, will you pray for me?"

Robert saw the tears well in his daughter's eyes and then slowly roll down her face. Robert's eyes filled with tears as well. Marjorie nodded her head.

Robert continued, "And each night, before I go to bed, I, too, will look up at that same star and say a prayer … that no matter where you are, God will keep you safe until the day you become queen."

"Oh, *Da*, I just want you to come home. I don't care about being a queen. I only want to be with you."

Robert gave his daughter a long, loving hug and a kiss, then promised her, "I will always be with you, Princess. Remember our star, and know that each night when you look up at it, I will be thinking of you."

Robert laid his young princess back on her bed, his tears rolling freely down his face. Princess... she was no longer his daughter but the daughter of Scotland. All the hopes for her future and for Scotland's lay in what he did over the next years. He would not let her down.

He walked back to Elizabeth, who had been listening. "I wanted her to have something that she could see when she woke up. But my brooch, it is gone as well as my cloak," Robert said. "How could I...?"

"Do not chastise yourself so on the brooch. I will get her one soon," Elizabeth said, crying as her husband held her. "May the men of Lorne find your brooch, and keep it as a reminder of the men they lost." Elizabeth looked sadly at her husband, and knew it might be months, even years, before he would see either of them again. "I, too, shall pray on the same star as Marjorie until we are together."

They lay together, Robert telling her how it will be for them in the future, until Elizabeth was finally able to fall asleep.

"Good-bye, my love," Robert said the next morning, as he kissed his sleeping wife. Then, walking to where his brothers and his men waited, he wished Abbot Maurice a safe return before they slipped into the morning mist and headed west.

# ELEVEN

## 1306: Marion Braidfute

After breaking their fast and saying good-bye to Abbot Maurice, Nigel and John led the way to Kildrummy. Lady Christian rode behind, barely keeping up with Marjorie.

"Come, please, Aunt Christian," Marjorie called out, trying to encourage her. "John says we must make haste."

"I know, sweetheart," Lady Christian replied. "I will."

"Did you know I was named after John's wife, Marjorie," she said, trying to make her aunt happy. "John just told me that this morning. That's special, don't you think?"

Lady Christian tried to smile, knowing that was half the truth, but each footstep weighed heavily, as though she were leaving her husband to die in some hidden part of the woods.

Her demeanor remained unchanged until the day before they arrived at Kildrummy. It was her brother Nigel's question that helped bring her back.

"Kerstie?"

"What is it, Nigel?" she inquired, not bothering to lift her face. Nigel couldn't bear to see her look of despair.

"One of our forward scouts says he has found Marion Braidfute. I've never met her, and I'm not sure."

"What?" she raised her head slightly. "Say again. Who did he find?" Her voice became clearer.

"Marion Braidfute. He says she is the wife of William Wallace."

"And he knows her how?" Lady Christian asked.

Nigel hesitated and asked, "Christian, what if this is a trap?"

"Who found her?" Christian asked quickly.

"Duncan," Nigel replied.

"You are doubting the word of your best scout? Bring him to me."

Nigel disappeared and shortly thereafter brought Duncan.

"How is it that you know Marion Braidfute?" Lady Christian asked.

"M'Lady, I was at a ceilidh* a few years back. It was when Sir William Wallace was made Guardian of Scotland and knighted. She was at his side. If I may say, m'Lady, make haste. I fear she is doing poorly."

"Take us to her immediately!" Lady Christian ordered. "Where is she?"

Duncan responded quickly, "She is north of here, near Loch Builg. She is very weak."

"Then do make haste," Lady Christian ordered. Then to her guards, "Have caution and be certain we are not played for fools."

They traveled a few miles before reaching a hovel securely hidden in the underbrush.

Lady Christian looked at Duncan. "Is this it?" she asked.

---

* A Scottish or Irish social event at which there is folk music and singing, traditional dancing, and storytelling.

"Aye," Duncan replied.

Lady Christian looked at another guard. "Make certain we are safe."

He opened the thatched entranceway and peered inside. "It is as he said, m'Lady. A wee bairn and a lady asleep on her bed."

Lady Christian pushed her way inside and found Marion Braidfute on the bed, close to death.

"Oh, dear God," Lady Christian exclaimed, going immediately to the child that lay asleep and then to Marion.

"*Mo cridhe*, why didn't you let us know?" she cried, sitting on the bed and pulling Marion into her arms. "We could have sent for you!"

Marion replied weakly, "You know the reason, Christian. If word got out that I or Wallace's daughter was alive, King Edward would leave no stone unturned until we were no more. Besides, you are now dealing with your own battles with King Edward."

"You know of this already?" Marion asked.

"Of Robert being crowned King of Scotland? Aye," Marion replied, "and at Scone."

"We are returning to Kildrummy," Lady Christian said. "Please come with us. We can take care of you and give your child a place to live in safety."

Marion replied, softly, her voice fading. "My time is short, and the peril I would add to those who would tend me is not worth it."

Marion drew quiet, her breath becoming shallow. "Once my husband was a Guardian of Scotland. It was not so long ago that your brother, Robert, honored me with a beautiful necklace and earrings in appreciation of my husband's sacrifice to Scotland."

Lady Christian replied immediately, "Yes, I remember!"

Marion tried to continue but began coughing, silent for a few moments. Finally, she looked hard into Christian's eyes. "And for the guilt he felt for fighting my William as he fought for Scotland. Even your daughter's husband betraying my William in Glasgow."

Christian lowered her head, ashamed.

"I recently heard of John Menteith's treachery," Lady Christian said. "But for Robert, he had no choice! He had to side with Longshanks and wait until he died, as Bishop Lamberton wanted!"

"Ah, but he didn't wait, did he?" Marion replied. "Remember, all Scotland has a choice, your brother included."

Marion coughed again before continuing. "My William was loyal to Scotland. He never claimed Longshanks his sovereign or switched sides as was convenient to save his skin."

Both were quiet. Then Marion said, "I need a favor."

"Yes, *mo cridhe*, anything!" Lady Christian replied.

"My daughter, Elizabeth, is asleep next to the fire. She is not yet three years of age. Take her. Raise her as your own." Marion grasped Lady Christian's arm. "Call her by her middle name, Marion, as I have, to hide her from Longshanks. When she is sixteen years of age, I want you to tell her of her father. When you do this"—Marion pulled at a small leather pouch she'd been wearing around her neck—"place this same necklace and earrings on her. Tell her of her father. And tell her she is a Scot!"

Marion slowly closed her eyes, relaxing for the last time, and passed into the welcoming arms of her husband, her Sir William Wallace, who had been put to death ten short months before.

"Yes," Lady Christian said aloud, "Sir Wallace would be so proud of you, knowing that you, too, had never sworn allegiance to King Edward." She kissed the face of her compatriot. "Your battles are over, my friend," she wept openly. "You will never have to worry about being found by the English or losing your daughter. I will take care of her, always."

Lady Christian called to Nigel. "There is a lady of Scotland who must be tended to!"

Nigel rushed in to see his sister cradling Marion's body in her arms.

"She has passed. We must give her all the dignity we would our king."

Nigel agreed and called out immediately, "Guards!"

They rushed in and picked up their matriarch, and prepared her for a burial befitting her station. "Do not leave a trace of this burial," Lady Christian said. "I won't have her desecrated."

Rising, she went quietly to the babe sleeping before her. "Oh, child," she said, tears streaming down her face. "All that your mother asked, I promise, and more." She picked up the child and took her outside. She whispered gently into her ear, "One day, I shall not only tell you of your father but of your brave mother as well."

"Who does the wee bairn belong to?" asked Isabella, the Countess of Buchan.

Lady Christian replied immediately, showing deference but also giving her a look that would defy any further questioning. "Her name is Marion, and she belongs to Scotland." Softening, she added, "She was in the care of Lady Wallace. Now that she has passed, I shall care for her."

Lady Christian answered no more regarding the child.

# TWELVE

## 1306: At Kildrummy

The sun touched the treetops and began its slow descent to the horizon as the gates of Kildrummy opened, welcoming their arrival. Declan, the warden, greeted them.

"It is good to see your safe return, m'Lord," he said, taking the bridle of John's horse. "Thank you. It is good to be home," John replied, as he stepped down from his horse, and into the welcome embrace of his wife.

Declan looked among the other riders as they rode up, taking in their numbers, then back to John. "M'Lord, King Robert ... is he not with you?"

John looked at him curiously, "No. Why do you ask?"

"It was just a question, Sire," Declan replied. "Our messenger has been kept busy of late with all the recent news, and I thought he might be with you."

John ignored his comment, and squeezing his wife's hand momentarily, said, "We are starving, my love. Have dinner served for us in the Great Hall."

Marjorie nodded and replied, "They will have to serve it in the courtyard, my husband. The Hall is filled with corn."

"What?" John asked. "When did this happen?"

"That was my decision," Declan stated, as Marjorie called to their servants. "With the news of battles being fought at every turn, I thought storing a large quantity of corn in the Great Hall would be wise. I hope you agree."

Nigel dismounted, and walking up, cast a quick look at John, and nodded his head appreciatively to Declan. "Your actions may be the only thing that keeps us alive. Good decision, Declan. Now, why did you ask of your king, and what news have you heard?"

"With the defeat at Methven and Strathfillan, I thought he would be with you, m'Lord."

"Nay, our king thought it wisest to split up," Nigel responded.

"Aye, m'Lord," Declan said and was quiet for a moment. "Sire," he continued, "we have had more distressing news. Both Bishop Lamberton and Bishop Wishart have been captured, and reportedly placed in chains and taken to England."

Nigel and John looked at each other.

"There is more, Sire. The Setons were captured at Loch Doon Castle. Our messenger says they were turned in by MacNab."

Nigel closed his eyes, recalling MacNab, a man who served under the new earl of Loch Doon Castle in Robert's absence. Nigel never cared for this man and was disappointed that the new earl had allowed him to stay on. Christopher and his brothers had indeed gone to where they felt safe, but had been turned in by those who should have offered them protection. Nigel was silent, crestfallen for his sister's loss.

It was John who broke the momentary quiet. "All this information … our messenger provided this?"

"Aye, Sire, our messenger is the marshal's son. You recall young Brian?"

John nodded. Brian was a good lad of about fifteen who had helped his father for years and, as of late, was always tending to the newest foal. John was pleased to hear he had been chosen as messenger.

"M'Lord," Declan asked, directing his question to Nigel, "Weren't the Setons with you?"

"Aye," Nigel nodded. "We became separated at Methven. All had hoped they would rejoin us or find their way to lands favorable to our family."

It was becoming clear to both men that there weren't many places left where one could hide without fear of being discovered and turned in. Most routes were being watched by those loyal to King Edward. How they had made it safely to Kildrummy, without their passage hindered or reported upon, was proving to be a mystery. Nigel and John exchanged glances and knew their options were becoming limited.

"I do not want you to tell Lady Christian about her husband," Nigel said. "I will find the right time. Do you understand?"

"Aye, m'Lord," the warden replied.

Both knew the likely outcome of the Setons' capture. Visions of Wallace's death the year prior flashed through Nigel's mind.

"M'Lord, I am truly sorry for her loss and that I was the one to tell you," Declan said.

"I know," Nigel replied. "Someone had to. You have done well in our absence."

There was a minute of silence before Declan continued, "Thank you, m'Lord. If I may ask, will King Robert come here?"

"No. We are to provide for the safety of his queen and daughter, no matter what it takes. I want you to post guards at each of the Interval towers, one in the Snow Tower, one in your tower, and two in the Gatehouse. Keep them on a continual rotating watch unless I say otherwise. Also, if Lady Christian has not summoned her son's caretaker, do so now. I am certain she is anxious to see her son."

"Aye, m'Lord," the warden replied.

John turned to his wife, "Marjorie, I hear the children crying. Can you check on our food? They have to be as hungry as the rest of us."

She cast a knowing glance at her husband and went to check on their dinner.

"I can never hide a thing from that woman," John said shaking his head. "After ten years of marriage, I swear she can read my mind."

"On this issue, it isn't hard," Nigel replied. "She too wonders if our travel here has been watched. If so, that means we should expect company soon."

"Yes," John agreed. "I think our young messenger needs to make another journey.

Nigel nodded. "I'll inform the marshal that I shall need to speak with his son."

Four-year-old Donald of Mar, Lady Christian's son by her first husband, had yet to hear of his mother's arrival. His caretaker, summoned by Declan, quickly came down from the Warden's Tower.

"My son," Lady Christian asked, "where is he?"

"M'Lady," the caretaker replied. "Young Master Donald has found great enjoyment playing in the corn in the Great Hall. He is there now."

"Since when have we begun using the Great Hall to store corn?" she asked, hearing this news for the first time.

"M'Lady, it was at the behest of Declan. With the news as of late, he felt it wisest."

Lady Christian nodded dismissively, wondering what news she was referring to, and let it pass. She would find this out later. First things first, she thought, as she walked to the Great Hall to find her son. The splendor of Kildrummy had certainly changed from when she was a young lady of nineteen. These troubling times would pass, and she would have it restored to its original beauty.

"Kerstie," Nigel called out, as he walked quickly toward her. Lady Christian, looking up, smiled faintly. *That was nice*, Nigel thought. *She smiled.* After so many days of seeing an almost vacant stare, it was wonderful to see something familiar in the sister he knew and loved.

"Ahh, pleasant memory?" he asked.

"Just happy to be home," she said wearily. "And I guess I always love hearing my brothers call me that." She was quiet for a moment longer, then added, "Nigel, if it's possible, I'd like us to stay at Kildrummy. I'd like to spend more time with my son and to pray. Maybe that's all I need. Since my Christopher ..." She stopped, knowing where those thoughts would lead her. "I guess I'm searching for things to be happy about."

Nigel replied sincerely, "I think we're all looking for that. But as to our staying..." Nigel hesitated. "On the morrow, we'll be sending out our scout. John and I think our travels were watched."

Nigel saw her look of disappointment, and pulled his sister close. "I know it's been hard. We'll see what we can do." Lady Christian leaned on his shoulder. "Thank you, Nigel." Her voice drifted off for a moment, then became determined. "I will take the wee babe with us, if we must leave."

"Are you sure she wouldn't be safer here at Kildrummy with your son's caretaker?"

"Maybe," she replied. "But I gave Marion my word that I would raise her as my own. If we leave and Robert wins"—she looked at her brother with determination—"then with his permission, I will relieve him of his duty as ward for my son, and I will raise the two of them as brother and sister."

She was quiet, then asked, "Nigel, do you think Robert will be able to win? No matter where he turns, he is faced with those who want to kill him."

"Kerstie," he said, "next to our brother Edward, Robert is the best fighter I know. With the help of our friends and brothers, he will do well."

Nigel pulled his sister closer. "There is more I must tell you. Something I have just learned."

Lady Christian pulled back and searched his face, afraid of what he was about to tell her.

"No," she said. "No ... no! Not Christopher!"

Nigel continued, softly. "Aye," he said. "Your husband and his brothers were caught at Loch Doon Castle. I know nothing more, other than they are said to have been turned in by MacNab."

She stared at her brother, disbelieving.

"It won't be good," Nigel continued, "not since they helped slay Comyn's uncle at Greyfriar's Abbey. Longshanks will not forgive any of us."

She knew her brother was right. She clung to him and cried uncontrollably. Slowly her tears subsided, and she pulled away from his embrace, finally able to speak.

"Oh, Nigel, I felt in my heart that he had been taken. I didn't want to think it, and I prayed and prayed that he and his brothers would come riding up, rejoin us, and tell us that Longshanks had died and his son had called his men back to England. I guess I wanted it so much that my naiveté got in the way."

"I would have liked to have seen this as well," Nigel said. "I prayed that the prophecy of Merlin would happen and the people of Wales and Scotland could come together as one and fight against his tyranny. Do not feel as though you are the only fool. There are others who could easily be accused of being naive."

They stood side by side quietly for a moment, silent in their respective thoughts. It was Nigel who broke their silence, and began to speak. "Robert mentioned that he wished he had not slain Comyn and had waited until Longshanks died, as our bishops wanted."

Lady Christian stared into her brother's eyes, questioning.

"Aye, 'tis true," Nigel said. "Robert shared this with me before we left. He says that he and Balliol should never have met. They despised one another so."

She nodded her head knowingly. "My son is in the Great Hall," she said, wanting to change the subject. "I'd like to see him now." They walked together, entering the hall, and Lady Christian's mind went back to a better time.

"Oh, Nigel, do you recall my wedding to Garnait, right here, just fourteen years ago? How splendid it was! The Earl and Countess of Mar, seated in the highest seats of honor, were next to my betrothed and me." She closed her eyes, cherishing the memory, and could almost hear the minstrels. "And there," she said, "would have been our father."

Hearing his mother's voice as they walked in, Donald ran from around the opposite side of the corn.

"Mother! Uncle Nigel! Aunt Marjorie said you might be coming home!"

Lady Christian bent low to take her son into her arms.

"Oh, my Donald!" she cried. "Oh, my baby, your mother has missed you so!"

Putting her arms around her son, she pulled him close and hid the last of her tears in his shoulder. Then she pulled back and looked at him appraisingly. "I swear it's only been weeks since I saw you and Aunt Marjorie at King Robert's coronation, but you are getting bigger each day!"

"It's all the good food we eat, Mother," he said. "You should see what she has our servants prepare. Pheasants, deer, even pig when they can get it. They were going on hunting trips all the time, until Declan closed the gates. Maybe Uncle Nigel and I could go hunting one day soon," Donald said. "Could we?"

Nigel laughed. "Absolutely! It shouldn't be much longer before you are old enough to go with us." He tousled Donald's hair and watched as he ran back to the corn.

"Did you see what I get to play with?" Donald asked and resumed throwing the corn against the wall, piece by piece.

Lady Christian continued her remembrances. "Here were the two long tables for our guests," she said. "Oh, Nigel, do you recall it?"

"I do," he said. "Garnait's father, Domhnall mac Uilleim, sat here in the seats of honor, next to his wife, Elen. And yes, our father and grandfather were on the other side. Here," he motioned to the opposite side, "were the seats of our dear John and his wife, Marjorie." He looked at his sister. "You are every bit as beautiful as you were then."

Lady Christian smiled. "Thank you, Nigel." Then, quietly, she asked, "Nigel, will we always be this way, father against son, brother against brother, even my own daughter's husband against us? Do you ever see us uniting as one ... a free Scotland?"

Nigel was pensive and then replied slowly.

"There will be many more who will give their lives before this happens. Robert is Scotland's hope for the future. This is why he must make it happen."

Both watched quietly as Donald continued slinging corn, before digging a small trench that allowed him to lay in it, undiscovered.

"Ah, to be four again and without worries," he said, and then suddenly remembered they needed to join the others. "We must go. The dinner they are preparing for us should be ready."

Nigel look down at his nephew and lifted him up onto his shoulders. "One day," he said, grabbing his nephew's hands, "this young man will be able to say, 'My uncle set all of Scotland free!'"

She smiled. "That will be a whole new beginning."

Nigel agreed, "A whole new beginning."

# THIRTEEN

## 1306: Of Loyalties

The next morning, Nigel arose early. He walked through the castle with John and their guards, checking their defenses. He had done this before, but now with special interest. They took note of everything, beginning with the usual: slits in each wall and tower for defense, with thick curtain walls that sloped out to keep adversaries in their line of sight. *All good*, Nigel thought admiringly, as they walked to the Gatehouse towers, a small group of men joining them.

"The door King Edward had installed should hold," he said to John, chuckling, pointing to it as they walked by. "I doubt he knew when he had it built that it would be used to keep his arse out."

They both laughed, knowing of its excellent construction. Nigel stopped, and turning to the men who had recently joined their group, became serious.

"Men, hear me. We are about to face those who wish to exterminate us from the whole of Scotland. If any of you do not believe this to be true, look back to Berwick. This time, it will be Kildrummy. When this occurs, we must defend our position completely or we shall perish."

All shouted their support and knew it was their land they were defending.

Osbourne, the blacksmith, listened and then pushed his way to the front of the group, his voice carrying through the din.

"After King Balliol ordered the Bruces to join Scotland in the fight against Longshanks, what happened? We who are here now know, don't we?"

He looked around the group, searching for support. One of John's men rushed forward and grabbed him. Nigel raised his hand, "Let him speak."

Osbourne shrugged the hand from his throat, and continued.

"Robert and your father continued their support of Longshanks! Not even for the benefit of Scotland would you change, would you? And, yes, I would have given your beloved Annandale to the Comyns, just as King Balliol did. It was shortly after that when Longshanks bloodied his blade on more than eight thousand men, women, and children. And for those who don't know, my wife and daughter were killed there. You, who were in the comfort of Longshanks's appreciation weren't concerned though, were you? You continued your fealty to Edward. Was the Bruce honor worth so little, or were your lands and title worth so much? Or was it just so you could see your beloved Annandale estates returned? My loyalty," he growled, "goes not to the spoiled son of a lord who slept in a warm bed and dreamt of being a king. My support goes to King John Balliol!"

Everyone was silent and looked from Nigel to John and then to Osbourne, his hatred filling the courtyard. Nigel raised his hand once more and provided the answer that was true for the Bruce family and hopefully for the men before him.

"Fellow Scots," he called out. "What our friend and blacksmith has said is true. Our father did swear fealty to Longshanks. But it was to bide time, to not attempt anything in haste. Scotland needed a king, and of what use is a future king if he is dead? Each of you needs to examine your own family and your own hearts. Did your decision to fight with our King Robert happen just now, or should it have happened a decade ago or a decade from now? Who has foresight to know what the correct time is? What I do know is that William Wallace forged our trail. He had only the title of knight to lose and his life. This he gave willingly for his country. No greater sacrifice can one give, and he will be remembered for this for as long as a Scot flag flies. My brother, King Robert, did have much to lose. We held many lands throughout Scotland and England. What he chose to do, as you have as well, is to put it all aside. We do this in hopes of regaining our freedom, our religious right to speak directly to the pope, and to never be subservient to a foreign king. Our hearts are with Scotland, but we had to wait. What Osbourne endured with the loss of his family, each of us may have to endure as well. Is this any less a sacrifice than what Osbourne endured or a greater one than what Wallace gave?"

John's men circled Osbourne. They pushed him into the wall and began pummeling him with their fists. Most were ready to end his life, and one tried to grab John's sword. "Men!" Nigel commanded, stopping their assault. "Why is it that we can see clear enough to know our enemies when they bear the English flag, yet are unable to see our supporters with the same clarity when they are our neighbors and brothers? Can we not see far enough to know who are our true enemies are?"

Nigel pushed himself into the group.

"Stop this immediately," he bellowed.

The men backed away, and Osbourne picked himself up off the ground. He grumbled vehemently as he walked into the courtyard, heading toward his shop. He knew the job that waited, to create coulters for their plows. One, however, was special. It would never touch the ground. Heated to its hottest, it would lay in the corn and set fire first to the Great Hall and then the castle. Now, fully justified with his decision made a month prior, he would await the signal from his old friend, William.

# FOURTEEN

## 1306: Two
## Months Earlier

Aymer de Valence and his messenger, William, talked softly, watching as the two nuns gently woke their king, Edward I. "Longshanks" had, for the last two months, been recovering from an unknown illness. His eyes fluttered slowly.

"What is it?" Edward asked, as he finally opened his eyes, bringing into focus the faces of the nuns and then the others in his room. He cleared his throat. "What is it that brings you here, interrupting my rest." It was not a question; it never was. The fire in his eyes, even with his illness, was always at a slow simmer, ready to ignite.

"My King," Aymer answered, walking to the side of his bed, nodding deference and then kneeling next to him.

"We have news that dared not wait. We have asked your son, Edward, the Prince of Wales, to be with us as well. He should arrive shortly."

Edward's eyes stared intently at Aymer and then wearily, closed.

The younger of the two nuns wiped gently at Edward's brow.

131

Waving her hand away impatiently, he said, "Get on with it."

"We have news, Sire, from Scotland."

Aymer pointed to William and said, "William is a Scot, Sire, loyal to the true bloodline of Scotland and a friend to the Comyn family. He traveled immediately once he learned the truth. I am sad to report, Sire, that John Comyn, the Lord of Badenoch, is dead. He has been slain by Robert the Bruce." Aymer waited a moment before adding, "At the high altar of Greyfriar's Abbey."

Edward took in this information, his blue eyes kindling with intensity.

William approached, "If I may, Sire?"

Edward lifted his hand and motioned him closer.

"Aymer says that during your illness, he informed you of a disturbance in Scotland. Forgive us, Sire, for taking as long as we did in getting you all the information you would require. It's far more than a disturbance. After Robert gave John Comyn a mortal wound, his uncle, Robert Comyn, came to his aid and was dealt a fatal blow, cleaved by Christopher Seton. From there, Robert and his men went to where Sheriff Court was being held at Dumfries Castle. He threatened to burn the castle down unless they surrendered, which they did. Afterward, Robert heard that John Comyn had not died. Hearing this, Sir Roger de Kirkpatrick went back to where the friars were taking care of him and killed him outright."

Edward listened, his rage becoming an inferno. Rising up as best he could, he asked, "All this is true? What you say, are you sure?"

William pulled back. Even ill, the king was an incredible force.

"You are telling me that, besides the challenge to my direct authority at Sheriff Court, they committed murder of a Scot nobleman at the high altar?"

The door opened suddenly, and the Prince of Wales and his

squire, Piers Gaveston, entered. King Edward turned his face away, disgusted.

The Prince looked at Aymer and asked, "How long has my father been here?"

"Since February, Sire. At the king's age, we dared not take any chances with his health."

"It is good to see you, father," the Prince said, bowing his head in deference. "Aymer has asked me to come. I understand there are issues that need tending?"

Edward looked at Aymer and William and said, "Help me up."

Each took an arm and lifted him so he was able to sit. Edward looked at his son and then at Piers. Piers and his father were of Gascony, and both had served Edward proudly at Flanders in 1297 and in Falkirk in 1298. Piers, his dashing personality aside, had not been the influential youth that Edward had hoped would guide his son in more kingly pursuits. Instead, the two had become closer, leaving many in the realm to wonder if they were beyond the fraternal friends they claimed to be.

"Yes," he glowered at his son, "there are matters of state that need attending. My loyal servant, Aymer, has informed me of something that you shall take care of in Scotland."

The prince was crestfallen.

"You do recall Scotland, do you not?" Edward said, ignoring his son's look of disappointment.

"Your highness," the Prince said, then added, "Father. Piers and I have plans of boating at Langley. We've been planning this for weeks."

Edward leaned forward, his fury rising, and glared at his son.

"Do you only assume the mantle of Prince of Wales when it suits you? And you dared to wonder why I did not make you lieutenant of Scotland, a country that had already been beaten into submission? As the next ruler of England, it is time you acted as the king you will become! Your boating trip be damned!"

Piers stood next to the prince and quietly offered, "Maybe we should leave."

"No, *you* will leave, and you will leave the prince to tend to the matters of state that need tending!"

Piers backed away, bowed, and left the room.

"By the Lord that lives …" Edward said, and let his sentence drop. There would be another time and day to deal with Piers. He turned to the group and began anew.

"It seems our vacillating 'Earl of Carrick,' Robert the Bruce, has finally chosen a side and now wants to be called 'King of Scotland.' Aymer, I have a special job for you," the king said. "John Comyn was your brother-in-law, and you are my cousin. I can think of no one more capable than you to become the next lieutenant of Scotland." Edward turned his attention to his son. He stared hard at him. "You will assemble the English army in Carlisle. From there, you will go to Bruce's Annandale Castle in Lochmaben. If they fight, kill them."

"I believe they will pose no resistance to your crown," the prince responded.

Edward ignored his comment.

"From there," the king continued, "you will travel to Perth and listen for news of the Bruce and his family. Aymer will arrive shortly, and from there, as my lieutenant, he will teach these stiff-necked Highlanders what the price is for disloyalty to their king. And Edward, you will once more learn how to punish total disobedience. William, you know who they are, yes? I want names."

"Yes, Sire. I have them here. From what I have learned, the names are many. Some were merely present when it occurred, others advised him, and others are his staunchest supporters."

"I want all their names," the king replied. "Their involvement and trial, if they are so fortunate, will determine whether they live or die, and more importantly, how."

"Yes, Sire," he said, and then began. "Roger de Kirkpatrick, Christopher Seton, John of Strathbogie, James Douglas, Alexander Lindsay, Robert Boyd, Alan Menteith, Robert's wife, Elizabeth de Burgh, and his daughter by his first wife, Marjorie, the Countess of Buchan ..."

Edward raised his hand. "John was there? Are you sure?"

"There is no doubt," William replied.

"And you say the countess was there as well?" Edward asked.

"Yes, Sire, my apologies. I meant to tell you this earlier. The Countess of Buchan and her husband are of divided loyalties. He is a Comyn and wishes to see a Balliol restored to the Scot throne. His wife, however, while her husband is here in Whitwick and you have her brother in custody, has taken her husband's horses and traveled to Scone to crown Robert, in her own right, as King of Scotland."

"In her right? In her right??" Edward's eyes blazed with hatred.

"Aye, my Lord," William said. "Their family holds the right to crown all kings of Scot—"

"Shut up, you fool! I know their rights!" the king yelled. "I did not know the baseborn whore had crowned him king of Scotland!"

A smile mixed with contempt and satisfaction crept across King Edward's lips as he recalled taking the Scottish crown and their coronation stone ten years earlier. "The traitorous Earl of Carrick shall be a king in name only. From henceforth, our king of no one or no lands is to be called King Hobbe."

King Edward leaned forward and tried to get into a better position. Aymer and William immediately came to his aid.

The king's gaze landed on his son. "Edward, before you leave, you are to contact my cousin, Joan, and send the king's condolences for the slaying of her husband at Greyfriar's Abbey. Say that all of England grieves for her loss. Let her know his killers will be hunted down to the fullest extent of the realm. And tell her that she, as well as their son, will be entrusted to the guardian of royal children."

Turning back to William, he said, "Now, finish telling me who is part of this."

"Bishops Lamberton and Wishart have become his staunchest supporters. Bishop Wishart, Sire, has gone so far as to absolve Robert of all guilt of the killing and is using the timbers given to repair his church in Glasgow to create siege engines. Word has it that he was heading to Kirkintilloch and Cupar Castles to destroy them. At every pulpit, he is preaching that Robert is their king and must be defended and supported."

"Defended, indeed!" Edward said. "And it is that damned Bishop Wishart once more." He looked at his son. "This is why I have pushed you. England can never become complacent with Scotland."

The king's mind raced for a moment. "Then I shall give them the opportunity to defend. I am certain Kildrummy will play a part. I want a full-time watch set for the west coast in case he has plans of going to Ireland, and one more in the north in case they plan on escaping to the Orkneys. His sister is the dowager queen of Norway, and he may seek sanctuary with her."

King Edward turned to William and smiled confidently. "Continue with the names of those who were part of this plot."

William did, leaving out no one. The king's thoughts grew ever more singular in intent. "Leave, all of you, except Aymer. I will summon you all on the morrow."

After the door closed, King Edward turned to Aymer and

slumped slightly in his bed.

"So, this William you brought before me. Tell me of him. He is obviously loyal to the Comyns and Balliol. I want to know more of him: his family, as well as his friends. Leave nothing out."

Edward listened intently as Aymer told him all he knew of William and his friend Osbourne who was the blacksmith at Kildrummy Castle, as well as the hate Osbourne bore the Bruces.

It was two days before Edward regained his strength and was able to bring the three men back to his sickbed. William and Aymer lifted their king up once more and leaned him against the headboard, as the prince stood off to the side.

"Edward," the king began, addressing his son, "you will have a letter sent to the pope. Inform him of Robert's actions. State that Bruce rose against his king and murdered John Comyn, Lord of Badenoch, at Greyfriar's Abbey and did so at the high altar. Include that John would not consent to the treason that Bruce planned, which was to resume war and make himself king of Scotland. We will then see what he has to say about Bishop Wishart's absolving Robert of murder and then attacking castles like a man of war. Include what you can of Bishop Lamberton as well. I'm certain there will be an excommunication in store for the three of them."

King Edward continued, this time addressing Aymer. "You are to find our dear Bishop Wishart and his friend, Bishop Lamberton. Have them arrested, placed in chains, and imprisoned. I cannot raise the dragon against them, but all will witness what happens to traitors, regardless of their position within the church. Now, here are my orders regarding the others who supported the Bruces. All Scots who oppose us are to be hunted down. Those involved in the murder, as well as those who consented to or advised Bruce, are to be drawn and hung. Anyone caught defending Bruce is to be decapitated or hung.

Anyone who surrenders is to be imprisoned until I decide their fate. The poor will be allowed to ransom their freedom, if they are able. You will make Berwick the center for all trials. A quarter of Wallace's body is still on display there, yes?"

"Yes, Sire," Aymer responded, "though not much is left."

"Good. I want our 'King Hobbe' to know what his treason has caused. When you catch the countess, I want her confined in an abode of stone and iron made in the shape of a cross. Let her be hung up in the open air at Berwick, that both in life and after her death, she may be a spectacle and eternal reproach to travelers. She will pay for crowning this king. For the rest of his family, I will let you know as you capture them. You have your orders."

Aymer and the prince bowed and left.

Edward, smiling, turned to William. "I have something very special that I would like your help with."

King Edward motioned for William to pull a chair closer to his bed.

"I understand you and your friend, Osbourne, have issues with the Bruce family. Your loyalty to the Scottish crown and true bloodline of Scotland, the Balliols and Comyns, is appreciated. How would your friend like to earn all the gold he can carry?"

William's eyes widened, as he thought of what Osbourne would give him. The king continued, "I hear your friend is a blacksmith at Kildrummy?"

# FIFTEEN

## 1306: Back at Kildrummy

Furious after the altercation with Osbourne, Nigel crossed the courtyard to where the marshal was repairing a cart that had come in the day prior with a broken wheel.

"I need to speak to your son. Where is he?" Nigel asked, his irritation clearly showing.

"He is retrieving metal for Osborne, Sire. He should be back this evening. I'll have him before you immediately upon his return."

"It is not necessary," Nigel replied, calming down slightly. "Have him before me after he breaks his fast on the morrow."

Brian arrived the next morning, out of breath. "I'm sorry, m'Lord! I would have been happy to come last night, after I got back. Father said there was something important you wished to talk with me about. I got here as quick—"

"Whisht, lad," Nigel said, laughing. "You need not explain. Sit, please."

Brian had barely slept the prior night, excited that Sir Nigel wished to see him.

"Brian, Lady Marjorie has told me of your love of our latest foal. She says you tend to him constantly. He's beautiful, isn't he?"

Brian's eyes lit up as he stood excitedly, then sat back down. "Aye, m'Lord, there's never been a more beautiful foal in all the Highlands!"

It was easy to agree. Solid black, with muscles that glistened in the sun as he moved, the foal would easily be as fast as his sire.

"You know," Nigel continued, "my father brought his sire back from Wales. I've seen his lineage. It's impressive. But my father has now passed. One of the things he told me is that a fine animal such as this can never be owned. They choose you, if you are worthy. As a young lad, I used to dream of being chosen by such a fine horse as this. Have you as well?"

Brian looked at Nigel, unsure of what he was asking. All his life he had dreamt of this very thing, and nothing less, from the first day he began working with his father.

"My Lord, sire, please do not jest. Do you truly mean the foal? I have dreamt of that and that alone for the last ten months," Brian replied.

"So, there wasn't another you were interested in?" Nigel asked, a small twinkle in his eyes. "I have heard there are donkey foals that can be found."

"No, m'Lord," Brian replied, anxious, barely able to breathe. "Only the foal."

"I thought so," Nigel said. "How would you like to earn him?"

Brian's eyes widened. In his entire life, he knew he would never earn enough to own a horse, let alone one of this breed and stature.

"My Lord!" Brian was speechless, uncertain what fortune had graced his life to earn such a gift.

Nigel continued, "This could be dangerous."

He shared with Brian what he expected his young messenger to do to earn such a special gift. "You will take the stallion," he concluded, "get me the information I need, and come back as quickly as you can. If you had wings, it would not be quick enough!"

Brian left by noon, riding as instructed, keeping the stallion restrained.

"There will be a time to unleash his speed," Nigel had told him before he left. "On your way down, you must stay off all roads but close enough to watch all movement. I am certain the English will be advancing, and every minute you travel must be treated as though you will be found. Make sure you go beyond where the roads join and funnel all to the north, and then stay on the road that leads north from Perth. Find an area where you can hide your horse and then wait. I want their numbers, how fast they are moving, their armaments, and if they have siege engines. Note anything you think might be of value. Then I want you to ride hard and return."

On his journey, Brian thought about the arrival of the royal family and the news he had previously gathered. This must be precluding something special. He had never seen so many people at Kildrummy at one time. The guards, their horses, the royal families, everyone, he thought, except the king and a few of his toughest soldiers. Even Lady Christian, her sister Mary, and the wonderful Countess of Buchan who had crowned Robert were there, along with the princess and a wee babe. He guided his horse through the forest and gave gentle nudges with his heels.

"Aye," he said to his stallion. "It's got to be important, just thirty-five more miles. We will need to stay steady. You can rest up once we get there. On the journey back, that's where we'll need your strength!"

The stallion snorted, seemingly with approval.

Brian arrived at his destination shortly after noon on the second day. His trip down was done as Nigel ordered. He took the stallion into the woods, tying him to a tree amidst a clearing with plenty of grass and a small stream within reach.

Doubling back to where the main road rose and climbed up and around a bend, Brian nestled in amongst a group of trees. Eyes never leaving the road, he pulled out the loaf of bread given him for the journey and began tearing pieces from it. He sipped water from a skin to wash it down. He continued to watch, even as the sun sank slowly, touched the horizon, and then disappeared completely. Still nothing. He laid his head on his forearms and watched the occasional passerby going north or south on some unknown journey.

Brian's eyes, heavy from the passing of the day, slowly closed. Blinking, he opened them, trying to ignore the call of sleep. He changed positions, trying to find one that was less comfortable. He watched the road and listened to the wind as it blew through the trees. Soon, however, he drifted off, and began dreaming of the new foal that would be presented to him by Nigel. Its beautiful coat shimmered deep black, with muscles that rippled with every stride. Its hooves beat a steady path to a time in the future when he would be presented with his father's job as marshal of the castle. That job would come about only when his father passed, and for that he could wait. The hooves continued their beat, although slower. But now there were many hooves, hundreds, and the foal was swept away with them, lost to the hills of Scotland.

Brian awoke suddenly and realized where he was. The sounds were not a part of his dream. Blinking to clear his eyes, he noted how dark it was and that he must have been asleep for a while. He sat cautiously erect, hidden behind the stand of trees, and watched as the procession moved past him, heading north.

"Your Highness, with your permission, we will camp in the clearing," the man in the lead said.

Brian had never seen the prince but could guess, with the procession and banners, that he must be King Edward's son, Prince Edward.

"Are you sure we've gone far enough? Father says ..."

The man in the lead turned suddenly, and Brian, recognizing him immediately from a prior errand to Aberdeen, jerked back in surprise. Aymer de Valence spurred his horse to where the prince was, then turned it sharply to reply.

"We will camp as I stated, Sire. In the morning, we will start early and split the remaining forty miles to Kildrummy in fewer than two days. Our king will be pleased, and our men will arrive ready to do battle. Besides, it will be at least ten days before William arrives."

Prince Edward urged his horse closer. Aymer called out an order to his senior officers, telling them to break ranks once they hit the clearing.

"Do you know, by chance, what my father wanted with this William? Will he bring the War Wolf?"

"A guarantee, Sire," Aymer replied, then spurred his horse away, allowing the prince's further questions to be lost to the night.

Brian remained hidden, noting when they would arrive and how many troops there were. There was no War Wolf, just bows and arrows and other handheld weapons. Watching cautiously until the last person went by, the officers broke ranks and spread out. It was a huge procession; Nigel must have expected it. Brian crawled away on his belly, until he was confident no one could see him. One never knew when or where a sentry would be posted. After one hundred yards, Brian got up and, still slouching over, ran into the woods where his horse was tied.

His horse whinnied, pleased that his companion had returned. Taking him by the bridle, he whispered soothing words into his ear. "My dark beauty, it is now that we must prove what we are worth. We've a job tonight and a fierce one at that. I know you can do it, and there won't be much of a chance for rest. For this you will be rewarded when we get home. Can you help me?"

The horse whinnied softly to the loving caresses Brian gave with his words.

Brian and his beauty walked in a huge half circle, giving a mile clearance from where the English had set up camp, to avoid any possible sentries. Finally, after almost two hours, they were on the opposite side of the camp, and he could now unleash his horse to do what it was bred to do. Brian mounted quickly, leaned over, and whispered, "Go!"

That was all it took; the stallion seemed to understand his thoughts and the urgency conveyed. Mile after mile went by, the boy's light frame barely noticed by the large stallion. By morning, all forty had gone by, and the ashlar towers of Kildrummy came into view.

Nigel was incredulous when Brian arrived back at the castle. "You rode him how far?"

"Forty miles, Sire, but he could do it! I walked him through the towns, and when we reached the other side, I could barely restrain him. He knew, Sire. He knew!"

Nigel could only shake his head. "You've done well," he said as he looked at the dark horse Brian affectionately called Beauty. "We couldn't have chosen a better messenger than you."

Nigel put his arm on the young man's shoulder, admiring the determination of character in a lad so young. "The stallion's foal is yours."

Brian beamed at first, but then looked down, becoming sad.

"I do not deserve her, m'Lord. I fell asleep. I stayed awake as long as I could and then woke to hear as they went by."

Nigel smiled. "Do not be harsh on yourself. You've done a man's job. We can be our own worst demon, can't we?"

Brian smiled, uncertain as to what Nigel meant, but nodded his head anyway.

"You've done well. I'd like you and your father to be with me if things get tough. Can I count on you?"

Brian beamed once more.

"Good," replied Nigel. "It could be rough these next few days."

Nigel left Brian and found John, sharing the messenger's news. "The Prince and Aymer de Valence will arrive in two days, maybe sooner. They've no War Wolf with them, but Brian did say it was mentioned, that and a man named William. They made camp last night forty miles away."

Nigel knew the decision that needed to be made and they had no time to waste.

John said, "We should do it immediately … this evening, if we can get everything ready."

Nigel agreed. "The sooner the better, I'm afraid."

"We will be able to travel quicker if we travel with fewer men," John said. "Can you use our extras?"

Lady Christian, after hearing the news, knelt next to the young princess. "You understand what this means, don't you?"

Princess Marjorie nodded her head, comprehension spreading slowly, but firmly, across her young features.

"Yes, m'Lady. John thinks that our journey here was watched, and he feels we must leave. Do you know where we will be going?"

Lady Christian sadly shook her head, but with quiet admiration for the princess's grasp of their situation. No longer was she just her brother's daughter; she was the hope for all of Scotland. Who knew what her future held?

"No child, I do not. Only John knows where King Robert wants us to go. I do know he wants us to be safe, and wherever that is, I know we will be. What I will need is help with baby Marion. Can I count on your help? She still cries for mother."

"Yes, Lady Christian," Marjorie replied. "I'd like that." Then softly, "Do you know if there has been word from my father?"

Lady Christian pulled Marjorie's head to her, kissed it, and replied, "No, child, there has not. But be vigilant, and do not stop your prayers. Your father needs them now more than ever."

Just after dinner, their procession lined up inside the gates. John said an emotional good-bye to his wife, and Lady Christian pulled Donald to her and held him.

"Mummy, when will you be back?" he asked.

She pushed her fingers into his thick, red hair. *He is so like his father. I won't let him see me cry*, she thought, and replied, "I am not certain. It may be awhile."

"But you just got here!" Donald said.

"I know, sweetheart. I don't want to go, either. But I do trust King Robert's decisions," Lady Christian said, "and as his ward, I know you do as well."

"Yes, Mother," Donald replied, sadly.

"Good," she replied. "All will be fine."

She held her son a moment longer and then released her embrace. Donald saw the tears she had wanted to hold back, and said, "Do not cry, Mother," and repeated her words. "All will be fine."

Lady Christian kissed her son and held him close once again. "You are right. Now, I need you to stay here with Uncle Nigel. Your mother needs to use the privy before our long journey."

She walked from the courtyard toward the Great Hall, thinking about the earrings and necklace Marion had given her. She knew if their party was caught, these would be confiscated and become English plunder, and likely placed next to the Stone of Scone that Longshanks had stolen ten years earlier. By stealing this stone, he had prevented Robert and all future Scottish kings from being crowned over it, as had been their tradition. It could be years, if ever, before it or the jewelry were ever returned.

Lady Christian sidestepped the entrance to the privy and walked inside the Great Hall. She looked around slowly until her eyes rested on what she thought would be the right spot. Sweeping away the dried corn with her foot, she marked off six paces from the two corner walls and began scoring with her blade between the tiles until one came loose. Prying carefully, she lifted the tile up and out and began digging out underneath. She hurried, knowing her presence soon would be missed. She dug to a depth of two hands, placed the leather pouch containing the jewelry into the hole, and, uttering a small prayer, packed the dirt back down and replaced the tile. Pressing her weight over the top of it, she then scattered the remaining dirt before covering everything with corn.

"I've not forgotten my promise," she said, "nor will I ever."

She could hear John's plea for expediency.

"I'm coming," she said, and hurried into the courtyard where everyone was waiting.

John gave his wife another long hug, and said, "Take care of our children, my love. Help with Christian's son, too."

Marjorie smiled and nodded. "I shall," she promised.

John walked over to his horse and called out to his men and their royal charges. "Is everyone ready?"

Each slowly nodded, apprehensive about leaving the safety of the castle for something unknown.

"John?"

It was Mary who spoke, asking what she knew the other women felt.

"Won't we be safer here, inside these walls?"

Nigel overheard and walked to where she waited in line with the others. He reached up and took her horse's bridle, and her hand, and addressed them all. "Our messenger reports they are heading north and they have many men. Will we be able to hold out? Absolutely, but our king feels another destination is where you will be safest."

Mary gave him a tentative smile, which was what he hoped for.

"M'ladies, have courage. We are going to win this."

It was Lady Christian's turn to break ranks, and she rode up to her son. Dismounting quickly, she knelt and hugged him once more.

"I love you so, Donald! Be good for your Aunt Marjorie. She will be just like you, missing her husband, John. Will you help take care of her?"

Donald nodded his head. "I will, Mother. I promise!"

She held him close once more, and then looked up at the Chapel, remembering her promise to pray there again. "Would you like to come with me?"

Donald nodded. They walked to the Chapel and said their prayers quickly before rejoining their group. Nigel hugged his sister once again.

"We will see one another soon," he promised. "I will help take care of Donald as well."

John and Lady Christian mounted their horses, exited the castle, and turned toward the destination that he alone knew.

On the afternoon of the second day, the English arrived at Kildrummy under the command of the Prince of Wales and accompanied by Aymer de Valence. Nigel, Donald, Brian, and Brian's father watched them begin preparations for their assault.

"I'm scared, Uncle," Donald said, his young voice barely heard over the din of men. "Are we safe?"

Nigel watched all they were doing. The English forces were disciplined and effective. They fanned out along the castle's perimeter, each man equipped with a bow. It was Brian who bent down and pulled the boy to him.

"Yes, we're safe," Brian said. "We've all the food we need, and their efforts will gain them nothing. Kildrummy is strong. Haven't you seen how thick our walls are?"

Donald nodded and looked up at his Uncle Nigel for affirmation, but Nigel continued watching their progress. Brian noticed his concentration and added, "Don't you worry. They will have your Uncle Nigel to deal with if they think of hurting his favorite nephew!"

Nigel remained focused on the scene unfolding before him. He knew if the English were able to breach their walls, there would be no quarter. Longshank's men were sure to deal with Kildrummy with the same tenacity they had Wallace.

Young Donald persisted, needing his uncle to confirm what Brian had said. "Our walls are really thick, aren't they, Uncle?"

"Some of the thickest," Nigel replied, finally hearing his nephew. "Let us go to the Chapel and say a quick prayer for your mother and our families, for all of us. I think God would like to hear our prayers, don't you?"

They all knelt before the altar, the bright sunlight streaming through the three lancet windows and lighting their faces. They crossed themselves after their prayers and walked outside to see the progress of the men as they steeled their defense for battle.

Nigel called out to his garrison chief, "Maintain our perimeter. I want continual guards around the clock."

"Yes, sir," was his immediate reply.

Nigel watched as extra men were dispatched to all corners and walls. *With the moat and all our preparations, we should be able to hold out,* he thought, sending out a silent prayer. *With your divine help, Lord!*

The English garrison attacked the castle for weeks. Nigel's men held them off, fiercely repelling them, meeting each attack heroically. Then, seemingly out of nowhere, flames burst out of the Great Hall. Nigel's men immediately brought all available water in an attempt to put it out, but it was useless. With the immense supply of corn in the Great Hall, the fire burned hotter and hotter and then spread throughout the castle. Now the English need only wait until the fire did its damage. Nigel, his heart heavy, despaired at this turn of events.

"M'Lord, come quick!" Brian called out to Nigel. "The garrison chief has Osbourne cornered in the Warden's Tower, and the men are ready to kill him!"

Nigel followed, running. The guards brought Osbourne before him, twisting with rage.

"We saw him run from the hall and then saw the smoke afterward," Declan said. "There was no one else in there, m'Lord."

Nigel looked at Osbourne, disbelief in his eyes.

"You did this?" Nigel asked.

Osbourne, his eyes alight, boasted menacingly, "Yes, I did. For one red, hot coulter of iron placed in the corn, I will be given all the gold I can carry. But know this: I would have done it for nothing. Your brother is a murderer, and your entire family traitors, siding with the English while mine died. He should have died at Methven!"

The men held Osbourne tighter, as he struggled to free his arms.

Osbourne continued, "The Bruce family will never rule Scotland, not as long as a Balliol or Comyn breathes Scot air!"

Nigel said furiously, "Balliol hides in France and has refused his kingdom! You did this, for what? We are here, fighting against a common enemy, and you did this? To all of us?"

"The Bruces could have supported King Balliol in his time of need," Osbourne replied. "What's the difference?"

Nigel felt sudden defeat, knowing that by the morrow, their gate would be burned and the English would be upon them. They could have held out, he was sure of it. It would have taken months before their food ran out.

"Remove Donald and Brian," Nigel told his men while glaring at Osbourne. "Get another fire going by the Gatehouse. Make it as hot as you can get it, and do it quickly."

He grabbed Osbourne's hair and added, "We will make it so you do not have to await the reward you so desperately covet. Men, this man says he will earn all the gold he can carry for the deed he has done. He should not be kept waiting. Gather all the gold we have and melt it down. If it is the last thing we do before we lose our lives, and the first thing the English see, I want his reward, all of it, poured down his traitorous throat!"

# SIXTEEN

## 1306: Voyage to Tain

John of Strathbogie lay his head on a moss-covered rock and watched as the moon framed the cathedral just two miles to the south, bathing it in a soft glow. Reconstructed after burning more than thirty years before, it stood proudly in the distance. It had been two days since they'd departed Kildrummy Castle, and their journey to Spynie Castle, so far, was unencumbered. John felt their passage to Brora would be equally uneventful, as would their journey to Orkney and then Norway. It was just the matter of obtaining quality boats at Lossiemouth, a task he had charged to the captain of the guard. He cautioned the captain against a craft that was too small; it would be best to find the largest available. The passage across the North Sea could be dangerous. With the young princess and their newest charge, baby Marion, he wanted to make certain their boats were not beyond capacity and all would be safe.

Just then the captain returned, and he stepped over Mary's sleeping form and went quietly to John.

"M'Lord," he said, "I have acquired the boats we need."

John got up, and they walked to the edge of the fire. Mary, now awake, listened quietly in the background.

"I have arranged with the captain of a small fleet to take us from Lossiemouth. He has committed himself to King Robert and assures our safe passage to Brora. He advises the waters can be rough, though, especially for the young princess and the wee wain."

"Aye, they can be," John agreed. As the Earl of Atholl, he had taken many trips over these very same seas and knew their potential.

"According to the captain, it's the sudden storms that are our greatest danger. He says by tomorrow morn, we should know if all is well enough for passage."

John did not see Mary get up or slowly make her way to the queen. "My Lady," she said and touched Elizabeth's arm gently to wake her. "If I may? The captain of the guard has returned, and Sir John and he are talking of going to Brora by boat."

The queen sat up, trying to awaken.

"To Brora?" she asked, unsure if she heard correctly. "By boat?"

"Aye, m'Lady. It will be from Lossiemouth straight across the North Sea. It seems dangerous with the wee wains."

The queen got up and walked quickly to where John and the captain were talking. Mary woke up Lady Christian and Countess Isabella, and they joined the small group at the fire.

Elizabeth said to John, "I believe you and the captain of the guard were talking of passage by boat to Brora? Is this true?"

John answered quickly, trying to assure her of the wisdom of his decision. "Aye, my queen. It is the safest way for us at this moment."

"I know my husband chose you to guide us in the safest passage, but I do not wish to travel by sea. I have seen sudden storms appear and know what they can do."

Isabella added, "I, too, have seen this, and prefer to go by Inbhir Nis."

Mary nodded her agreement.

Lady Christian did not. "I do not like the thought of going any further west toward Inbhir Nis," she interrupted. "It is too risky. Besides, those lands—aye, even the ones we are on now—are favorable to the Comyns. With every footstep, we stand the chance of being caught and turned over to King Edward. At least while on open water, we have a better chance of avoiding them. Brora is perfect, and from there our travel north would be amongst villages more favorable to our passing."

"If I may," said the captain of the guard, looking at Lady Christian and then addressing John and Queen Elizabeth. "My contact is a quality man of the sea. It is how he earns his living. He can get us through to Brora." He turned to the others. "Ladies, the going should be easy enough and take but six hours."

He turned once more to the queen, trying to plead John's case on his behalf. "It's the wisest, my queen."

John felt his goal to keep their destination secret throughout their entire journey was slipping through his fingers. He doubted he could get them on any boat, let alone to Orkney or Norway. He felt he was losing the battle. John walked over to Elizabeth and took her arm.

"My queen, if I may have a moment alone?" He led her away from the group. "My Lady, we need to be further north of Tain. We are still in Comyn territory. They will leave no stone unturned 'til they find us. They will go so far as to side with the English before allowing us to escape. Please, my Lady," he pleaded. "If there were a way we could travel entirely by sea, I would have the captain arrange it and be damned the children's inconvenience! They can live through that! Let us not go through Inbhir Nis!"

Queen Elizabeth listened quietly, but in the end, John knew she had decided.

"Was it not our dear Maid of Norway who died en route to Scotland? I will not have our next princess suffer the same fate! John," she continued, though softer this time, "remember, Robert was afraid of our crossing from Scotland to Ireland. He knew there was a chance of being seen by Longshanks's men. I will not allow our crossing at Lossiemouth. I will, however, allow our passage from Kinloss to Balintore."

John knew there was no option. The queen's decision trumped Robert's orders to him. Assured that their horses would be waiting for them north of Tain, they departed early the next morning from Kinloss. The captain, pointing to the size of the waves in the distance, shouted quickly, "Get the wee wains secured, and then yourselves as well. Do as you are told, and all will be safe."

Once secured, they pushed into the bay, and then into the North Sea, where the captain's prediction quickly became true. Their craft was buffeted by heavy rain and pushed about by strong winds and currents. Wave after wave lifted them up and then careened down into the trough, only to be lifted up for the next wave, threatening to capsize their craft.

"We should have stayed on land," Mary cried, as she laid her head over the side of the boat and emptied her stomach into the sea. Each of her companions did the same, as well as their guards in the other boats. Only Lady Christian and John, despite feeling the same sickness, held firm in their belief that what they were doing was better than traveling by land.

"Alas, but for a ship," she said to John.

John only nodded. All were thankful when the sun finally came out and brought calmer waters. The shores of Balintore became more pronounced, and the waves slowly pushed their boats ashore. Queen Elizabeth, feeling the firmness of land beneath her feet, said happily, "The remainder of our journey should be blessed. Let us stop and find shelter for the evening."

"We mustn't!" Lady Christian stated immediately. "We must push on. These lands are still unfavorable to us!"

"There's a new sanctuary I know of," Countess Isabella offered. "It is St. Duthac, in Tain. We can make it there, even with the children, shortly before dinner."

The thought of a sanctuary, especially a church, appealed to most.

"I'd like this, Aunt Christian," young Marjorie implored.

Looking down at her niece, she felt outnumbered, but compassionate. *She's been incredibly strong on this journey,* Lady Christian thought. She couldn't imagine being nine years old and going through what she had … her mother dying shortly after she was born, and now her father, who may never know a throne, could well die for his efforts. Lady Christian closed her mind to negative thoughts and pushed them in a better direction.

"Yes," said Lady Christian as she pulled her niece to her and kissed the top of her head. "Let's. It will be nice to clean up before we go on."

All were excited at the thought of a rest and a small amount of fresh water to wash away their travels. They began walking, cautiously talking, until they saw the sanctuary in the distance. Marjorie began to run.

"Be mindful of the nettles, lass!" Lady Christian shouted.

"I'm gonna find some fresh water," Marjorie replied, her voice trailing off as she ran. "I got mud everywhere!"

All were thankful upon their arrival on sanctuary lands. St.

Duthac had been recently built. Though small compared to the Cathedral at Elgin, it was still beautiful against the backdrop of the North Sea.

"We should be safe," John offered, but then quickly added, "Guards, make certain that it is."

The guards ran forward and then disappeared, the woods obscuring them from view. Moments passed.

"Guards?" John called.

Uilleam, the Earl of Ross stepped into the clearing. "Seize them."

# SEVENTEEN

## Kildrummy;
## Twenty-Nine Years Later
## Lady Christian's Revelation

ady Christian reflected sadly to Marion. "Uilleam, the Earl of Ross had been told that a band of royals were heading north, and he was waiting for us. Sanctuary meant nothing to him, church or no. We never made it to the church and were caught on sanctuary grounds. His guards were well-hidden and surprised us. They killed our guards immediately. You and I were sent to the Gilbertine nunnery, where I told them we had found you and your name was Marion. When I was released in 1314, in spite of my inquiries, I was given no information regarding you. It was as though Gilbertine had claimed you, and refused to share anything more, especially with a Scot. Though I never quit trying, my search always ended the same way."

Marion looked at Lady Christian. "M'Lady, I never knew anyone was searching for me. And now, I know much of Scotland's history. Our history. All but one person, and he is the one I want to know above all! Please, m'Lady, who is my father?"

"Yes, *mo cridhe*," Lady Christian replied. "I have fulfilled only part of the promise I made when your mother died. It is now time to tell you of your parents, and to present you with the gift I promised."

They went to the Great Hall, alone. Lady Christian, spying a sword, grabbed it, and said, "This will do." She measured off her steps, six from the north and six from the west walls. "I believe this is where it is."

Lady Christian, at over sixty years of age, knelt down and began digging around the edge of the tiles with the sword.

"M'Lady, please, allow me!" Marion got down on her knees and began digging at the edge of the tiles, packed hard after thirty years, until one slowly released. "What are we looking for?" she asked.

"You'll know it when you find it," Lady Christian replied, as she wiped the sweat from her face with dirt-covered fingers.

Marion dug down deep, until the blade hit something soft.

"Be careful," Lady Christian cried excitedly. "Now, hand it to me."

Pulling the pouch from the ground, she gave it to Lady Christian.

"I am sixteen years late, *mo cridhe*," Lady Christian said, as she wiped the dirt away from the bag. "I hope you can forgive me."

Marion looked at her quizzically. "M'Lady?"

Lady Christian carefully opened the leather bag, pulled out the necklace, and gasped softly. It was still as beautiful as the day Marion Braidfute gave it to her. Lady Christian stood, and then gently took the hand of the young lady before her. "Arise, Marion, and know the generations before you."

"Now turn around." Lady Christian said, as she gently pulled her hair back, and put the necklace on her.

Then, turning Marion around once more, she cradled her face

in her hands "You, Elizabeth Marion Wallace, are the daughter of Sir William Wallace, our Guardian of Scotland. Your mother was Marion Braidfute, the bravest lady I have ever known. You now have the necklace I was supposed to give you so long ago. It was given to your mother shortly after your father passed, in appreciation of the sacrifice he made for Scotland."

Lady Christian softened slightly, and continued, "Longshanks never knew of you. Your mother protected you and this secret to the end. She knew if he ever found out he would kill you both. I found her, by God's grace, on her deathbed. Before she died, she asked that I raise you as my own, call you Marion, and give these to you on your sixteenth birthday.

"I failed her, *mo cridhe*, until this day. Now, my child, by sharing Scotland's history and telling you of your mother, I have fulfilled the promise I made to myself. There is but one promise left. Lady Christian pushed back Marion's hair and said, "And it is the one that I am the proudest to do." She put the first earring on, and then the second, and proclaimed:

"You, Marion Wallace, are a Scot!"

Two days later, Lady Christian and Sir Andrew Moray assembled the more than one thousand survivors of the Battle of Culblean outside the gates of Kildrummy. Sir Andrew spoke first.

"Honorable men," he said loudly, "it is because of your caliber that we won this battle. Men of Merse and Lothian, I thank you. Your numbers, barely eight hundred, together with the three hundred men of Kildrummy, have soundly defeated David of Strathbogie and the Comyns, whose numbers exceeded three thousand! With this victory over the English, we have once more gained a pivotal battle for our independence. Your actions have put asunder any sense of victory Edward may have felt. And further," his voice rose to a shout, "our victory has ended any prayers Balliol had of regaining the throne of Scotland. May he live his life in the company of those who love him: the English!"

The men cheered, the pride of Scotland in their hearts, as they looked at Sir Andrew Moray and his wife. Then Lady Christian stepped forward and began speaking. All were quiet.

"I have a special gift to present to you. One that, until my arrival, I did not know I would be sharing. We know of Sir William Wallace's gifts to Scotland, do we not?"

All cheered again, even louder and longer. Sir Andrew raised his hands, and the crowd quieted.

"Today, we are honored with the presence of a young lady I knew many years ago." Lady Christian projected her voice so that all could hear. "It was after the battle at Strathfillan, when the royal family and I were escaping for our lives to Kildrummy Castle. Our guards had gone ahead to make sure all was safe. At Loch Builg, they found Marion Braidfute, the wife of William Wallace. She was weak from sickness and in hiding to protect her wee daughter.

"I made a promise to her before she died that I would take care of her daughter and raise her as my own. When she reached her sixteenth birthday, I was to give her the gift that King Robert gave to her mother for Sir Wallace's supreme sacrifice. It's a special gift," Lady Christian added, as she turned to accept the necklace from her guard. "But I failed her. When we were captured at St. Duthac's sanctuary in Tain, the English took us to the Gilbertine nunnery, where we were separated. I thought her dead until my arrival this week."

Lady Christian turned to the couple off to her side and beckoned Marion to come forth. Marion stepped up to her and knelt.

Lady Christian whispered to her, "We do this now for Scotland!"

She clasped the necklace around Marion's neck and then reached for the earrings. "My friends and fellow Scots," Lady Christian said loudly as she gently placed each earring on Marion, then stepped back. "Arise, Marion, so the people of Scotland may greet you." Turning to the crowd, she proclaimed, "Allow me to present Lady Marion, the daughter of Sir William Wallace!"

The crowd had been listening quietly as Lady Christian spoke. All of Scotland knew of Lady Christian's imprisonment at Gilbertine, as well as the fate of the royal family. Now they burst out with cries of joy, their excitement uncontrollable. Their cheers echoed around the castle as the daughter of William Wallace, lost for twenty-nine years, had come home to her people.

That night, Ian held his wife close as they talked of all that had happened. Marion never felt happier. She still wore the necklace and earrings that Lady Christian had put on her earlier, and imagined the day when she would put them on Elizabeth and tell her who she was and about their struggles for independence.

"My love," Ian said, pulling his wife close, "control your beating heart, or neither of us will be able to sleep for a week!"

# EIGHTEEN

## 2005: A Lineage Discovered

"Ian," Marian said gently, as she watched him slowly waken. He had been asleep for much of their long flight and had barely moved.

"Ian," she repeated, as he fluttered open his eyes.

"Have I been asleep long?" he asked.

"Oh, not too long," she replied. "Maybe six hours."

Ian sat up abruptly in his seat, allowing it to come forward.

"Six hours?" he said, disbelieving.

"Yes, I'm happy to say." She smiled, pleased that he had gotten so much sleep. "Look," she said, pointing out the aircraft window to the northeast. "See, the sun is coming up over the horizon."

Ian dry washed his face with his hands, trying to get the sleep out of his eyes. Suddenly he paused.

"You aren't having any dreams?" he asked.

Marian looked at him quizzically. "Why do you ask this?"

Ian looked at his wife, closer this time. "I'm not sure. It's just …

things are opening up. With my dreams and all." He reached into his travel bag and pulled out a pen.

"How do you spell your name, baby? Show me, here," he said, as he handed the pen to her.

"Ian, you've been asleep for the last six hours and you wake up to this?"

"I know," Ian interrupted. "Just show me how you spell your name."

Marian wrote out "Marion," then looked at it quizzically and crossed it out. She looked at Ian.

"That's strange," she said. "Why did I do that?"

"I don't know," Ian replied. "In my dreams, Ian's wife is Marion, spelled with an 'o.' I've no clue what the connection is, but I believe your father misspelled your name when he named you Marian. You said it was your mother's dying wish to call you that? That it was part of a lineage of names shared through the years?"

Marian nodded her head, and said, "Yes."

"Then we should start our vacation at Kildrummy Castle. For whatever reason, my dreams are becoming clearer, and I believe that will continue now that we are here. Sweetheart, I do know there are things in life that will never be understood. We've all heard about how people can heal themselves and the doctor stands by, mystified. You, as an archaeologist, can sometimes piece things back together just from following your innate instincts. What we've been through these last few weeks is one of the things we may never understand. I believe your past and mine were intertwined in some fashion."

Marian, disbelieving, just stared at him.

"Hear me out," he said. "Did you ever think of your lineage before you got your earrings from your aunt and uncle?"

"No," Marian replied, "though I did dream of my true mother and father.

I wished I'd known them, but I doubt it was more than any other child who had lost their parents."

"Exactly," Ian replied. "And once you received your earrings, did you think of your lineage more?"

Marian replied, "Almost every day. I became so obsessed with it that I would wear the earrings, and stare out my window for hours and dream of where they had come from and who originally owned them. When I was younger, I would even have the knife in my sock, same as the pictures of men in kilts would do. Often, I'd ..."

Ian interrupted. "The earrings have been in your family for over seven hundred years."

Marian stopped, and stared at Ian, not bothering to finish her sentence.

"Sweetheart, for whatever reason, I think you and I were destined to be together. And now, we are being pulled to Kildrummy to put together two ancient gifts that should never have been split apart. One of those gifts you own already, the earrings. The other is a necklace that goes with the earrings."

Marian sat back in her seat, at a loss for words. Never did she dream there could be more to her heirloom than her earrings.

"Ian, are you sure?" was all she could ask.

He nodded. "From everything I've seen in my dreams, yes, though I've no idea where or how they got separated." Ian could sense her sadness at this news. "Sweetheart," he said, "two months ago, we knew nothing of your heritage other than the earrings and the knife, and that they had been passed from mother to daughter for hundreds of years. Now, we know of a necklace. For whatever reason, I believe you and I were destined to find one another, to put together things that never should have been separated. The hard part is that it's not our timetable. Never has been."

Marian nodded her head, and then suddenly brightened. "Ian, remember that visiting student from Scotland? The one who came to our university? He has since graduated from the University of Glasgow, has his PhD, and is now famous in his field of ancient archaeology, especially Great Britain's. I know you want to go to Kildrummy, but Niall might be able to help us or at least point us in the right direction."

Ian reflected on this, and agreed. He thought of the other things that had been revealed to him in his dream, but decided, for now, he would wait. Hopefully, with their meeting Niall, and going to the castle, all would become clear.

"Are you sure this is the way?" Ian asked Marian as he drove their rental car along the M9 motorway, heading north.

"Niall once told me he lives north of the town of Bridge of Allan, by a golf course," she said.

Ian knew that most times her intuitions were right. She picked up her phone, searched through her list of contacts, and pressed Call. The line rang for what seemed an eternity but finally was picked up.

"Hello," said a child's voice.

"Is your father home, sweetheart?" Marian asked.

The young girl dropped the phone suddenly, and Marion heard it thud on the floor. She then heard her call out, "It's for Da, and it's a lady. She sounds funny, like the ladies on the telly!"

Niall picked up the phone from the floor where it had dropped and muttered a quick "Hallo?"

"Niall?" Marian asked.

"Marian!" Niall replied, instantly recalling her voice. "What a pleasant surprise! Where are ya, lass?"

166

Marian replied that she was in Scotland, on a vacation of sorts.

"Of sorts? That's nay kinda holiday in my book. Will ye have a chance to stop by?"

Marian answered quickly, "Niall, I was so hoping you would ask! It's all so sudden, and something has come up that I could use your help with."

"Aye, it must be important. I dinna ken if I can help, but we'll do our collective best. Besides, it's always a pleasure to see you. Have ye got your husband with ye?"

"Yes, I do," Marian replied.

"Well, it's *aboot* time I got to meet him!" laughed Niall.

She hung up, and they carefully followed the directions Niall had given them.

"I think this is it," Marian said quickly. "He said the road would be barely visible from the main highway."

They began the slow drive up a small, narrow road. Trees were everywhere. Around the last bend, the trees formed an archway, and the road opened up to a beautifully maintained cobblestone home, with thick vines almost concealing its walls.

"It's beautiful!" Marian said excitedly.

Ian let out a soft whistle. "Do you think he'd mind if we moved next door?"

Marian smiled, "Niall said it had been passed down in his family for the last two hundred and fifty years."

"Two hundred and fifty years! We're lucky if some of our newer homes last eighty years in the States."

Marian only nodded in agreement, as she stared at Niall's home.

They parked the car and walked up the cobblestone path to a door that was promptly flung open by an excited three-year-old, followed by a beautiful, white West Highland terrier, and then the girl's father.

"Niall!" Marian exclaimed, as she gave him a big hug. "My god, it's so good to see you!" Stepping back from their brief embrace, she added, "You look well. I don't believe you've met my husband, Ian."

Niall shook Ian's hand and introduced his wife, Becka, pregnant with their second child, and their daughter, Ellie, and the barking Angus. Quieted by Becka, Angus crawled under their BMW, reproached, but still curious as he feigned new interest in the passing of a small beetle.

"Don't be worried," Becka said, smiling. "He doesn't get to see many visitors and really won't bother a soul. Not even that beetle, as you can see."

Marian smiled, as she watched Angus lick the beetle appraisingly. Becka continued, "I take it you are the famous American archaeologist Niall has talked of?"

Marian blushed slightly. "I believe it is your husband who is on the fast track to Scotland's collective hearts. Hasn't he begun a documentary for the BBC, or was that another famous Scot who just happens to look like your husband?"

Becka smiled at the compliment. Marian could sense her warmth, and her desire to talk. "Boy or girl, do you know yet?"

"We're both hoping it will be a boy," Becka replied. "Someone who will keep our Ellie company."

Marian smiled, inwardly hoping for her and Ian to have a child someday. *Professional careers be damned. We've waited long enough!*

"Would ye care to come inside?" Becka asked. "We never know when a sudden rain can appear."

The entire group, including Angus and his beetle, followed her inside.

"Where you from?" Ellie asked immediately, hoping to hear more of the strange accents but not waiting for a reply. "You sound like the ladies on the telly."

"I'm from the same place as those ladies," replied Marian. "We're from the United States. We all talk like that there."

Everyone began to chuckle, while Ellie looked at them, not fathoming why.

"Maybe one day you can come visit us with your dad and mum? Would you like that?" Marian asked.

Ellie nodded her head excitedly.

"Maybe we will have a little girl for you to play with by then," giving her husband a nudge.

Ian caught her subtle hint, and winked.

With that, Ellie ran off, and Niall offered them chairs in the living room. "Please, make yourselves at home."

Ian began the conversation, with a twinkle in his eye. "So Niall, just how did you meet my wife?"

"Ahh, where did we meet?" Niall smiled at Marian, sipping the tea Becka had just poured. "I was on loan from the university back in the late eighties. I swear it was a gambling debt." Everyone chuckled. "Your professor and mine were both notorious soccer fans, and I'm sure my professor lost, so he sent me to your university to assist with research on the pre-Clovis period of ancient Missouri. Besides being the novelty and all, I was really out of sorts. But your wife," Niall nodded to Marian, "made me feel welcome. We even went out once, where I met Michael and Anna." Niall laughed, "I even recall their conspiring to set you and Marian up. Those two, I understand, are now in Colorado, and he's your business partner?"

Ian smiled and added, "And best friend." Ian reached over, and took Marian's hand. "Once this wonderful lady got us to agree to check out Colorado as a location for our clinic, we were hooked. We knew where we wanted it, and even had it built so we could see Long's Peak from our office windows."

Marian squeezed Ian's hand, and asked, "Niall, with the time you spent in the States, did you ever consider staying?"

Niall laughed. "Noo, I had my Becka then, was madly in love, and desperately wanted to return to Scotland. I will admit, it was an enjoyable summer, and I even took a trip to Las Vegas. That trip, through Colorado and Utah, was stunning."

Ian and Marian looked at one another and smiled in agreement.

"Niall," Marian chuckled, "we thought the same thing when we came around the corner and saw your home. It's beautiful! It brought to mind the adage about how we always view with myopic eyes the heaven we are from as compared to the heaven we are visiting."

"Hear! Hear!" Niall said, raising his cup of tea to a small toast. "The next visit will be ours. I promised Becka a few years back I would take her to Colorado, so she could meet you. Maybe we could revamp our trip, so she could see your wonderful west." Niall smiled at his wife, "And with my schedule and delays, let's hope we do it soon enough that we don't need to rent a larger car!"

They raised their cups to Niall's toast, "To your visit, and that your rental doesn't end up being a van!" Ian added.

"*Sláinte!*" they all said, honoring the toast.

"Now, for your story." Niall requested, as he took a bottle from a small tray on the table. "This is my favorite scotch," and poured a small amount in all but Becka's glass.

"I hope you enjoy it. It's from one of our islands, and it's called Bruichladdich. Highly flavored with peat, it comes from ..."

"Islay," Ian interrupted, "and it's my personal favorite as well!"

They clinked glasses together, and Becka, getting up, said, "I'll be getting their rooms ready."

Niall smiled, "It's settled. The missus lets no one leave the house, even after a wee dram. And there's no arguing with her, either. If you're like me, you'll need a good night's sleep, and a place to do it soon. East to west flights, or vice-versa, are always the toughest. Time zones mess with me for days. Besides," Niall added, "Becka makes the best breakfasts. You are in for a treat!"

Ian and Marian both gave an earnest "Thank you," and Marian began.

"It started the night Ian and I began making plans for Scotland. He started having dreams, small ones at first, but before long, they grew in intensity. His most recent one was on the flight over. He's still trying to piece them together."

Ian continued, "My dreams began as if they were unveiling portions of history lost through the ages. So much revolved around Kildrummy Castle. I was able to piece together the lives of ..." Ian hesitated, unsure if the others would believe him, and he began again. "I was able to see the life of an Ian de Airth, and his wife, Marion. I even dreamt of King Robert of Scotland and his brothers and sisters!"

"My," Niall said. "That is quite the dream. Do either of you know much of Kildrummy?"

Marian shook her head and said, "Only what Ian has shared. I had never heard of it before that."

Ian added quickly, "All that I dreamt, I never heard of or experienced in any way.

And, other than a few tales from my grandmother when I was younger, I knew almost nothing about Kildrummy. I've since learned that it was heavily damaged by the Jacobites in 1690 and then abandoned in 1716."

"Aye, it's true," Niall said. "Since then, it has gone to ruin, with many of its ashlar stones removed and used in local construction. Thankfully, there was a gentleman who had started cleaning and restoring her over a hundred and twenty years ago. Then it passed to his daughter and then to the care of Historic Scotland. They protect it and many other castles, as well. It's a good thing it went to Historic Scotland, and a shame it went the route that it did. But then, it's our history. There was so much that happened at Kildrummy from the time it was built until its demise. From Uilleam, the Earl of Mar, who many think had it built, to Domhnall, Lady Christian's father-in-law, to Christian herself, and then Alexander Stewart, but he is a story unto himself. From there, it went to the Elphinstones for a hundred years and then finally returned to the Mar family, who were now Erskines. What did you say Ian's last name was in your dream? Did you say de Airth?"

"Yes," Ian replied.

"That is something," Niall said, sipping his scotch, and then was silent as he searched his thoughts. "Back then, the Elfynstun clan were said to have originated from the lands of Airth in Stirlingshire, hence the 'de Airths.' The Elfynstuns, as time progressed, became the Elphinstuns and then finally Elphinstone," he said, spelling aloud the different names. "But it took the marriage of Lady Christian's daughter, Margaret Seton, to an Elphinstone to forge their alliance to King Robert. This naturally included others loyal to their cause. Were you aware of this?"

It was Ian who said, "My dreams did reveal that Lady Christian married a Seton after her first husband died. Christopher, I believe."

Niall looked at Ian appraisingly. "You are having incredibly accurate dreams." Then he pressed further. "Ian, do you know where your family came from originally?"

"We are Scots," Ian answered. "From as far back as I can tell. My family departed from Aberdeen, but where they were before then, I've no idea. They immigrated to Canada and then to America. I just know they changed their name before they left Scotland, and some time later, hid their original name from their children. I believe all this may have been due to their sudden need to escape, and their ties to the Jacobites."

Niall leaned forward in his chair.

"Have you considered the possibility that your last name, Dirks, may be a derivative of de Airth?"

"Honestly, my mind has gone there, especially since my dreams began, but, again, I've no proof."

"Ian, with my background as a researcher and archaeologist, I've learned many things. Of importance to our discussion is this: Immediately before the battle at Bannockburn, there was a defector in Bruce's army. His name was David of Strathbogie, the Earl of Atholl."

Ian looked at Niall, curious. "The name John of Strathbogie has come into my dreams a few times. He was a supporter of Robert the Bruce who was caught leading Robert's family to the Orkneys, and the other, a grandson named David, attacked Kildrummy. Is this the same family?"

"Yes. David was the eldest son of John and his son, David, was the man who attacked Kildrummy in 1335. In 1307, this David defected from Robert the Bruce to the English. However, in 1312, he had enough of what he perceived to be King Edward II's ineffectiveness, and he returned to the Bruces."

Niall continued, "King Robert always needed support from the Scottish nobility. He readily accepted him back and returned to him his family estates ... and made him constable of Scotland. Unfortunately, the love interest between Robert's brother, Edward, and David's sister, Isabella, proved to be their downfall. Their tryst yielded an illegitimate child. When the relationship soured, Edward turned his attention to the daughter of Uilleam, the Earl of Ross. David felt his sister's honor had suffered and was angry that his political clout with the Bruces was damaged, so he once more made plans to return to the English."

"It's the same thing as King Robert did, if you think about it," Marian said, "going from one side to the other. Except this David and his lineage stayed with the English."

"Absolutely." Niall said. "But it's what happened the night before Bannockburn that almost had Robert turn away from his greatest victory. David, having made previous plans to return his allegiance to England, struck that very night. He led an attack on Cambuskenneth Abbey, and stole all Robert's provisions. One of those killed in their raid was the knight in charge, a William Airth."

"One of my ancestors?" Ian asked. "Are you sure?"

"The names are a part of history, Ian. What I am certain of is, if the name Dirks is a derivation of de Airth's, then you could be related. From what I've been able to surmise, it was William's being related to Lady Christian and his loyalty to King Robert that secured your family's future through the entire Stewart line. That is, up to the time your family fled Aberdeen in 1716."

"I had no idea," Ian said. "My grandmother used to say we were royalty, but she had no proof. All knowledge of our family's history was lost within a generation." Ian pursued further. "You mentioned that the battle at Bannockburn almost didn't occur. What happened that kept it going, do you know?"

"I can tell you this one, Ian," Marian responded. "Lady Christian's second husband was Christopher Seton. His brother Alexander, I believe, had sided with the English. On the same night David killed your relative, Alexander crossed over to the Scots and was immediately brought before Robert. He told Robert that the English had lost heart and expected nothing but an all-out assault from the

Scots. It was his words of assurance, even in spite of Robert losing his provisions, that guided Robert to battle and victory the next day."

"So," Marian continued, "if Niall is correct, your family name was de Airth.

"All this, finally revealed," Ian said, amazed. "And I thought we were here trying to solve the riddle of your family. My only question now is, why did they have to leave Aberdeen?"

"And," Niall interjected, "how does all this tie in with Marian?"

Ian and Marian shared what they had gone through over the last few weeks: the restless nights, the intensity of Ian's dreams, and the story of Kildrummy. Niall listened closely and, when they were through, offered a suggestion.

"Back when I was at the university, there was a student whose passion for knowledge about Kildrummy exceeded his desire to become an archaeologist. We still stay in touch, though he has changed his direction entirely. He quit pursuing his doctorate, and he and his wife run a travel agency. He uses his knowledge of Scotland to help others see the hidden Scotland, the side of it many have never known. But his passion has always been Kildrummy. I think in this area, he will have more knowledge."

The next day, after Becka's wonderful breakfast, and a small basket of food for the journey, and armed with the name and number of their next contact, Ian and Marian said their good-byes.

"He's a remarkable man," Ian said of Niall as they drove off.

Marian smiled and agreed.

Ian looked at her closely. He could tell she was pulling up memories.

"Did you and Niall ever go out on a second date?" Ian asked.

"He's a very dear friend ...one I admire very much."

"Hmm. I'm not sure that's an answer."

"I might have," she replied, "if he didn't already have Becka, and I hadn't met you."

"I think you picked the right doc, baby," Ian said, as he winked at his wife.

"I completely agree," said Marian.

He pulled over and took her hand, then kissed her lovingly. "Have I told you how fine you are to me?"

Marian beamed. They held each other, savoring their togetherness, before Ian put the car in gear and pulled back onto the road.

"Ian," she said, "I'd like to see us start our family. Don't you think so, too?"

"Ian took his hand off the wheel, and held hers. "I've thought the same thing, especially now that the clinic is up and running. I just don't know why you wanted to wait so long." Marian whacked Ian's arm, and Ian laughed, before quickly putting his hand back on the steering wheel.

They were quiet for a few moments, each lost in thought, before Marian asked. "Ian, all that you've seen. Everything is from your dreams?"

"Everything," Ian replied. "It's like," he searched for the words that would make sense to him as well, "in the beginning I didn't understand. But later, it's like you were the conduit to my dreams. Remember when you went to Denver University for that lecture?" She nodded. "Well, that night you stayed there, and I didn't dream. Same thing happened the next night. However, when you came home, I began dreaming again. The more it happened, the more I began to understand that it only happened when you were near me. Then, finally, I started getting used to it. No," he reflected, "I don't think I ever got used to it. But it did seem to unravel things that needed to make themselves clear, so I could share it with you. I think your family's past needed to find the easiest way to make itself known, and I was it. I'm still clueless why it is coming through to me and not you."

Marian shook her head, finding it hard to believe. "Okay, let's go back. Who was the first Marion?"

"Her real name was Elizabeth Marion. Her mother, however, on her deathbed, asked Lady Christian to raise her as her own and call her Marion. Unfortunately, as Lady Christian was trying to escape to the Orkney Isles, she was caught at a sanctuary in Tain, called St. Duthac, and lost touch with baby Marion for many years."

"They were caught at a sanctuary?" Marian asked. "Was there a church?"

"Yes," Ian replied, "but I'm not sure they made it. Seems, back in those days, sanctuaries were known for how many were caught seeking sanctuary than were actually given it."

Marian replied with a "Wow" and remained silent as they drove through the town of Perth.

"Hon," Ian asked, "can you pull up the number for the gentleman Niall told us about? What was his name?"

Marian pulled out her day timer. "It's Russell, with Scot Tours," she said, and punched in the number on her phone.

"Ask for the easiest way to get to Kildrummy, and then ask if he has any time in the next few days to take us on a tour," Ian said.

Marion was on the phone with him for the next five minutes, getting directions, and then exclaimed, "You will? Oh, that would be wonderful!" She hung up the phone, "Russell says he is in the area and would be delighted to meet us now and share as much of its history as he can."

They exchanged glances, smiling broadly, then she added, "He says to step on it, though, as they close the gates at 5:00 p.m."

They were quiet for the next ten minutes, deep in their own

thoughts. Marian broke the silence, suddenly remembering, "You said there is a necklace as well?"

"Yes, from what I saw in my dreams. But I don't know where it is or to whom it went or anything. They are a matched set, your earrings and the necklace, and were given as a gift to Marion Braidfute."

"Will our going to Kildrummy help?" she asked. "I mean, if you know nothing more than what you've said, why are we going there?"

"Because," Ian responded, "I don't think we have a better place to start. Not yet at least."

# NINETEEN

## 2005: North
## to Kildrummy

arian saw the sign for B974 shortly before Laurencekirk. "Turn here!" she said.

They anxiously held hands, knowing it was getting closer.

"It's hard to imagine all this was once completely forested," Marian said, as she surveyed the countryside, dotted with the occasional farm, house, or business.

Ian agreed. "I think the same thing at times when I drive on I-70 and imagine that sixty million bison once roamed our plains."

She looked at Ian. "You don't think, after seven hundred years, that my necklace has gone the way of their forests and our bison? I mean, lost forever?"

Ian squeezed her hand a little. "I don't know, sweetheart. I hope not."

They headed north, through the town of Banchory, following Russell's directions.

"Russell said that once we get to Alford, we're within ten miles of it," Marian said. "We should see road signs once we get there."

They held hands the final minutes, until they came around the bend and were finally able to see the castle. It was magnificent and grew more so as they paid their admission, walked up the path, and came face-to-face with its weathered walls.

"It's like I really have been here," she said in amazement, taking in everything. "I can almost see it as it once stood. Oh Ian, it's beautiful!"

Ian nodded his head. "Yes, sweetheart. You have ... and it is." He walked to the left. "Here's where the Snow Tower once stood, just like in my dreams. From what I remember, there were five private quarters, one atop the other. They even had water they could bring up from a well in the center, and each had a privy."

Marian looked at the signs that described what was left of a once magnificent structure. "What you are saying seems so much more modern than what I imagined for a castle built seven hundred years ago. I mean, my degree aside, look at those church windows, even the stonework. It's so much more than I ever imagined."

Ian nodded, his thoughts the same. "Yeah, I agree. It is beautiful. Hey baby, what time is it? Wasn't Russell supposed to be here by now? It's getting close to five."

Marian looked down at her watch only to hear her phone ring. "It's him."

She talked with Russell briefly, then hung up. "Something came up, and he can't make it until tomorrow morning. He's not sure exactly when, but he said he'll be bringing his wife, Hayley. He'll call when they are within minutes of the castle."

"Sounds good," Ian replied. "How about we spend the night in that hotel you mentioned at home. Kildrummy Castle Hotel. Is it far?"

Marion smiled happily. "I think …" She ran a few quick steps to the side of the tower. "Yes, it's right behind here! Oh, Ian, I'd love to! It would be so romantic!"

As they began their walk down the long path to the parking lot, the lady who had sold them their tickets called out, "I'm sorry for your quick visit. If you'd like, I'll be staying here a few more minutes, and you can look a wee bit more?"

"We'll be staying at the Kildrummy Castle Hotel, if they have a vacancy," Ian responded. "Either way, we will be back here in the morning. Thank you, though, for your kind offer."

"Can I offer you a suggestion if you get to stay there?" she replied. "Ask Miss Fiona if she has any sticky toffee pudding."

"Fiona?" Marian asked.

"Aye, she is the assistant manager. Tell her I personally sent you over. She will take good care of you. Her staff and service are second to none."

Ian and Marian pulled out of the parking lot and took the first left that led them to the hotel. He parked the car while Marian ran inside and Ian waited patiently until she came out.

"Oh my God, Ian, it's beautiful!" she said breathlessly. "There's an incredibly beautiful wooden staircase that leads to the second floor. It's amazing! Fiona took me on a quick tour, and she's given us her superior room. It's called Stronagaich. One of its windows looks out to the castle, and the other looks out over the gardens. Ian, even the windows are leaded glass! And you should see the room. It's huge and has a beautiful blue carpet, and …"

Ian laughed and interrupted her. "In all this, did you get a chance to ask her about the pudding?"

"Yes! Tonight, she will have some ready for us, and a wee dram of … Oh, Ian, I so love Scotland! Do you think Michael and Anna will move here with us? I'm sure with Niall's recommendation I can get a position at a local university. We can get excellent prices for our homes on the lake!"

Ian smiled at Marian. "I think I'd like that wee dram about now, and … if you could grab one of these suitcases?"

Marian reached over and grabbed one, barely listening to his reply. "It might take a few drams to convince them to move. He still has Norway mixed up with Denmark!"

Ian couldn't help agreeing that Scotland was incredibly beautiful. It must have been something drastic that made his and Marian's ancestors leave so many years ago.

That night, after enjoying a wonderful dinner, they relaxed in the Gordon Lounge, while Ian sipped his scotch.

"Fiona says this room was named for the Gordon Clan," Marian said. "She said Kildrummy is on the edge of what was once their lands, and it was one of the strongest clans in the region." She leaned against Ian's shoulder. "Do you think we will find out anything more? It would be ..." She stopped, knowing that for them to learn anything more would take a small miracle. "How about the knife? Ian, did your dream show you anything about it?"

Ian shook his head. "Sweetheart, I wish the pieces were more cohesive, something that could be added that would join everything together. I'm hoping Kildrummy is the link we need. Maybe something, like runes written on the castle wall. Something ..."

Marian could tell by the tone of his voice that he was frustrated, and squeezed his hand. She knew, and so did he, there wouldn't be any stones that held secret clues. Intuition, at least to the level Ian had mentioned before they landed, rarely happened. Marian sighed; maybe there wasn't anything more to learn.

Ian, sensing their spiraling disappointment, placed his drink down. "Hey, ya know what? We've come this far. No, we've been guided this far, and we're not about to give up. At least not without getting an answer somewhere. What I do know is Glasgow has a wonderful university, and we could spend the last few days of our vacation researching. Would you like that?"

Marian agreed, then asked, "What if we find something? Or don't? Do you think Michael would mind if we had to extend our vacation some?"

"I think he'd be happy just to know we're getting things figured out. We'd just need to call him so he knows. He's here for us, and I've never had a better friend. Then we could spring the idea of moving the clinic to Scotland!" Ian chuckled, "I'm not entirely sure that would work, though."

Marian looked at him curiously.

"It seems they have socialized medical care here," he said. "It could be tough for us to get our first customers."

They both laughed. Marian took Ian's glass, set it down, and said, "Dr. Dirks, sticky toffee pudding aside, I think it's time for our romantic evening to start. That is, after we thank Fiona for a wonderful dinner and dessert."

Ian smiled, agreeing. "And before we leave, you've got to get that recipe."

Marian reached into her purse and pulled out a piece of paper. "Done! I stopped by the front desk an hour ago and asked Fiona for it. She even assured me it could be made without a microwave. You know how I hate those things! We'll just need to find a place that sells treacle."

"Treacle?" Ian asked.

"That's what I said!" Marian replied. "When I asked what it was, she said it is like our blackstrap molasses. The cutest thing was when one of her guests in line said, 'Not quite. Here in the UK, we eat treacle. Our cows get the molasses!' Fiona grabbed her broom and teased like she was going to hit him. I gather he's a favorite customer, but she did threaten to charge him double!" Marian chuckled, "It was so cute! I just love her!"

"I've never heard of treacle," Ian said, "and I have never seen one of these!" He pointed to the coffee carafe with a plunger in the center. "The filter holds the grounds in a center ring. We'll have to get one before we go home!"

Ian then took Marian's hand and kissed her. "And while you were getting the recipe, I went upstairs to our room. The moon is incredibly beautiful, and you can see the castle below it. I'd like to be around for our daughter's sixteenth birthday and can't think of a more special time than now." Ian set his drink down, and picking his wife up, carried her upstairs.

Fiona smiled, and exclaimed, "Newlyweds!"

Later, they lay in each other's arms. With a final kiss, and Kildrummy Castle just outside their bedroom window, they both drifted off to sleep. Ian enjoyed his best sleep in months, dreaming of their life in Colorado and the beautiful daughter he hoped would soon be in their lives. This time, it was Marian, the daughter of Scotland, who was called home, to learn the missing pieces of her lineage in the only way it could be shared. Breathing deeply, she felt the guiding hands of Lady Christian as they pulled her into her dreams.

# TWENTY

## 1746: Culloden

Young Marion looked out at their glen. She watched as the wisps of fog slowly lifted and imagined each of the flowers lifting their heads to the sun, pushing through the last vestiges of the morning mist. It was spring, and it was going to be another beautiful Highland day. Marion was excited that her father would be coming home soon from helping Prince Charles regain his throne. She smiled, smelling the bacon her mother had just finished cooking over their brasier, as it wafted on the breeze in her direction.

"Come, child," her mother hollered, in Gaelic. "Set our table."

"Coming, Mum," Marion called back.

She scanned the trees as far as she could see. The glen had been their home for years. Beautiful oaks and maples lined their path, hanging low. Moss grew on most of them and on the rocks that lined the road as well. What wasn't covered in moss was covered in vines. Ariel House had been theirs for years, built more than a hundred years ago by the Elphinstones and Mars for her great-grandmother, and she knew every tree for miles. She could never imagine living anywhere else. Where else would be as beautiful? Marion continued looking for him, scanning farther up the road to where the path was not covered with trees. She saw nothing.

Marion skipped up to the gate and closed it behind her. He would be back soon and their home would return to what it was before, with mum singing as she made the evening meal. Theirs was a quiet single story stone home, set back in the glen, with a fence made of the same stone. It surrounded their land in a large V as it opened up from the front, and closed at the far end. And their cattle, Och! They were beauties, each with beautiful brown shaggy coats. No others in the Highlands looked like their breed. Marion turned and continued skipping toward their home. Their thatch roof, heavy with the morning dew, hung over the edge of the house, protecting the interior from rain. Around the house thick vines covered all the outside walls and required trimming each year so as to not cover the window's completely. The main room was where she slept and where each morning the smell of her mother stirring the prior evening's coals would greet her, and together, they would make breakfast. The other room was her father and mother's.

Elizabeth watched her daughter approach. She brushed back a strand of hair that had straggled free and dangled in her face. A tear formed in her eye as she too thought of her husband, and she turned as she continued her cooking, wiping it away before her daughter could see it.

"Has there been any new word, Mum? He should be home soon, don't you think?"

He had been gone now for the last nine months, and she missed him terribly. Their clan, this part of the Gordon clan, was the only one in this glen. Many did not know of its location, and most had never even heard of it.

Elizabeth reflected quietly. Not since the Reverend James Hay came by a week ago, saying that the prince and his men were heading north toward Inbhir Nis, had they heard a word. Elizabeth kept her tears to herself and tended to the things that needed doing. There was nothing her crying would help, she knew.

"No, Marion, I've not heard a thing beyond that," she replied, then tried to distract her daughter from the fear they both felt.

"Tell me our lineage," Elizabeth asked her daughter.

Marion looked at her mother, and quietly and stoically recalled all that she knew. Her mother often did it when she grieved, and Marion was happy to oblige her.

"Marion Braidfute of Lanarkshire bore Elizabeth Marion," she began, and continued reciting their lineage, covering almost four hundred and fifty years, until she came to her mother. "And then you married Papa!"

Elizabeth smiled. "Aye, child. Nicely done. And you will remember to tell this to your daughter when you have your first bairn, yes?"

Marion blushed a little. "Aye, Mum. I will nay forget. But I need to find a husband first!"

Her mother smiled, and repeated, "You will be sure to teach her our lineage as I have taught you?"

Marion replied, exasperated, "Aye, but it's all Marions and Elizabeths. There's nay much at all to remember, is there?"

Elizabeth smiled, recalling when she told her own mother the same thing.

"'Tis true," she said. "But it's the lives lived that make us who we are and who they were. Ye are never to forget."

Marion looked up, hearing the hooves of a galloping horse.

"Mum?"

Marion knew that most Highlanders could not afford a horse.

It was Reverend Hay, and he was riding hard, even up the last of their path.

Elizabeth went out to greet him. "'Tis a fine day, Reverend Hay, when we see you a com'n up our path. But ride'n a horse?"

She stopped when she saw the blood, dried and matted, that had run down from a large gash on the side of his head.

"Elizabeth, Marion, please. Come into ye home," said the reverend. "I have news." Marion and Elizabeth both rushed inside, with the reverend limping behind.

"Tell me it's good news," Elizabeth asked, as she grabbed a bowl and then some rags. "And look at the likes of ye," she exclaimed and began cleaning his wound.

"There was a battle," he began. "It happened at Culloden Moor. The clans were there, but why in that miserable marsh? Only our Lord above knows, but they fought bravely, nonetheless. It was a terrible battle, and though he made it away from the main battle," he looked at Elizabeth and softly touched her hand, "your Ranald, thankfully, died from his wounds. He was with others of his clan, many whose lives ended too soon."

Marion gasped and fell into her mother's arms, crying. The reverend continued, "A volunteer for the English, a real butcher of a man by the name of James Ray, came knocking at my door afterward, searching for any of our men who escaped the carnage. None had made it to my home, but he made himself available to what he pleased. He said, 'Reverends always have good things.' For that, I can forgive. But what they did to our men afterward, to the boys, young ones, old ones, women, too. It made no difference." He shook his head. "I've never seen anything like it."

"What happened to Ranald?" Elizabeth asked. "What happened to my husband?"

The reverend continued, "I tried to see if he was alive still and pull him from where he lay. That's when the same rogue James Ray took his musket and bashed my head. He said, 'You will leave them lie unless you wish to add your body to their likes.' I ran, but I saw him shoot anyone who had come to watch the battle.

"Elizabeth," he continued. "Your Ranald ... I went back that night. The guards were there to make sure no one came in or was taken out. It was terrible. Many were still moaning," he continued, "and when the guards heard them, they bayonetted them to finish them off. I bribed each guard sixpence, and they let me bury him. He died in my arms."

Elizabeth and Marion looked at the reverend, horrified.

"It's what the lobsters are doing afterward that is unforgivable."

He looked at Marion. "I beg, let the child leave while I tell you the rest."

Elizabeth looked at her daughter and then back to the reverend.

"No," she said. "She needs to stay. I want her to know, to be afraid if necessary, afraid enough to protect her life. Go on, we need to hear this."

"It's the most terrible," he said. "They are looking for clansmen. I heard the Duke of Cumberland say to his men, 'If you think they are in a home, burn it down. If you think they are protecting a clansman, kill them. If they have food, take it. Take their cattle as well. We will soon occupy Fort Augustus, and all cattle are to be brought there to be sold. All soldiers will share in these profits. Tell your men this.' I heard this from Cumberland himself. They are trying to take away all our food, cattle, grain, chickens, anything, so we Highlanders die. They are trying to starve us out of existence!"

"Mum," Marion asked, "the lobsters, the English troops ... they are to be rewarded for stealing all we have and burning down our homes?"

Reverend Hay looked at Elizabeth and answered, "Aye, child. And raping is an extra that they do for free. When they leave, if you are not lucky enough to be dead, you may soon be."

The reverend looked at each of them. "Please, insofar as your dear departed Ranald, forgive my comment earlier, that he thankfully died, but his wounds were mortal. I am sorry for your loss and all of Scotland's, too. What I meant is that I am thankful they could do no more harm to him."

Elizabeth understood and held Marion's hand.

"You will need to leave, and soon," he said. "You may have a day or two, possibly a week, longer than the others. To most, your glen is still unknown, but not for long. If you can get to your clan, they may help you get to the colonies, though this may no longer be possible. Most of our clan leaders have died supporting Prince Charles or are running for their very lives. If you are lucky enough to escape, you may be indentured for a few years to pay off your fares."

He was quiet and thought more. "If not the colonies, maybe to France. They are our allies and know of our prince's attempts to regain his throne. If all else fails, I may be able to enlist the help of a lord who is sympathetic to our plea."

The reverend shook his head. "I wish my life were taken as well. I have prayed, asking for strength. Why was I spared when all others have lost their lives?" He began to weep. "Even surgeons who I saw help the dying, they rounded them up and put them in prison. Young boys, as well!"

He stood up and laid his hands on each of them, and said a prayer. "God be merciful," he said at the end.

He got back on his horse. "I will remain in contact, I promise, though it may not be directly. If you leave, stay off the main roads. Travel at night, but be wary of the soldiers who sneak out on their own."

Marion, crying, watched him ride off and looked at her mother. "What are we to do?"

Elizabeth dried her own tears and said plainly, "I do not know. But we must think. Come with me."

Marion went inside with her mother, her young world crashing inward. Her father, gone. Her home, their home for over a hundred years, would soon be burned. Their cattle would be captured and sent to slaughter to feed the English. Marion's tears turned to sobs.

"Marion," her mother snapped. "I need you." She looked sternly into her daughter's eyes. "We must stay strong and think clearly." Then she hugged Marion to her. "It's what your *da* would want!"

"Now, again tell me of our lineage," Elizabeth said, hoping to bring clarity to her daughter's thoughts.

Marion sniffled, at first unable to speak, then took a deep breath. The words stuck briefly in her throat. "From Marion, to Elizabeth, to ... Oh mother, again?" she said, her normal stubbornness coming back momentarily. Her mother smiled, pleased at her daughter's strength.

"Then tell me of the life of Lady Christian. We must always be as strong as her. "

Marion began, still sobbing occasionally. "She was born in 1273 at Turnberry Castle to Robert the Bruce, the Sixth Lord of Annandale."

"Excellent," Elizabeth said.

Marion continued, recalling each piece of Lady Christian's life as her mother asked. "She lived through the Great Cause and Scotland's struggle for independence. She was captured at Tain as she tried to escape to Orkney and then to her sister's in Norway."

"From there?" Elizabeth urged.

"She was taken to the Gilbertine, where she was held prisoner until freed by her brother, King Robert, after winning the Battle at Bannockburn."

"Good child," Elizabeth said. "After this?"

"She defended Kildrummy Castle at the age of sixty-two until her husband, Sir Andrew Moray, arrived, and he and his men defeated David III of Strathbogie at the Battle of Culblean, forever removing King Balliol or his sons' attempts at regaining the throne of Scotland."

"Yes. And how long did she live?"

"She outlived all of her brothers and sisters, except the dowager queen of Norway. She even survived the great sickness, until she died at the age of eighty-four," Marion replied, her voice no longer shaky.

Elizabeth smiled. "Good. That's my girl. Your knowledge of our lineage is as good as my own. Your father, as the leader of our clan, would want us to be strong, to one day strike back, even if it only means that we survive when all others perish. We must do this. Can you help me with this?" Elizabeth asked.

Marion nodded her head.

"Och, *mo cridhe*, daughter of my heart! How I love thee!"

She held her daughter closely, cooing words of love into her daughter's hair. Then, pulling away gently, Elizabeth knew what she must do next. Going inside, she took an aged walnut box from its hiding place. Marion watched with interest, knowing what it contained. For more than four hundred years, it had been passed from mother to daughter. She watched as her mother opened it reverently, then, looking over at her daughter, closed it.

"This is for you, Marion," she said, as she handed it to her.

"But, Mum," she replied, "it's not my sixteenth birthday yet."

"I know, *mo cridhe*," Elizabeth said, "but our plans have changed."

Marion took the box gently from her mother and opened it. Inside, nestled on soft linen, were the earrings and necklace that were now to be hers.

"Oh, Mum!" Marion said. "They are so beautiful!"

"Aye, child, they truly are. I know your da wanted to be here for this special day. He would be so proud! But alas, that is not to be. Now, kneel down."

Marion obeyed, kneeling on the rug before her mother. Elizabeth took out the necklace and gently clasped it around her daughter's neck. Then she picked up each earring and placed them on her daughter's ears, proclaiming as was done to her seventeen years before: "Arise! Daughter of Scotland, and know the generations before you and those that go through you. Know you are descended from their love and their love of Scotland. You, my daughter, are a Scot!"

Marion beamed with pride. She would never forget this day or the memory of her mother placing the necklace and earrings on her. Nor would she ever forget her words. Marion would remember and share this joy when it was time to pass this birthright to her own daughter.

Elizabeth took Marion's hand and said, "Now, *mo cridhe*, I must ask of you something that no other mother in our lineage has ever had to ask her daughter. Your earrings we can hide. But your necklace ... I fear it is something we may be caught with and lose. Or even worse."

Marion sensed her mother's meaning as she said this. Being caught with their jewelry could lead to their death. "Oh, Mum, are you sure?" she asked, "I've only had them a few moments!"

"Child, I am not sure of anything! But these are only things, no matter how important they are to us. What I am sure of is that we must leave immediately. You heard the good reverend. Now, I want you to take off your *leine* and sew the earrings into the hem. Do it well, so they will be difficult for even you to find."

Marion gathered what she needed, and then spent the next hour slowly and carefully doing what her mother had asked, pushing the material around each, until it was done. She eyed her work, then handed her *leine* to her mother for inspection.

"Nicely done. Beautiful! Now, hand me the necklace."

Marion did, and watched sadly as her mother placed it into a small leather bag, and then set the bag into a small crock. She then heated up some pitch and slowly poured it over the bag, hiding and protecting it.

"We shall wait till it cools, and then we can pack it," Elizabeth added.

Marion put her *leine* back on, made lunch, and then gathered food for their journey. After lunch, Elizabeth took her mallet and smashed the crock, exposing the congealed lump of pitch. She placed it inside a small bag they were packing. Marion's eyes filled with tears, and she saw her mother blinking back her own as she did this.

"I know this is hard, *mo cridhe*. But know our very lives may depend on hiding this. And we will come back for it if at all possible!"

Marion nodded but felt in her heart that neither of them would see it again. She ran her hands over the walnut box, lovingly oiled over the centuries since Lady Christian had given it to her ancestor almost four hundred years ago.

"Come, child, we must go," Elizabeth said. "We must try to get to Lossiemouth, but first we must go to Kildrummy. That is where we will hide the necklace."

Sadly, they walked away from the only home they had ever known, leaving the walnut box on the mantle.

"With luck," Elizabeth said, "we will be out of Scotland very soon. Reverend Hay said for us to stay off the roads. He fears for us, to be sure, but I doubt anywhere will be safe. With the Duke of Cumberland setting up headquarters at Fort Augustus, the entire area will nay be safe for a while."

They talked quietly as they walked.

"Mum, if our prince is trying to escape, where do you think the safest places would be?"

Elizabeth thought a moment. "I guess our prince would do best to get to the doorstep of France. But getting there from here is directly in the path of where everyone will be searching for him."

Marion interrupted her mother. "Isn't that like us now?"

Elizabeth smiled. "Thankfully, not quite. They are looking for him and not us specifically. We will be caught only if we are not careful. Or," she shuddered, "if they do something we don't anticipate. Oh, child, I don't know. But we are safer trying than waiting at home for the day they discover us."

It was not a long journey to Kildrummy, and they talked quietly as they traveled. Elizabeth shared what it was like when she had received the necklace and earrings from her mother.

"It was on the night of my sixteenth birthday. We had come home from a huge ceilidh, it was. Da and Mum were there, and so was my granny. Aye, it was wonderful. They had always told me I was related to someone very special in our past, but never said who."

Elizabeth curled a wisp of her thick auburn hair in her fingers, as she recalled that night.

"It was the same box. The same place behind the mantle where we hide things. That night, when Da reached up and handed it to Mum, I thought my heart would burst! In all my years, I never knew it was there! Mum had me kneel before her, just as you did, with Da and Granny watching. I could barely catch my breath! Then Mum knelt and held my hand as she began telling me our story. She stood and put the necklace on me and then the earrings, and then said, 'Arise, Daughter of Scotland!' Mum then told me how they had been passed from mother to daughter ever since. Each daughter had been named Marion or Elizabeth in honor of our ancestors and our heritage."

Elizabeth took her daughter's hand. "I never felt like that again … not 'til the day you were born. But I made a promise shortly after: that when it was my turn, I would tell you the whole story as you grew, so it would be a part of you …something you would memorize forever, so when it was your turn to pass on our gift, you would do the same thing for your daughter."

Marion smiled, happy that her mother had shared this. Then she asked, "Why are we going to Lossiemouth? We know no one there."

"I have never told you this," said Elizabeth, "but before I was married to your da, there was a young lad of title from Lossiemouth. He and I were," Elizabeth smiled at the memory, "fond of one another. He wished to marry me, but his parents knew our family had willingly given up our title."

Elizabeth continued, "He would have married me anyway, but there was a lady from Aberdeen. His parents pushed the idea of marriage to her, as her family had money and he the title. So, it was arranged, and once they were married, she moved from Aberdeen to Lossiemouth. He with his title, and she with her family's money."

Elizabeth reflected back on this time, seventeen years ago. "When we parted, he told me I had his undying love forever. I knew this to be true, though I thought I would never see him again. In some worlds, lass, money is the only language. I understood this, and within that year, I met and married your father."

Marion thought of this before she asked, "Do you still love him? Do you think he will help us?"

"Och, child, I nay think of him in this fashion any longer. Your father was the only man in my life. To answer your other question, I know not, but we can hope."

They continued talking through the night, until they saw Kildrummy Castle slowly materialize through the morning fog. Drawing nearer, Marion heard her mother's sharp intake of breath and the quiet word that said all she felt. "No!" Her sadness became mixed with anger as they drew closer.

"It's in ruins now! Oh, child, her walls were so beautiful! My granny used to tell me how it looked when she was a wee lass. She would never have dreamed that it would one day be scavenged."

She saw a cart full of blocks recently dug out and left by someone. Elizabeth knew they would be back to finish taking what they needed. From the way it looked, it seemed it was an ongoing process of stripping down the castle. They walked slowly through the ruins, overgrown with vegetation.

"When was it abandoned, Mum?" Marion asked.

"Before I was born, child," Elizabeth replied. "Bobbing John Erskine was the last tenant, and aye, child, I know your next question. He was called that because he changed from one political side to the other. Not unlike our King Robert, going from side to side until he took the Scot crown. I do know John Erskine led the battle of Sheriffmuir for the Jacobites before he was exiled to France. That's all I can tell you." Elizabeth continued staring at the castle. "I never would have guessed it would be treated so."

She pointed to an area at the rear. "This is where the Great Hall was. Around two hundred years ago, they built the Elphinstone Tower just to the west."

Elizabeth took her daughter's hand and said proudly, "This is where we are from, child. Not directly; we were not Mar. But our family precedes the Elphinstones."

Then Elizabeth walked to where she thought Lady Christian had buried the jewels.

"Here we are," she said, pointing to the ground between them. "Six steps from here, and six steps from ... Och, child. I dinna ken! It should be in this area!"

"Mum," Marion replied. "If the new tower is here, and ..."

Suddenly, they heard voices. It was a group of soldiers who had started their day early and were heading west. They had no intentions of stopping at an old castle that was being torn apart for its stonework. There was money to be made, and they needed to get to Fort Augustus as soon as possible.

"Shh," Elizabeth said, listening as the men's footsteps grew closer and then started to recede.

"They are not interested in us," her mother finally said softly, "but we shan't let them prove otherwise. Let's stay here for a moment longer, to be sure." They passed without incident.

"We were careless," Elizabeth said when they were finally beyond hearing range. "We must always think and be careful. We may not be so lucky next time."

Resuming their search, Marion found the likely spot. "Mum, I believe it should be here, in this area."

Elizabeth nodded. "Yes, you are right!"

Both got down on their knees and began digging with their fingers, looking for a tile that was a little looser than the others. After a few minutes, Marion's fingers began aching. She looked for something to help her dig. Finding a rusted piece of sword blade, she began anew, searching for a tile that had long ago been loosened from its foundation. Prying at each, she found one.

"Mum," she called softly yet excitedly, "I've found it!"

Elizabeth came to her and smiled.

"Do you think this is it?" Marion asked.

"I don't know," she replied. "But we need to make haste, child, before the scavengers return. Let's dig down now and bury the necklace so we can be gone!"

Marion looked at her mother with sadness. "You don't think there's a chance we can get it out of Scotland with us? Oh, Mum, I just got it and I don't want to lose it!"

"Och, child, I know, I know. I don't want to leave it here, either! I have only had it for a few years myself. But I do know that many will kill for it."

She took Marion's hand. "Know this in your heart: We will be alive! One day, hopefully, you can come back and claim it anew. It will always be yours!"

Elizabeth felt she needed to remind Marion of all she still possessed. "Show me once more where you hid your earrings."

She looked closely at the hem of Marion's *leine* and admired her needlework.

"Nice, child. Very nice! No one can even tell there is anything there. And, sweetheart, know this: You will be alive to pass them on to your daughter!"

"Thank you, Mum, I know." She gave her mother a hug. "I did my best so no one could tell they are there."

No one—no man especially—would be caught touching a lady's leine. And for the ones who didn't know this, Marion had a surprise for them. She reached down to touch her father's *sgian-dubh* she had hidden under her leine. Elizabeth saw where her daughter's hand went and what it outlined.

"What have you got?" she asked immediately. "Show me."

Marion pulled out her father's prized knife—the one he always wore in his stocking.

"I took it before we left. I didn't want to leave it. I thought we might need it."

Elizabeth looked disapprovingly at her daughter, then reflected. "Keep it. Your *da* would be pleased to know we have it. Hopefully, we won't need it."

They buried the necklace in the hole they had dug. It was deep … more than four hands. They covered it with dirt, packing it down before covering it, almost reverently, with the tightly fitting tile. They tapped everything down and brushed away any remaining dirt. Hugging each other, they looked down and admired their work.

Marion looked at her mother, and said softly. "It will be ours again, Mum. I promise this to you and our family. If I am not able, then I will tell my daughter, so she can tell her daughter, until the day we can reclaim the necklace that is ours."

Elizabeth looked at Marion and knew what she said would one day be true. "I know this, my love. I hope to be with you on that day."

They walked from the castle and did not look back. They ate their breakfast in the woodlands to the north of Kildrummy. Pulling their *leines* up around their shoulders, both fell quickly asleep.

They awoke just before sunset and enjoyed a small supper of bread and cheese, both silently thankful that the cover of darkness would be upon them soon. In the distance, they could hear the voices of men scavenging the castle.

"It will take us an extra night to make Lossiemouth," Elizabeth said, "but I don't mind trading an extra night's travel for one of safety."

Marion knew her mother was right. It was better to take their time and, if the surprise at Kildrummy taught them anything, they would need to be quiet. That night, they traveled quickly and easily, avoiding the occasional escaping Highlander, darting from tree to tree en route to safety. They also avoided the occasional soldier who had snuck out in search of bounty and anything else he could find.

The next night they ate lightly, conserving their food, and had gone only three hours before Marion stopped quickly. She put her hand out to stop her mother and touched her finger to her mouth. "Shh," she motioned, and then pointed.

Listening intently, they heard the occasional laughter of men and then the sounds of cows complaining as they were being moved. They waited until the cows could no longer be heard and all was silent. Walking quietly, they came to a small Highland home that was now smoldering. The thatch had fallen inside the walls hours earlier and covered the interior in a black, crackling charcoal. All signs of life that had made the small house a home, were now gone.

"Mum, why?" Marion asked softly.

Elizabeth had no answer. They and their clans were simply to be uprooted and discarded, like flowers that were no longer desired from a well-tended garden.

"Let us be gone from this place," Elizabeth said.

They walked away until they saw a section of fence that had been depleted of its stones, and then piled anew, directly in their path. A hand, pale and withered, stuck out from the stones, as though trying to catch their attention.

"Oh, Marion!" Elizabeth said, as she ran to the cairn and tried to feel for life in the nameless man's hand.

"Help me, child," she said. They both began moving rocks aside until Elizabeth could touch his wrist. Searching for a pulse, she found none; his hand slowly losing the warmth of life. He had been stoned and left to die. They looked at the haphazard pile of rocks strewn around him, thankful he was beyond pain.

"Let's take more rocks from the fence and cover him. It's the least we can do to provide him a better resting place."

They carefully laid stones one by one over his head and chest until he was almost covered.

"This will keep the animals from him."

It was Marion who noticed the small object that caught the light of the moon. Peering down, she called to her mother. "Mum, what is this?"

Elizabeth came to her daughter's side and looked carefully at what had caught her eye.

"How did we not see this before? Let's get these rocks off him," Elizabeth said.

They did, until the pin was fully exposed and Elizabeth could grasp it. "It's the pin of his clan," she said, removing it from his shirt. "It may have been the reason he was killed. If we see Reverend Hay, we should give it to him. He will surely know who he was and can give his soul a few words of comfort. Let's cover him back up."

They resumed stacking the stones over him, completing the burial.

"Rest in peace, clansman," Elizabeth said, and they both crossed themselves.

They traveled the rest of the night, with little to interrupt their journey except the occasional flapping of wings from a startled bird or the patter of a rabbit scurrying for cover.

The third night began nicely, with only a fox scampering across their path, unfettered from worry as he carried a rabbit home to his family. They were almost to the town of Elgin, where the smell of oak burning over nightly fires wafted the smell of dinners, enticing them to stay.

"Come, child," Elizabeth said. "We are so close. We could be there by morning if we don't stop."

Marion looked back toward the fox and imagined the rabbit slowly turning on a spit, its juices dripping into their fire. Elizabeth smiled, reading her daughter's thoughts, "I'm sure the fox would put up a fight."

They both laughed for the first time in days and pushed on, ignoring the reminders of their home in the evening fires of Elgin as best they could. Seeing no night travelers, they decided to keep with the main road, though near the woods, for the rest of their journey.

Then softly, barely audible, a twig snapped, as though someone had shifted their weight.

# TWENTY-ONE

## Peavey: Intro

Peavey of Southwark was born in the year of His Majesty, 1721. He had no last name, just Peavey. His mother and aunt, both strumpets who worked the streets, had a rented flat where they alternated shifts and shared the raising of this little "accident." Such things as this happened in their profession, and both looked forward to the day when he turned five and, the good Lord willing, he could be sold to the master sweep, one of their better customers. Most sweeps were aware of children born to the local doves and knew that most were anxious to be rid of the extra mouth to feed as soon as possible. And for only a few shillings, a sweep could get a young lad small enough to climb all the chimneys.

It was just three weeks after Peavey turned five that his mother died from the pox. His aunt, due to recent enforcement by the local constables, was unable to sell him to their sweep, and was forced to keep him. Peavey's aunt had little time for the raising of what she had been stuck with. She would make young Peavey earn his keep.

That was for certain. She despised the extra work he caused, and was frustrated that there was no father who would claim him. That option, however, was exhausted long ago, like the quick deed that had caused him in the first place. His father could be almost anyone in Southwark.

Peavey had always felt her animosity and instinctively stayed clear of her as much as possible. Hungry most of the time, the six-year-old wandered the streets, dreaming of having parents who loved him and gave him a warm meal and a kiss good night.

Soon, his dreams faded, and the reality of having to work became his constant companion. Most of the orphans he knew were working and were not given the option of schooling. Learning a quality trade with a printer or an apothecary was equally out of the question. Their lot in life was mud larking at low tide, where they collected anything of value from the foul-smelling Thames, into which everything was thrown to rot and rarely made it to sea. Or, as he did now, collecting shit and piss—or, as his mates called them, pure and pish—for the tanneries, which they used to make leather.

Each morning began before dawn, with a small portion of a loaf and water to wash it down. Luck would occasionally supplement his meager breakfast with a bit of potato that was beginning to spoil or even an apple that he could steal from an unwary vendor. Peavey grabbed the small leather bag he kept outside the door. It swarmed with flies, attracted by the remnants of bird and dog excrement from prior days. He whistled as he began his day and thought anew of his dream. He would be apprenticed by his father to the owner of a boat that traded between France and England, just like Sir Francis Drake did a hundred and fifty years ago. The boat would one day be willed to him when his master died, and Peavey would travel around the world, claiming all things in the name of England. "Sir Peavey," the papers would exclaim, "has found a new land and treasures he has claimed in the honor of His Majesty."

Peavey loved this dream, and it helped to while away his day as he watched for the occasional friend and searched out the areas where dogs typically relieved themselves. Throwing their droppings into the bag, he would then run to the bridges and buildings where the pigeons roosted and add their droppings as well, before heading to the tannery. Most times, he would have it gathered before the other boys had even gotten started. Then he would switch over to street sweeping.

At that job, he would tip his hat respectfully and quickly clean the path before a rich customer crossed. "Good day, sir," or "Good day, m'Lady," he'd say, as he bent low and quickly whisked away any dirt that might soil the fabric of a rich lady's dress or the bottom of a shoe. "If there's any service you need, please feel free to ask for ol' Peavey!" he'd say and hold out his cap, hoping for a pence. Industrious and hardworking, young Peavey learned how to earn as much as possible and how to get customers to remember him.

It was a slow process, and it was never enough money. If he could only add to his day by chimney sweeping, but he knew he had to wait until he was at least seven to do that. It was dirty work, and most of the lads who did it coughed for days afterward. Thankfully, Peavey thought, it did not smell like the tannery, where his friend Cyril worked, processing the pure and rotting skins. Nor did it smell like the Thames. Peavey still recalled the time he cut his foot on a piece of glass when he first started "larking," and it festered something terrible. His aunt was forced to call a doctor to visit him, Peavey reflected; one could mistakenly have thought she cared.

"You can get used to anything," Cyril would say, when Peavey asked him why he worked at a tannery. The tanneries were generally located on the outskirts of town, where the stench would not offend the rich folk. "It's not just the pure and the skins, either. It's the brains and the pish that we use, too," Cyril would say, shrugging his shoulders, as he ate his morning loaf. "It's not so bad after awhile. I don't mind it. You can get used to anything."

Nineteen years later, Private Peavey was still able to recall his friend's words. *Yes, one can get used to anything,* he thought.

He had come to watch Private Hendricks be hanged for the crime of spying for the rebels, a charge that Sir Francis Drake had whispered into Peavey's pox-ridden thoughts. Peavey liked it immediately and put it into play. He placed his last month's pay inside Hendricks's clothes and then informed the major of the "spy" in their ranks. "I saw Hendricks talking to the Highlanders," he had reported, "and then he took some money." This would teach him, Peavey thought—permanently. Never again would he snitch on another, as he did on Peavey in Southwark.

Ten minutes after the rope dropped, Hendrick's body had settled down. It usually took a few minutes for them to quit moving about. All was going well, until that damn minister's plea for mercy—using the Duke of Cumberland's birthday—got him cut down. Rank has its privileges, he knew, especially when it comes to life-and-death decisions. The same type of decision, Peavey reflected, is what got him stuck in His Lordship's army. He watched as Private Hendricks slowly came to, though dazed for quite a while, even after the surgeon let his blood to expedite his recovery.

Peavey didn't care, and left. There was still Culloden that had to be fought, and no one knew who would survive, not yet at least. He would find another way to end that snitch's life. He was thankful that his being sent to Drummossie Moor had led him to Hendricks, and that they were both in the duke's service. Peavey would pray on it again tonight. Hopefully, Sir Francis would guide him once more. With his help, Hendricks would not survive the battle. Peavey would pray extra hard, to make certain of this.

"It's as I say, sure enough," Peavey overheard one of the corporals tell his buddy. "After we take on these stiff-necked Highlanders"—he used the same words as the Duke of Cumberland to describe the clans of northern Scotland—"we're to exterminate them once and for all, beginning right here in Drummossie Moor. After that," the corporal added, pleased to see the audience that was beginning to surround him, "His Lordship thinks they'll run north. We're to stay here, while our troops chase after them. Afterward, we're to march to Fort Augustus and begin gathering up their cattle, horses, and sheep. 'Starve 'em out,' says His Lordship. And what we don't eat ourselves, we can sell and get a cut of the profits. Can you imagine our names alongside the duke's and being remembered for an eternity?"

*Sir Peavey, you need to listen.*

The voice of Sir Francis Drake passed clearly through Peavey's mind, cutting through the fog that had been present since his mercury treatments. *The duke has heard your plea. That strumpet Maggie and those like her will pay for giving you the pox. The duke wants to help you. We can take care of them after we take care of Hendricks. You'd like this, wouldn't you?*

Private Peavey smiled and listened intently to the corporal's speech. He liked the fact that the duke and Sir Francis had Peavey's interests at heart. They would help him with Hendricks and Maggie and make things right. The Highland women would be theirs for the taking, their men killed, and anything of value kept. Then they would burn their homes. The rest, still hiding in the hills, would be starved out. Yes, Sir Francis must have shared Peavey's plight with the duke. Things were going to be better. Much better than he first thought when he was put in His Lordship's army.

*Sir Peavey*, the voice echoed in his head. Peavey looked from side to side, curious if others heard the same voice that he did. *I only wish there were more men of your mettle. You'd have made a good sailor.*

Peavey stood taller as he walked toward his solitary tent, saluting the soldiers he passed. The soldiers all gave him a wide berth, the stench of his pox assuring this. They watched him, each shaking their head. A weird, absent smile formed across Peavey's lips as he listened to something only he could hear, nodding his head to a silent, invisible tutor.

It was shortly after Peavey turned seven that he approached Master Higgins about becoming a chimney sweep. He had heard of Master Higgins from his aunt and, summoning his courage, approached him.

"What's this? Young Peavey has finally come back? How old are you now? I imagine you still want to be a sweep, yes?"

"Aye sir," Peavey replied. "I do. I'll be eight soon enough."

Higgins recalled turning Peavey's aunt down more than two years ago. There was no way he could take in her sister's bastard, even though doing so would curry favor from one of Southwark's best strumpets. His lads were typically indentured to him through the church for a full seven years, until they became journeymen. It would be his duty to provide a place for them to sleep, plus their meals. Higgins looked at young Peavey, impressed with his ambition, and considered his request.

"Well, now, it's quite the job you will be learning, and my time is valuable. You come back in a week, and I'll let you know my decision."

"If you please, sir," Peavey replied, "I could start tomorrow. I need the work, sir. Me aunt, why, I'm the only money we gets to eat off of, now that she's sick and can't go out at night. I already collect the pure, lark, and street sweep, but it's not enough."

Peavey stared at Master Higgins and waited for an answer.

Higgins stared intently at the young lad, as visions of himself passed through his head. Visions of Peavey's mother didn't hurt either, and he smiled at the recollection.

"Well, my little shite collector, you have a way about you. Here is what I can do. Because I knew your mother, bless her departed soul, I will train you until the day you become a journeyman. At that time, I will release you, and you can work for any master in Southwark. I'll not pay you, nor will you live here with me and the other sweeps, but for every chimney you clean, you can keep the soot to sell on your own. You should make a little for every bushel you collect."

Peavey happily agreed, and that night, he stood before the hot fire in Master Higgin's tub of brine, his tears quelled with determination as he endured his first "lesson."

"Stand closer. You'll need to toughen up those knees and elbows."

Higgins scrubbed each until Peavey's flesh was raw.

"You won't want your first lesson to be like mine," he said. "My master didn't do this, and by the time I was halfway through, I was bleeding like a stuck pig, I was. Now, we'll give your skin a couple days to heal, and then do it again and again 'til you get some callouses built up."

Every other night for almost three weeks, Peavey returned to get his elbows and knees scoured until they were raw and, finally, turned to calluses. On the final night, Higgins pinched Peavey's knees and elbows, making sure they were tough enough. Pleased, he said, "I've got you your first job, tomorrow night. Good Mr. Baker makes bread every day, starts early, and demands a good job. We need to be done by the time he comes in."

That next night, as they laid out their tools, Higgins reminded Peavey. "Remember what I've told you. Never let your knees get to your chest. Always keep them below you. You get your knees up by your chest and you'll suffocate. If it happens on the way up, you'll knock down more soot, and it will get in your lungs. You don't want to die in there, do you?"

Peavey adamantly shook his head and remembered this for years, even after Master Higgins died.

"It's cool enough now," Higgins said, though Peavey thought the chimney was still quite hot from the baker's fire earlier in the day. Peavey looked at the small opening that he was to crawl up.

"You're lucky this is a bigger one. My first ones were smaller, barely a nine by nine brick," Higgins said, proud of himself and his prior work. "Remember, scrape on the way up. I'll have the soot gathered and bagged as you do. Then, on the way down, you can use the brush and it will be easier to breathe."

Peavey crawled through the entrance and, like a worm, shimmied sideways. Immediately the soot fell into his eyes, and he stopped. Clearing them the best he could, he pulled his cap down low and began using the scraper ahead of his body, loosening the soot before he went any further. Then, at the spot where the flue turned up sharply, he began using his knees and elbows to lodge his body against the walls before he started scraping. He loosened the soot in small sheets to fall to the bottom, until he had reached the top and the blue sky. Breathing in the cool air for a few minutes, he began his journey down, occasionally using the brush to get the loose deposits he missed on the way up.

"A clean chimney, mind you!" Higgins hollered up to Peavey, his voice echoing. "You make sure you get every bit. I don't want any complaints of fire due to shoddy work."

Peavey didn't need the reminder. He did a quality job the first time.

For three years, Peavey continued learning from Higgins, giving each chimney his best work, and did so until the day Master Higgins died.

"It were the sweepers' cough," Peavey said to young Tommy, the newest apprentice.

"I heard tell he had the soot wart downst below," Tommy added. They both heard of this malady and how it went inside a body.

"What the bloody 'ell do I do now?" Peavey asked. Tommy would go to Master Arthur and continue his apprenticeship there. Peavey had not become an apprentice, but knew how to do it as well as any apprentice ever did. Unless other options presented themselves, Peavey, at the age of ten, had to find other work to do, and soon.

For two weeks, Peavey approached every shopkeeper, only to be turned down. Broke and hungry, still carrying the tools left to him by Higgins, Peavey pleaded with the same Mr. Baker whose chimney had been his first job.

"I'll give you a try, but I will need it completed before 5:00 a.m.," warned Mr. Baker. "I open up for business at 7:00 a.m. and"—he slammed the oven door shut to punctuate his point—"I need two hours to get the oven going and my breads ready. I'm only hiring you because you worked for Higgins. It had better be ready, or I'll take it out of your hide."

Peavey promised it would be and, meeting him at midnight, once more reassured him it would be done. Laying out the canvas, scraper, and brushes Mr. Higgins had left him, he stripped down. Off came everything, until he was naked. He eyed the chimney carefully, recalling its shape. It was the first chimney he had ever done with Higgins, a large one at that, with a two-foot riser. Standing on a chair, he first threw his brush and scraper into the flue. Then, reaching up to the chimney that was still warm from earlier in the day, he grasped it as best he could and pulled himself into the first ninety-degree angle. This part was easy, and he began scraping each inch ahead of him, before pulling his way into the next section and the next, to where it went straight up. This was the tight part, and Peavey recalled its difficulty from when he was seven. He was glad he had stripped naked, needing the extra room that his larger frame now took.

Turning his body diagonally into the flue, he angled himself slowly into the vertical shaft. Peavey could see the stars overhead. This was the part of the job he liked. It was a pleasant view and distraction from a dirty job. Plus it always smelled better than working for the tannery. He paused a moment, pulled his hat down over his eyes, and put his mind to the sea, where he was sure he would one day find gold and silver for the English crown and be knighted for his efforts, like Sir Francis Drake. *Sir Peavey*, the papers would say.

Smiling at his favorite dream, Peavey grabbed the scraper and started. He scraped each side before pushing himself up three inches at a time, and resumed his scraping on a new segment. It had not been cleaned since he'd done it three years ago, and because it was used daily, the soot fell down thick over his shoulders in huge sheets of black powder, dropping to the bottom of the flue in soft thuds. Occasionally, he would find a deposit of creosote that needed a little more work, and he took the time to get it perfect before moving on. Peavey worked quickly and quietly, and two and a half hours later, he reached the top, thankful for the fresh air he was able to breathe. Now all he had to do was go back down, bag up the soot, clean up his mess, and go home. Peavey was pleased with a job well done, knowing he would now have a little extra for the soot that he could sell, plus what this job would pay. He was tired and sore, and his knees, back, and elbows were scraped raw by the interior of the flue. He would collect his money tomorrow.

Shimmying down the flue and brushing the occasional spot that needed it, Peavey hadn't concerned himself with the soot that built up at the bottom. There had been no one, no Mr. Higgins, to stand on the chair and reach in to pull it out as it fell down the flue. The entire bottom of the flue of this sixty-foot, four-sided chimney, which he had carefully cleaned, was now filled, having built up with each scrape of his tool. Unthinking, Peavey dropped the last three feet into the soot, sending it immediately into the air, surrounding him in a thick black cloud. Peavey panicked, tried to stop breathing, and tried to outlast the powdery soot cloud as it hung in the air, but he could not. He opened his eyes, quickly covering them in a coarse, dry layer. He cried out in fear, inhaling the soot deep into his lungs, and began clawing at the bricks, ripping off his fingernails in a desperate attempt to get away from the cloud and inch his way back up the shaft to fresh air. But his coughing, a long continuous hacking, slowed his every attempt. His thoughts raced as he climbed. *Why didn't I think of the soot?*

Inch by inch, he crawled, until he could go no more. The light of the stars was now peering through the black veil that was trying to consume him and pull him back down. Peavey felt the coolness of the air above him, and he lodged himself tight against each wall to keep from falling back down. Then he did the one thing Higgins told him to never do: he pulled his legs upward toward his chest. It was Peavey's lucky day, however, as the chimney above him had already been cleaned, and no more soot could fall down on him. Peavey, weak and faint from the exertion and lack of air, passed out, his knees wedged tight against his chest, locking him in.

"Peavey?" Mr. Baker hollered up the chimney. "Damn it, boy, answer me!"

He had come into the shop at 5:00 a.m., ready to begin his day, when he saw the empty bag and the chair propped in the chimney.

"God damn it, boy," Mr. Baker called a last time, angry. Peavey's eyes fluttered open, slowly coming to, his chest compressed tight against the back wall and his knees. With the scraper still on his chest, and barely able to draw a breath, Peavey slowly extended the fingers of his right hand until he was able to push the scraper over his side. It clanged on each wall until it hit bottom, landing with a soft thud in the soot.

"Damn you, boy!" Mr. Baker called up. "I told you I had to start at 5:00 a.m.! Damn you!"

He rushed out of his bakery to get help.

After a work crew took apart the chimney and pulled him to safety, Peavey lay naked in the dirt, each of his fingernails ripped off. The lash from Mr. Baker's whip went down and down again, each time cutting him deeply.

"You pathetic, little bastard, I'll take the repairs for the chimney and my lost day out of your hide!"

Afterward, Peavey lay on the ground, too weak to move. For the first time in his life, he cried. He was taken home, where his aunt stayed with him for the first week of the three that it took for him to get better. Peavey's lungs and eyes were never the same, and he wore the marks on his back from the lash for the rest of his life.

It was a slow process, the lessons in Peavey's life, but they took hold. Things that were not of his control, he learned to deal with. Things that he could control, he made work. He had no control of the way his aunt felt toward him, nor of the "bastard" label his mother had left him. Peavey did learn, however, that even a bastard could make money, and he would do this no matter what it took.

Peavey began to see opportunities in everything he did. It became more than just needing to stop the pangs of hunger; eleven-year-old Peavey became calculating. He knew there were other boys who faced the same challenges as he and were equally hungry and desperate. Peavey would use this need. He began spreading the word that he would train any boy from the age of seven and up to be a sweep, and that they could live with their parents instead of being sold to a sweep for a few shillings. He would charge only a small amount of what they earned, and he would always send out two boys at a time: the younger boy to do the sweeping and the older boy to tend to the cleanup and help as needed.

It took a while to change perceptions, but Peavey showed them where each boy could bring in money on a daily basis, instead of a cash price for being sold. It wasn't long before he was given a grudging respect and even admired by some of the parents. "There's young Master Peavey. For a bastard, he's done aw'right for 'is-self." He was equally despised by the master sweeps for stealing young boys who would normally go to them. Peavey didn't care; he would make money for their service, as would their parents.

Soon, he was making more than two guineas a week—more than most orphans his age ever dreamt of. He even hired a group of older boys to protect him. By the age of fourteen, he was making enough to afford his own flat at the local pub and was known to spurn the advances of the strumpets.

"Er'll be no bastards on my account," he was heard to say on more than one occasion.

# TWENTY-TWO
## Peavey: Scapegoat

Peavey sat back in his chair, loving the darkness of the tavern and the coolness of the ale as it went down his throat. He had already dispatched his friends with their work for the morrow, and after finishing their ales, they left. Peavey slumped noticeably in his chair. The hot days of August could make his occasional headaches unbearable, and today the twenty-four-year-old had endured one of the worst ones. Emily, his dearest friend, could see the strained look on his face and came up behind him, rubbing his temples.

"Still bad?" she asked.

Peavey nodded his head, and relaxed as her hands did their magic. This year had been particularly warm, which had made it worse.

"How are your eyes?" Emily asked.

Peavey had complained occasionally about his eyesight, beyond the usual weeping from the soot he had gotten in them years ago.

"The headaches are always worse," Peavey replied. "It makes it hard to think."

He had grown into a man who was thick of body, with short arms that seemed to cheat his large height. His blue eyes, no longer clear, still felt the continual wipe from the back of his hands. His breath came short, never deep, his lungs laboring to fuel a frame much too large for their diminished ability. Other than a couple of abscesses in his remaining teeth and a small bulbous growth on the side of his head, life for Peavey had been profitable, though not perfect. He'd done well for a bastard. Tipping his ale back to get the last drop, Peavey nodded to Emily that it was time to go.

"Not a word more," said a voice at the tavern door before it opened to allow ten sailors inside. The leader eyed the patrons. Emily started to get up, but Peavey touched her hand and motioned her to sit back down. He recognized the men as the crew of the ship that had embarked for India months ago. They had taken Devon, one of his best sweeps from years past, who, like Peavey, dreamt of going to sea. It was good to see him and to see that he was growing into a young man. But something was amiss; Peavey felt it immediately.

After months at sea, sailors were a riotous bunch and, having made home port, were ready to drink and tear apart every tavern before heading out on their next voyage, conscious or not. Peavey watched as they walked quietly to the back of the tavern and took two tables. Emily looked frustrated, wanting to leave. Flo and Molly, the two strumpets who tended clients upstairs, winked at one another and got up. Pushing up their bosoms and opening their cleavages, they walked suggestively toward their newest customers.

"Welcome home, mates," Molly said. "Can ya buy a couple lonely ladies a drink?"

The biggest man, Flanders, looked up and replied, "Get us each a pint, and keep yur damn pox to yurself."

Molly and Flo exchanged disappointed glances and walked back to the bar to get their ales. Flo elbowed Molly, whispering softly, trying to see a smile no matter how small.

"Don't worry, sweetheart. They've been at sea too long and 'ave been buggered regularly. We won't get a quid out of the lot of 'em!"

They both laughed loudly, and Molly hugged her friend. Returning with the beers, the women laughed once more between themselves, almost spilling the ales before serving them. Flanders waited impatiently until they were gone, before beginning. Peavey listened, hearing only the occasional sentence.

"Quiet!" the stocky guy said, the one with the heaviest of beards and a dark tan from years at sea. He looked at the patrons in the bar, then back to Flanders. "We don't want half of England 'earing what we got's ta say."

Each stopped talking and waited for the leader to begin their earlier conversation. Satisfied that he had their attention, Flanders began anew.

"There's no way we can get at it," he said in hushed tones. The conversations in the bar had lowered somewhat, letting Peavey hear a bit more. "And I'll be damned if I'll let a crate of jade slip away."

Each murmured their assent. "I got's me a farm already picked out, I does," the stocky man added.

His partner on the opposite side, a scar running down the side of his deeply tanned face, added, "Other than us and the captain's boy, there's no one else awares."

From what Peavey could make out, they had planned and waited patiently until they got near England. Once they were on the Thames, they made the captain's boy steal the key to the ship's locker.

A large crate of jade, destined for the finest jewelry stores in London, was thrown overboard and then carried upstream by the tide. The tide would soon go back out, and unless they acted quickly, it could be swept out to sea.

"It was the most expensive thing on board, and I'm sure the captain will know it's gone by first light," Flanders said.

He looked at the man on his left, a burly fellow of about five foot three and just as wide.

"You, Smithe. After we get this crate, you remind young Master Hendricks of what's in store for him if he blabs."

He pulled his knife from his side and laid it on the table. "Let him know what 'appens to those who snitch. How they're oft' times lost at sea, with never a soul to see wat 'appened."

Smithe nodded his head, the point made clear.

Seaman Devon Phillips, the youngest in their group and the one who Peavey knew, added quietly, his voice barely heard over those of the older sailors, "I know someone who might help. He's here now."

Each continued talking, and then, his words slowly sinking in, they turned their heads toward Devon, waiting for him to add more. He thumbed in the direction of Peavey. "He has a larking business 'ere, on the Thames. 'E could 'elp us get it."

They began arguing quietly among themselves.

"I've known him for years," Devon interrupted again. "He gave me my first sweep job 'ere in Suderk, he did," he said, pronouncing "Southwark" the way all native boys did. "Me dad trusted him for what he did for me, letting me stay home wit' me family."

"'E'll tell," said one of their group, and then another to his right, "'E'll want a cut as well!" Their voices quickly rose in volume, the ale taking effect and adding to the noise of the tavern.

"It's worth a small fortune. I'll be damned if I'll share," Smithe added.

At this, Peavey walked up, his eyes going from sailor to sailor, and each became immediately quiet. He pulled out a chair next to Devon and asked, "Mind if ol' Peavey has a sit?" He patted Devon's shoulder as he did so. "Good to see you."

Devon smiled up at Peavey. There was no reply from anyone ... just meaningful glances exchanged as Peavey sat down.

"He's right, I'll want a cut," Peavey said. "The way I see it is you can let it sit, and the longer it does gives the other larkers a chance to get it. That or the local constable."

He dabbed at his eyes with the back of his shirt and continued, organizing his thoughts. "Then no one has to worry about giving me a cut. Or, you can wait for the tide to take it back out, where it's likely to get washed out to sea or buried in the mud for years. Same answer. Or, lastly," he paused, "we could get it tonight."

He looked from one to the other, watching their faces. "We'd bust the crate," he said, now with an audience, "and lift, say, half of it. In the morning, 'Endricks—is that his name? He can run to the captain and say pirates came aboard and he was forced to give 'em the key. He can even say that a big, strong brute held 'im as they took it and then it fell overboard, hitting their boat in the process. You hear 'Endricks's cry for help as they escape, and seeing 'em, all dive into the water and try to catch 'em."

He leaned over Devon's chair and continued. "Sadly, they get away and are lost in the fog. The captain gets the broken case, 'appy as a lark to get 'alf. The rest we sells and split the profits between us. I think it being split twelve ways is not much different than it being split eleven ways. As I said, we does nothing and no one gets a thing. The only worry I see's if young 'Endricks blabs to the captain."

An assenting murmur went through the group.

"All he has to do is stick with the story. And mates," Peavey added, "if I may add one more thing? Things like this 'appen 'ere on the Thames. Accidents, we calls 'em. If it 'appens again in the future, feel free to contact ol' Peavey. I guarantee that mum's the word, and I'm always here. I'll leave you for a few minutes to decide. I'll be waiting outside."

He called to Molly and Flo to bring each of the men a pint before going out.

It didn't take long before they agreed. Shortly after midnight they arrived at a small dock on the Thames, the moon shadowing Somerset House in the background. The spring tide had carried their crate further than they'd thought, lodging it into a dead tree. They drew lots, and Flanders, Devon, and four others were left at the dock. Smithe, Dawson, Peavey, and two others rowed to where the crate was being held precariously in the tree by the strong current.

"Full moon," Smithe said, as he looked up at Somerset House, its shape easily distinguished in the light. "We could as well be doing this in the middle of the bloody day."

He shook his head. Peavey nodded agreement as he stood on the edge of the boat, the current pushing it quickly toward the dead tree.

Bringing their boat closer, the rowers fought the current until they were able to throw a rope around the tree. Peavey carefully balanced himself and threw a rope around the crate, pulling until it was freed from the branches. He could feel its weight grow as he hauled it from the water, and called to Dawson, "Give me a hand. This thing is 'eavy!" Maintaining their balance, they finally cleared the edge of their boat and were able to lower it inside.

"I 'ope you feel you got your money's worth," Peavey said, relieved that the first half of their evening's work had gone well. He tried to push away the headache he felt coming on. Smithe and Dawson both grunted as they headed back to shore, slightly downstream.

"Once we get ashore, I will," Smithe said. "We still 'ave to break 'er open and take the 'alf that our captain has so kindly given us."

His mates chuckled at this.

"Then we waits till the tide goes out, and we drops what's left of this crate on a sandbar."

Peavey smiled anxiously. He would be happy when this night was over, having been up for over twenty-two hours. Besides, other than Devon, he didn't trust this group. He had larked the Thames for years, and this was the first time he had worked with a group outside his own men. He wouldn't do it again. That said, a half crate of jade, divided by twelve, would be the most money he had ever made in so short a time. Maybe he was being a bit hasty. They continued rowing, each quiet in their thoughts. Peavey was dreaming of what he would do with his share of the money once they sold the jade. He thought of Sir Francis Drake, and smiled. Peavey's thoughts of late were about him. Drake would have been happy to have a man of Peavey's qualities at his side. If only Peavey had been born then!

Drawing close to the dock, Flanders stepped out of the shadows, his hand outstretched to take the rope from Smithe and secure their boat.

"We'll just pull our boat out of the moonlight and wait," Smithe said. "It won't be but a few hours." He looked at Flanders, and anxious to break open the crate, asked, "Do you still 'ave the 'ammer we brought?" Peavey, not hearing a reply or seeing any of the other sailors, looked up to see their boat being pulled to the dock and a constable stretch out his hand.

"You won't be needing a hammer now, gentleman. We have it under control. You are all under arrest for suspicion of pirating."

The next morning, Peavey was taken before the magistrate, where he learned that he was blamed for the entire plot. Young Hendricks had apparently gone to the captain and told him everything; the captain, in turn, had told the constable.

"'E's the one we saw, coming up the side of the ship," Smithe said, pointing to Peavey. "'E had a whole group with him, and they threatened young Master 'endricks and made him hand over the key. They made us 'elp 'im get the crate. If we didn't return with this Peavey, unharmed, they'd kill the rest of our group. We were just waiting our chance. We didn't know for sure what was in the crate, but knew our cap'n would be pleased to get it back."

Hendricks, hearing this, spoke for the first time, quickly agreeing. He pointed to Peavey, and said, "It were 'im, it were. All along. 'E's the one who sneaked on board and threatened me life if I didn't give 'im the key, and tell 'im where the cap'n's private goods were stored. I 'ad no choice!"

Peavey was dumbfounded, tired, and his head was exploding. They were saving their skins at his expense. The crew was pointing to the expendable rat on a sinking ship, and it was easy enough. All they had to do was make Peavey the guilty one, and once they were set free, they'd get Hendricks and send him overboard on their first voyage out.

Peavey wondered why. Hendricks could have kept quiet and made his fair share. Or he could have told the truth and said Peavey had nothing to do with it, that his shipmates had threatened his life if he hadn't given them the captain's key.

With one look, young Hendricks could see his future. He knew he made a mistake by squealing to the captain. But worse now, as a snitch, he knew if he went to sea with this same crew, his life would be over. Peavey was the perfect scapegoat, and the sooner Hendricks got off the ship, the better.

All agreed, except Devon, who signed a paper against their lies. But, it was ten against one.

"'E's likely in it, too," Flanders declared, pointing at Devon. "'E's just trying to protect his ol' employer is all."

Each nodded his head and was thanked by the court for saving the cargo for the captain. They were cleared of all charges. The next day, Peavey was brought before the magistrate to hear his sentence.

"Peavey," the magistrate said. "Is that it? No middle name, no last name, just Peavey?"

"Yes, sir, m'Lord," Peavey said. "I was born a bastard and was given only the one."

"Well enough," the magistrate continued. "As to the crime of piracy, I find you guilty. As to the accusation that you were the one who thought up the theft of the jade, whether you did or not, there is no crime for thinking, only doing. The accusation of the ten, however, against young Master Devon's declaration of your innocence, causes the court to either believe him and that you are innocent and that the ten lied to save their skins. Or that he is lying as well to protect his former employer. Which, sir, is the court to believe?"

Peavey wiped his eyes and responded, knowing he was close to being hanged. He tried to formulate thoughts that, combined with the headaches, were becoming more and more difficult.

"Sir, I am guilty of larking the Thames with the men this court thought wise to set free. This, I did, sir. I did not think up the crime, only helped in gett'n the crate. It is true, that Master Devon did work for me, and ol' Peavey appreciates 'is words, 'onest ones that they are."

Peavey hoped the truth would help save his skin, and said no more.

The magistrate looked at Peavey. "And you have no more to say in your defense?"

Peavey held his hat in his hand and remained quiet. Finally, he said, "No sir, I do not. I always 'opes the truth speaks in my defense."

"Then, Mr. Peavey," the magistrate said, his gavel banging down on his bench, "for your admitted involvement with the piracy of said cargo, the court sentences you to hang by your neck until dead. Sentence will be carried out tomorrow. Next case."

Two large men of the court took Peavey by each arm and led him out, placing him in jail to await his hanging.

The next morning the sun rose, its light shining into Peavey's cell, causing him to blink repeatedly. He awoke and swatted a fly that buzzed around his face. He stood and relieved himself in the dirt, looking out the bars of his cell as he did, only to see the East India trading ship pull away from the dock and set sail. There was nothing he could do.

"You bastards," he said vehemently. "If it takes my finding you in the next life, then you 'ave that much waiting for you! If there be a God," and Peavey prayed the only prayer in his life, "me life 'as not been easy, Lord. Allow me vengeance at getting these men what wronged me."

Peavey hoped if he couldn't get them hanged, he would surely aid their passing.

It was but an hour more when his door opened and the jailer took Peavey outside to the gallows. Peavey had seen hangings all his life, and there was already a crowd waiting. Now, he would be a witness to his own. The rope went around his neck, and the minister said a few words before walking off, uncaring.

"Peavey, you have been found guilty of piracy and shall now be hung by your neck until dead. Do you have any words you would like to say?" asked the hangman.

Peavey stood quiet, his eyes closed, and repeated his only prayer.

"I do," interrupted the magistrate, who walked into the courtyard. "Bring him to me."

A collective murmur went through the audience, now saddened at being deprived of the morning's entertainment. Peavey's head was released from the noose, and he was brought to the magistrate's office, where Emily was waiting.

"Have a seat, Peavey. It seems this lady, whom I met this morning, says she saw and heard the entire thing. I know for a fact that you have not had the chance to see her since that night, and her story confirms what the two strumpets said as well. They all state that you had nothing to do with the pirating of the crate, of which the court agrees. However, the court does find you guilty of aiding in the transport of pirated goods. Does that seem to be the straight of it?"

Peavey nodded his head quickly, amazed at how fast some prayers get answered. "Yes, m'Lord!"

"Then you have it to these ladies' credit for saving your life. Your sentence of hanging by the neck until dead has been dismissed."

Emily interrupted, "Your Lordship, if I may add? After the court had dismissed the crew, young Master Devon found out that if their plan failed, Peavey was to be blamed for all of it. They knew their ship would be leaving this morning, and they would either be incredibly rich or be aboard. They had nothing to lose."

Peavey looked at Emily, the news of all she said finally sinking in. "What happened with 'Endricks?" he asked quietly.

Emily shook her head. "He was not on board the ship as it left port this morning, but I heard talk of His Majesty's army recruiting in the area. He may have enlisted, just to get away from the ship's crew."

The magistrate stroked the side of his face, wrote something on a piece of paper, and turned to Peavey. "With this new turn of events and the disclosure by this young lady, the constable will be prepared for the return of their ship and will arrest the entire crew involved. Peavey, you will be sentenced to ten years in His Majesty's militia and sent to Stirling, where you will serve in Howard's 3rd, effective immediately."

Peavey felt happy at first, then angry. His accusers had gotten off scot-free and at his expense. Even Hendricks had slipped away. If not for his dear friend Emily, plus the two strumpets and Devon, Peavey would be swinging from a rope at this very moment. He closed his eyes once more, and prayed the constable would be waiting for them on their return trip. There would be only Hendricks to find after that.

Peavey was allowed a minute to say good-bye to Emily before the same two deputies took him to the king's army auxiliary in London. From there he was then taken by the next ship to Edinburgh and transported to Stirling.

# TWENTY-THREE
## Peavey: The Cure

"Where will they place you? Any idea?" the young volunteer next to Peavey asked, as they waited in line for their medical exams. The young man was excited. "I'm hoping to be placed with His Lordship, the Duke of Cumberland. I hope he gets back in time from France. If not, then I'll likely go with General John Ligonier's group. He's the top man, and some say equal to His Lordship."

Peavey turned away, not caring to banter. He'd been played for a fool. He closed his eyes momentarily and prayed once more for revenge against those who had put him here.

"Next," Dr. Edmund called out. Peavey walked inside the tent to see an older man, his back curled in an odd manner.

"Stand there and strip," the doctor said, as he pointed to a table with hands that were incredibly gnarled.

Peavey did as he was told and stood naked, waiting for his first medical exam ever. The surgeon, straightening as much as he could, looked into Peavey's eyes, curiously, and then looked at his knees before telling him to turn around.

"Uh-huh," he said, as he grabbed first one elbow and then another. "Turn back around."

Peavey did so. The doctor pushed into his lower abdomen, feeling for any abnormality. "No pain?"

Peavey shook his head no.

"Hmm," the doctor said again.

Peavey was becoming annoyed.

"You were a sweep," the doctor said.

He then pointed to the small mass that had begun growing from the side of Peavey's head, and asked, "How long have you had this?" Not waiting for an answer, he continued, "You had any headaches lately?"

Peavey looked closer at the misshapen gnome of a man who was slowly gaining his respect.

"I have," he replied.

The doctor continued, "Down below, in your privities, you have any sores?"

Peavey answered, "When I was younger, I got the soot wart when I were a sweep. It went away and only come back once as a rash. It went away after a few weeks."

The surgeon took Peavey's hands and looked at each, flipping one over and then the other.

"Did it ever appear anywhere else? Maybe your hands?"

Peavey looked at the doctor, curious at where his questioning was going.

"Yes, sir," he replied, "on both me 'ands and on me back. It were bad, but it went away."

"Boy, you may have had soot wart once, but I doubt it. Your

lower parts would be infected. What you have is the pox, and you've had it for years."

Peavey sat quietly. He'd only been with one strumpet, ever, and that was years ago. Peavey recalled her with disdain. He was drunk and she had grabbed him through his breaches, pushed him onto the floor of the bar, and finished him quickly. What followed were her public insults and barroom laughter. Peavey had slowly pulled up his breaches, humiliated. Yes, he remembered her.

"Your eyes," the doctor continued. "Have they been like this for years?"

Peavey blinked self-consciously, returning to the conversation. "Yes, since I was a sweep. Same time as I breathed in the soot. It were an accident."

"Your vision … it's been getting worse, hasn't it?"

Peavey heard the question and thought back over the last year. How long has it been? A year? No, more. It had occurred slowly, over the last two years. Peavey nodded his head in response. His eyes were much worse than they had been when he was a lad.

"I'm surprised your pox isn't more visible, but it can take on various forms. The growth on the side of your head is from the pox. Your nose will be next. We'll have to bleed you, and then we'll begin treatment. I hold no stock in the newest cure, guaiacum. That holy wood be damned. We'll use mercury. Your saliva will turn black, but that's a good sign."

"Mercury?" Peavey asked, curious. He had heard of it for years, as well as the childhood rhyme, "One night with Venus, and a lifetime with Mercury." Other than this, he knew nothing of it.

"Not to worry," the doctor said. "Hopefully, we've caught it in time, and you won't end up like that French painter, Lairesse. You don't want to end up like him, do you? If he'd had his humors balanced and been administered the proper medications, he'd still be with us to this day. But first things first. We'll take you out of His Majesty's service and then begin your treatments."

Peavey nodded his head slowly, not comprehending completely, and thanked him. He wasn't anxious to be a part of an army, traveling to the colonies or north to Scotland to deal with the Highlanders. Anything was better than either of those options. Besides, with luck, his pox could be cured.

"Now lean your head back," his doctor said, as he felt for his jugular vein, "and you'll feel a stick…"

Peavey felt the lancet as it pushed into his neck. Warm blood dripped out in a steady stream.

"We'll need to do this regularly," the doctor said after a few minutes, and he put pressure on the wound, letting it coagulate. "Be at the treatment center in the morning, right after breakfast."

Treatments began that next morning, after the surgeon had let his blood once more. The attendant, a young soldier with very shaky hands, was busy adding wood to the fire, making the room almost unbearable.

"I … I am to apply this several times a day," he said shyly, holding a tin-glazed earthenware jar, "but it has to be next to the fire, where you need to stay and sweat. It absorbs best this way."

He guided Peavey to the chair and began rubbing the elecampane and mercury ointment vigorously onto his body with his fingers.

"After a while, the ointment will make you sweat on your own."

Peavey endured it all, hoping it would work. He certainly felt light-headed afterward. Three times a day, over five months, he tolerated the treatments, even beyond when sores appeared in his mouth.

The black saliva didn't bother him, but one by one, the teeth he had trouble with fell out, and others loosened. Peavey suffered through the treatments until the time he began having dreams and dark thoughts. He wasn't sure if his pox was cured, but it didn't matter any longer. He wanted to join the troops and go to the colonies or the Highlands, where Sir Francis Drake could appreciate a man of his talents. One day, he would become the newest knight of England: Sir Peavey.

Dr. Edmund, Peavey's physician and a captain in King George's army, entered the major's tent and touched his cap wearily. After twenty-five years in the medical field, he didn't care to salute, nor did he even attempt it.

"You understand why you're here, yes?" the major asked.

"To determine fitness for duty for Private Peavey," the doctor replied.

"That's the short of it, yes," the major said. "He's been assigned to the duke's militia and will be leaving for northern Scotland. We need all the available men we have. Is he ready for duty?"

Dr. Edmund replied, "He's beyond what modern medicine can do for him. I'm afraid he's in the last stages of the pox, where it has entered his brain. Not even the heavy doses of mercury I have given him have helped."

"Damn you, man," the major said, impatient. "Answer my question. Will he be able to hold a weapon and fire at the enemy?"

"I'm sure he can do that," Edmund replied, "as long as you have him at a lucid time and one points him to where he needs to shoot. When he isn't lucid, he will have visions of grandeur. His memory is already failing, and he will become quite deranged. His skin is sloughing off in spots, and he smells."

"Then his stench will blend with the other eight thousand men," the major said. "With any amount of luck, he'll die fighting for his king. Sign his release, and you are dismissed."

"I do it under duress, Major. Peavey should be retired from service. Hell, he shouldn't have been put here in the first place. He's a good man. I've even taken a liking to him. Damn magistrates," he said. "They administer law any way they see fit."

# TWENTY-FOUR
## Peavey: Madness

It was early evening, and it was cold. Private Peavey of Howard's 3rd laid down his losing cards. He looked beyond the entrance to the tent to where the clouds wrapped around their camp and promised rain. The dampness permeated his mind with long, cold fingers. Peavey pulled his jacket around his shoulders, trying to stay warm, and smiled. *Sir Francis Drake knew I would find Hendricks here. He knew!*

But now that Hendricks was dead, it was time for Peavey to leave.

He looked down at his card hand and grumbled, "It's never warm."

Private Alexander Campbell of the Royal Scots Army laid down his cards, showing them to Peavey. "You almost got me this time," he said.

He didn't want to rub it in too much. He had seen Peavey's malevolence only once, and he didn't care to see it again. "But you're right. My father and I used to come here when I was a wee lad. It can stay on the cold side 'til June."

Peavey's thoughts went elsewhere, as he pushed the winnings to Alexander.

"I'm heading east tonight," Peavey said, conspiratorially. "Every day since Culloden, the subaltern has had us going north, always with a commanding officer and always under escort. Tonight, I'm heading east."

Alexander looked at Peavey. He could barely stand his stench, but with the tent flap open, he could tolerate it. Pocketing his winnings, he gathered up their cards and put them in the deck. Lowering his voice, he said quietly, "What the hell you saying? You trying to get yourself hanged? They'll take you for a deserter if they catch you."

Peavey went to the tent opening to see if there were any listening ears. He lowered his voice, conspiratorially. "Most Highlanders head north to get away. Tonight, I will go in a different direction" He touched Alexander's hand, as he looked to the left and right. "Ol Peavey knows they're trying to mix with the Lowland Scots. They thinks they is wise, but ol' Peavey is wiser. I even gots me a horse lined out to stake the main road."

He touched his forehead with his finger, repeatedly. "They can't hide from me."

"What do you think you'll get if you find them?" Alexander asked. "Money? They've got nothing as it is."

Peavey was quiet for a moment, then mumbled something to himself, and smiled. "They'll knight me one day."

Alexander shook his head at what he heard and pressed further, hoping to bring him back to clarity.

"If not money, what? Women?"

Peavey's eyes lit up, his remaining teeth showing as he grinned a hollow grin.

"Sir Francis wants them Highlanders to pay for what that strumpet Maggie did. What she did to ol' Peavey."

Alexander looked at Peavey and shook his head. He was sinking lower, way beyond what anyone knew. Something wasn't right, something that went beyond having the pox or being born a bastard that shaped his life. Hell, almost a fourth of the men in His Majesty's army were bastards, and they were all fine. Even with the surgeon's treatments, Peavey was beyond delusional. His Sir Francis Drake? He had been dead for more than a hundred and fifty years; yet Peavey was talking to him daily. And the whole camp had seen his madness.

It was after Culloden that Alexander knew he had to talk to the sergeant. A Highlander had raised his claymore, going for Private Hendricks. Peavey had ample time to use his bayonet, but he didn't. He just smiled and watched as Hendricks was cleaved. Afterward, Peavey killed the Highlander and then bayonetted Hendricks over and over.

The strangest part, Alexander told the sergeant, was when Peavey started talking to Sir Francis Drake, saying, "We did it, m'Lord!" And then in another voice, Peavey answered back, "Didn't I tell you there would be another chance?" And Peavey had smiled and said, "That you did, sir. That you did." He had carried on this conversation for minutes, as the rest of the troops continued fighting.

"It's over my head," the sergeant responded after hearing Alexander's story. "'E'll be dead soon enough, anyway."

"Sir?" was all that Alexander could say, and went back to his tent.

"Ya gotta be daft, man," Alexander said, continuing his conversation with Peavey. "We've got all the strumpets here at the back of the camp. You wouldn't be getting anything more than what you got already. What the hell you doing, wanting to find stray Highland women? Haven't they had enough of a run of bad luck already? Why take the chance of getting hanged?"

"I've gots my reasons," Peavey answered. Yes, it was payback time, and Sir Francis Drake would guide him once more.

The pretender to the English throne, Prince Charles, had caused all this, and it was Sir Francis who would guide Peavey's next steps. From now on, it was Peavey who would do the laughing. The fruits of war were to be taken, and he was deserving. Wouldn't it be the other way around if they had won at Culloden? It was this way throughout history: to the victor go the spoils of war. The Duke of Cumberland, now that his hands were incredibly full with the Highlanders, would need his and Sir Francis's help.

Peavey reached for his knife and felt the cool comfort and sharpness of his blade. His head pounded with the return of another headache, and the blade cut his finger deeply as he drew it across. Yes, it would be his personal job to diminish the Scot arrogance. All of them, he knew, were related to that Glasgow strumpet, Maggie. Her memory infuriated him. He'd make Sir Francis proud. He smiled at that thought and pinched his finger to stop the flow of blood. The ones he let live would become his personal servants. He might even let them live on his estates.

"Sir Peavey."

The name flowed easily from his lips as he said it, and Peavey could imagine a whole countryside under his control. Yes, he'd settle here one day, maybe down by Aberdeen, where it didn't rain as much. He had seen the countryside there, before they headed west to Kildrummy and then north to Drummossie Moor.

Peavey reached into his pocket and pulled out the only money he owned, clenching his fist around it in anger. After a half year of service, the pittance he had saved wasn't enough to buy the socks an officer wore. Yes, tonight was the night. He put the money back in his pocket. The magistrate who put him here was a long ways away and would never know. It was going to be a busy night.

It was an hour past tattoo, and Peavey lay in his bed, waiting patiently for the sentry to walk by as he made his rounds. Peavey heard his footsteps and listened as they faded into the distance. Fully dressed, he threw off his blanket and opened the tent flap to make sure all was still clear. It was, and he walked quickly past the other tents, to the rear of the camp where the horses were corralled, with one that awaited him, freshly saddled.

"Not a word, or I'll get the noose next to yours!" the guard said, as he handed him the bridle.

Peavey reached into his pocket and pulled out the tuppence their earlier agreement required.

"Not a word from you, either, or you won't make it to the noose," Peavey threatened. Flipping his remaining coins that were bloodied by his thumb, he added, "I'll be back by reveille."

Peavey guided the horse out of the corralled area, whispering soothing words as he tried to calm the beast, leading it down the dirt path.

"Good horse," he said, softly. "You be extra quiet for ol' Peavey, and I'll find you some hay to eat. Maybe even a new home with a warm barn. Good horse," he said again, pausing, now confident they were outside of camp. He patted its withers and, stepping into the stirrup, threw his leg over the saddle, quickly and easily. Turning the reins, Peavey guided the horse east to the main road that led to Elgin.

Peavey had no intention of returning by early morning. He had mulled it over and over, and finally made up his mind. He would head to Aberdeen, to a better clime and better money, and enjoy the fruits along the way. He was rich beyond belief while he lived in Southwark, and he knew he could do it again. Yes, Peavey was going to get over the pox that the strumpet Maggie had given him, and enjoy this trip and his new life. Finding nothing of interest in Forres, he continued towards Elgin.

# TWENTY-FIVE

## Peavey: "You Were a Good Sailor"

"Shh," Elizabeth whispered to Marion, and they both came to an immediate stop. They waited a few minutes more, a space of forever as they stood motionless, their breath seemingly loud in the night, their hearts beating wildly.

Elizabeth nodded to her daughter, relaxed, and smiled. "I don't see anything. I think we're safe."

Marion looked at her mother and said what they both felt. "That scared me!"

They took another step. Without warning, a hand reached out and grabbed Marion by her leine, while the other arm grabbed Elizabeth around her neck and held her.

"Don't move, either one of you," a man growled to them both. "If you know what's good for you, you will stay ... right ... here."

They both could smell his stench and feel the incredible strength in his arms and hands. Everything became worse as he spoke, from teeth long ago ignored, clothes seldom changed, and something else.

Elizabeth's face was inches from his, and she was forced to breathe him in with each ragged breath.

"If you move," he said slowly to both of them, looking specifically at the young girl in his grasp, "I'll snap this one's neck like a stick."

Elizabeth panicked, knowing Marion did not understand the King's English.

"She doesn't understand you!" Elizabeth said hoarsely through the grasp he had on her throat.

She said to her daughter, "He is of Cumberland's army and doesn't want you to move, or he will kill me," she said in Gaelic.

Marion nodded her head quickly.

The soldier growled, "I don't care what she understands," as he tightened his grip around her throat. "I won't have either of you speaking that shite unless you have my permission. Do you understand me?"

He pulled Marion close to him. "Sneaking over to Culloden, are ye? Trying to help your clansmen, I'll warrant."

Elizabeth's throat was locked tight in the crook of his arm, and she fought to breathe.

"Speak up, you pathetic tart!"

Marion's heart beat wildly. She heard his words and waited for some sign from her mother as to what they meant. She thought of the knife in her leine and wished she could grab it.

"I'll bet the Duke of Cumberland would like to see you two, personally. Especially when he hears ol' Peavey has found the strumpet that did me wrong. He has a special place for tarts in his jail. That is," he added, "unless you and Maggie here want to play nice with ol' Peavey?"

Elizabeth glared at him, her words forced as she spewed out the Scot hatred of hundreds of years. "Her name is not Maggie, and you

241

will keep your filthy hands off my daughter, or I'll …" Elizabeth shut her mouth, knowing she had said too much.

"Ah, but you're a feisty wench. Your daughter, is it?" he said with a leer. "But then, her and ol' Peavey … why, we've met once before. You should be proud."

Peavey looked at Marion again, then back to Elizabeth as he tightened his grip around her throat. "I don't think you are in any position to make threats, do you?"

He then pulled Marion forcefully to him. "No one understand how lonely it is out here for a man in the king's service. All day long, killing you pathetic Highlanders. You know what I meant by 'play nice,' don't you?"

Elizabeth, still in the crook of his arm, had worked herself toward the front, and kicked him hard between the legs. It was a glancing blow and did nothing but infuriate him.

He turned around and slammed Elizabeth up against a tree, and held her there, growling in her ear. "Ol' Peavey was hoping this could be done differently."

Marion could see the fear in her mother's eyes and was unsure of what to do or how she could help. She was terrified.

"Tell you what I'm going to do," Peavey began. "You are going to tell Maggie to get the rope from my horse on the other side of those trees. If she does not return, I'll slit your throat. Tell her now!"

Elizabeth was still trying to catch her breath, then slowly translated all, telling her daughter to do exactly what he wanted.

Looking at their captor, she begged, "Please, take me instead. Do not hurt my daughter. She is barely a young woman."

"Trust me." He smiled hatefully into her ear. "I'll be real special with her. Why, before the night is over, she and I will renew our old friendship and she might want me as her husband. You'd like that, wouldn't you? To have ol' Peavey as your son-in-law?"

This time, Elizabeth, eyes glaring with hatred, controlled her anger. Marion returned with the rope.

"You," he said to Elizabeth, "put your back to the tree and then put your hands around it, backward. Yes, just like that. Now, give her your wrists."

He watched as the young girl tied up her mother.

"That's it, just like that. Tell her to make it tight. I don't want you joining in with me and Maggie. Not yet, at least."

He smiled at Elizabeth, still feeling her glancing blow between his legs. *The bitch,* he thought. *I'll teach her. Neither of them will be missed.*

Suddenly, his headache reappeared with malicious intensity, then, confusion.

*Peavey,* Sir Francis said. *Have you forgotten our plan? They would make excellent servants, wouldn't they? Your estates could grow, with just these two. And their children would know their father. Peavey, Peavey, a quality sailor always remains in control.*

"Yes, sir. Thank you, Sir Francis. I almost forgot." A smile of satisfaction rolled across the stumps of his teeth, and he nodded his head with infantile repetition. "Thank you for reminding me, sir!"

Elizabeth looked at her daughter and said, "There is something wrong with him. He is sick in the head. You still have your knife? Do not answer me. Just nod your head."

She smiled at her daughter, trying to alleviate her terror. "Listen, *mo cridhe.* You know what he wants to do, don't you?"

Marion nodded her head.

"Once he does that, he'll likely kill the two of us. You can see this, yes?"

Marion nodded again.

Peavey stopped nodding and interjected, back to his malicious self, "I told you not to talk that shite. Just tie the knot and be done with it."

Elizabeth looked at him. "Ours is a different language, and it takes longer for me to tell her to tie my hands. I'm sure you knew this already?"

"Yeah, yeah. I know," he said, but didn't. "Just make sure she ties your hands tight; then have Maggie come over. Ol' Peavey has something he needs to show her."

Elizabeth smiled deceptively. "You're really not as bad as I first thought, and I'm sorry I kicked you. If you'd like, I can tend to your sores after you are through. Would you like that?"

Peavey muttered angrily, wiping at his eyes. "Just tell her to get it done and get over here now. I'll deal with you later."

Elizabeth smiled again and with a lightness in her voice said to Marion, "He says for you to make sure my hands are tight. When you do this, grab your father's *sgian-dubh*. Keep it hidden, but ready. You know what we do to our sheep, yes?" Then, lowering her voice to a tone that only Marion would understand, "Remember what they did to your father."

Marion walked around the tree after shifting the knife. Trembling, she knew what was next and what Peavey was going to do. He grabbed her and pulled her down to him.

"Now, Maggie, let's you 'n me 'ave some fun. Jus' like the ol' days. Then, after we do that, why ... ol' Peavey'll let your mother go."

Elizabeth listened and remained quiet. Peavey began pulling at Marion's leine, shoving his mouth on her neck, the foulness of his disease incredible. She felt him reach his hands under her leine, touching her body.

*Yes, Maggie, just like old times,* Peavey thought angrily. The memory of that night came back. When she gave him the pox. And humiliated him. His breeches were already loose, and he pushed them down to his ankles. "I'll teach you, Maggie!" Peavey said, hating her anew.

*Peavey!*

The headaches, his failing vision, the growth on his face, the treatments for months at the hospital... he brought his hands up and placed his fingers around her throat, and slowly began to squeeze.

*Peavey!* He could hear the voice of Sir Francis Drake.

Marion felt his grasp slowly tightening, and as he did, she reached in between the folds of her leine and grabbed the handle of her *sgian-dubh.* There would be but one chance. Carefully concealing the knife, she reached up through his arms as though to caress his face. Then quickly, she twisted her wrist to reveal the hidden blade and then savagely drew it across his throat.

Peavey's eyes grew wide with the sudden knowledge of what had happened, and he instinctively grasped at his throat, blood squirting from his neck and over the top of her.

Marion scurried out from under him. She could think only of the hatred she bore for this man for what he and his kind had done to her father and her clan, and for what he had just attempted to do to her. She hated him with all her might, and she stabbed him three times before her mother's voice cut through to her.

"*Mo cridhe!*" Elizabeth said to her daughter, crying. "Stop. Shh, it will be all right. It will be all right! Shh, be quiet, my child. It is all right."

Marion fell to the thick leaves, curling up.

"Please, child, come cut this rope off me."

Marion watched as Peavey, still grasping at his throat, tried to get up and then fell, his voice silenced as he lay on the ground, dying. Marion looked at him with hate in her eyes.

"That was for my father," she said, in a language that he never understood.

Peavey laid there, hearing the voice of Sir Francis Drake. *You were a good sailor, Peavey, one of my very best.*

# TWENTY-SIX

## 1746: Dreams of a New Home

"Please, come quick, child," Elizabeth called to Marion. "Cut the ropes. We must make haste from here and get you to the nearest stream. You need to be cleaned up, and we need to be on our way."

Marion's fingers trembled so she could barely cut the bonds from her mother's hands. She sobbed uncontrollably.

"*Mo cridhe*, you have saved your mother's life and your own as well. It was for your father's life, too, that you did this."

Freed, Elizabeth hugged her close, and Marion clung to her mother, trying to regain the security of her childhood.

"Let us be gone, child," Elizabeth said gently. "He will be missed come morn, and they will come searching for him when he does not return. Let us cover him with leaves, then we will think on him no more."

They did this and then, grasping the horse by the bridle, began backtracking, staying on the same path as before until the path was clear of their tracks and they were in an area covered with rock.

"I want them to think we are escaping Highlanders heading south, may our Lord in heaven forgive me!" Elizabeth said. She then slapped the horse hard on the flank, and it ran full speed away from them. "Now, child, look for places where we can turn around and leave no trail."

It took them a short amount of time to resume their journey. Stopping at a stream, Marion stripped and washed herself and her clothes carefully.

"*Mo cridhe*," her mother said softly, "If you were a soldier, what you have done would be nothing. To me, my love, you have saved my life. I will never forget what you have done for us."

Marion replied quietly, "I know, Mum."

Elizabeth saw the pain in her daughter's eyes and knew it would take time before the memory of what happened no longer weighed heavily on her heart. She prayed her daughter was strong enough to bear what she had just endured.

Elizabeth waited as her daughter put her leine back on, and asked, "Can you travel? We must make Lossiemouth by daybreak."

"Yes, Mum," Marion replied.

They traveled quietly, going through fields and tall stands of trees, staying off the roads until they arrived at the earl's home. It was shortly after daybreak when they knocked on the door of the stately mansion. Marion looked around in quiet amazement, saying nothing.

"Aye, it is big," Elizabeth said, hoping someone would open the door soon. Elizabeth knocked again, and after a few moments more, a servant opened the door cautiously. A look of disdain crossed his face as he saw the Highlander women.

"Go away," he said, "or I shall be forced to call the sheriff."

He pushed on the door, trying to close it.

Elizabeth pushed her shoulder against it with all her weight, and said, "Tell my Lord that it is Elizabeth, the lass of his youth. Do it now, and be quick!"

She pulled away, letting the door slam hard against its frame, securing against their entry.

Elizabeth and Marion waited. Within a few minutes, the door opened, and the servant ushered them to a room off to the side of the main parlor.

"His Lordship is detained at present but will be with you soon. He requests that I provide you shortbread and tea."

A tray of warm shortbread was brought soon thereafter. Elizabeth and Marion devoured it hungrily, washing it down with delicious tea. It was another forty minutes before the huge door opened.

"Elizabeth, as I live and breathe! It is so good to see you! Forgive my taking so long, but as you are likely aware, all of the Highlands are in turmoil."

William Atherton, the Lord of Lossiemouth, gave Elizabeth a heartfelt hug and motioned for them to sit. He sat down across from her.

"Aye," she began. "We do know, m'Lord. That is the reason we are here."

William looked at her inquisitively and remained silent, urging her to tell her story.

"My husband fought at Culloden Moor and has perished."

He looked at her, his sadness at her loss etched across his face. "I am so sorry, Elizabeth. Please accept my deepest sympathies." He shook his head and continued, "There has been such devastation this last week, since the battle, that the world should be hanging its collective head, and aye, should never forget. I will personally make sure of that."

William took a sip of the tea that his servant had just brought him and looked at Marion. "Who is this young lady with you? By chance a daughter?"

"Aye, m'Lord," Elizabeth replied. "Please forgive my rudeness. She is my daughter, Marion. She is almost sixteen now."

William smiled and said, "She looks just like you. Has it really been that long? How the years pass. But, now, dear Elizabeth, how can I can help you?"

"We need to go north," Elizabeth continued, "to Orkney and from there, if we can, to Norway. Anywhere besides Scotland."

"That is a tall order," William replied. "The English are searching every coast, every firth, until they find Prince Charles. I doubt he will leave Scotland alive."

Elizabeth stopped to translate William's words to Marion and, when finished, apologized to him.

"Forgive me, m'Lord. We tried to teach her English when she was young, but she is a strong-willed lass and refused to reply in anything but our native Gaelic. It became harder to do as she got older, and honestly, we gave up."

William laughed heartily as he heard this.

"I'm sure she is! She reminds me of someone else I once knew," and then winked at Elizabeth.

He became serious once more and said, "For you to escape now would take a miracle. All craft of any size are inspected. Many foreign ships are fired upon and sunk. They are watching Scotland's seas as much as her land."

"I see," Elizabeth said. "Is there no chance for getting from here to Brora?"

"Even when the English are not a concern, the seas from here to Brora can be difficult," William replied. "Foul weather can happen quickly, and I've seen waves high enough to sink a small craft."

Elizabeth pleaded, "We need to leave, m'Lord, and in spite of your concerns, I would appreciate a small boat so we can at least try. Can you please help?"

"Lass, are ye daft and nay been listening? Any boat at this time is almost impossible!"

"M'Lord, we are desperate," Elizabeth replied.

William was quiet. Then he said, "A boat is out of the question. I will need to think on all you have said. But if I am to put my life and my title to the test for you, I need to know why, beyond 'desperate.' We both know these are desperate times." He then raised his voice and became stern. "Elizabeth, if you need my help, you must tell me everything. I won't put all at risk for a prior love, especially one who I have not seen in almost seventeen years. Besides," he said, lowering his voice and trying to smile, "you would almost need an English flag and ship to take you, and I dinna ken if anyone can get that."

Marion remained quiet and listened to their animated conversation, then the translation. She looked at her mother and said, "Tell him all, Mother. Tell him of father and Reverend Hay and what happened at Elgin. Then ask once more if His Lordship knows of anyone who could help."

Elizabeth stared intently at her daughter and raised her eyebrows.

Marion asked again, "Please."

Elizabeth began, sharing their story with William.

"It's not what we have done. It's what we as clans were made to support and fight for, whether we wanted to or not. It's the reason my husband gave his life. He fought as a Gordon at Culloden. Now that the battle is over, the English are butchering all Highlanders, whether they were there or not. If they live, then it's to jail one goes, until they sort it out, and the good Lord knows when that will be. Even our homes are not sacred. They burn those as well and then steal our cattle and food. The women ... they have their way with them to bear English wains. If they are not killed, they will likely starve."

Elizabeth told him how Reverend Hay had buried her husband and then rode out to advise them to leave. She spoke of the burned-out home of the old clansman who had been stoned. And she told him of how Marion and she had almost lost their lives to an English guard.

"My daughter wishes to know ..."

William looked at Marion and then said in Gaelic, "You need not translate."

He looked back at Elizabeth, reaching out to take her hand. He spoke to her in their native tongue.

"Until now, I did not know if you were a spy sent by the English to test my loyalties by playing upon the love of an old friend. I grew up here and have known Gaelic all my life. I learned it as a child through Dougal, our gardener and caretaker. It would have been an offense to speak it, though, as my father was an English major for the crown. I could never speak it, even to you, Elizabeth. My mother, the countess, knew the language as well. You say you saw an old clansman north of Kildrummy by about a day's journey?"

Elizabeth suddenly remembered the clan pin she had pulled from his shirt. She reached inside her leine and handed it to William.

"I pulled this from his clothing, m'Lord. I wanted to give it to Reverend Hay, if we had the chance, so he could say some words over him."

William gently took the pin from her hand, and his eyes filled with tears. "He was the best friend I ever had. Aye, even as a child, I learned more from him than anyone."

He wiped his eyes with his handkerchief.

"By this pin, I am certain it was my dear friend. I thought it strange that I had not heard from him in days. This now explains it. I guarantee he would have taken his own life before he confirmed anything with the English. We became emissaries to the clans, the French, and occasionally to Prince Charles. I have done this for the last two years. The English know someone does this, but they do not know whom. That is why the need for secrecy."

William continued, "There were gentlemen here this morning. One of them is to contact a man of considerable influence. He will be here soon on a different matter and may be able to assist."

Marion was thankful they had switched to Gaelic, and she could follow their conversation.

"Would you consider the colonies if we can arrange it?" William asked them.

Marion looked at her mother excitedly.

"Yes!" they both exclaimed. "Yes!"

That same day, William received word of an English soldier who had been reported missing at reveille. He had apparently snuck out during the night and was found dead, his pants around his ankles, his neck slit, and bearing other stab wounds. From what the English had reported, he was performing his necessaries when a Highlander had stealthily come upon him, killing him instantly. There was no sign of struggle, with only leaves covering his body, his horse loyally by his side, eating peacefully. A search was mounted and then quickly thereafter was halted.

When William told Elizabeth of this news, he said, "More Highlanders will pay for Peavey's death, though I really don't see how they can add to their current pace of killing, pillaging, and burning. We will be safe here. The Duke of Cumberland will not be concerned with upstanding English lords with holdings in Scotland."

He watched Marion's and Elizabeth's faces and quickly understood their unspoken question.

"'Aye, my being an English lord in the Highlands of Scotland is not a guarantee of safety from an avenging Highlander. Quite the contrary. I am, however, protected by the heads of the clans for services rendered, as it were. If all works as we hope it will, our benefactor will be here presently, and we may have an answer soon thereafter."

Marion looked at the man whom her mother loved at another time. She saw his wisdom and kindness, and understood what it was she once saw in him.

They each hugged him in thanks and walked outside. Looking across the North Sea, they could see two ships patrolling the coastline. The sea was peaceful, their sails full; their beauty hiding their true purpose.

"Mum, those ships are beautiful! His Lordship says those are the ones that are watching every coast. What is it they do?"

Elizabeth knew the English military might was foreign to her daughter. "Those ships have conquered lands the world over. They have cannons that can sink a whole ship at one time. What his Lordship says is true, and his words are wise. He wishes only to protect us."

They walked back to the mansion, its shape silhouetted by the ancient trees, the shadows of their leaves meandering endlessly across its weathered front.

"Mum, if the earl can nay help us, would you still want us to try to escape on a small boat?"

Elizabeth looked at her daughter. "If we've no other choice, then aye, we must. Even if it means we must take our chances against those ships, *mo cridhe*, even then."

# TWENTY-SEVEN

## 1746: Help ...
## From Both Sides

J ames Douglas, the Fourteenth Earl of Morton, arrived at Lossiemouth Estate a week later. He left his carriage and walked
through the cool evening rain, toward the open door and his
longtime friend, William, the Lord of Lossiemouth.

"'Tis good to see you," James said, "and I apologize that it took
so long. It seems one needs special dispensation from the Duke of
Cumberland before one can travel, even from Inbhir Nis to your estate." He shook his head in disbelief. "Thank God I wasn't requesting
to go to London."

He pulled out a paper, briefly showing it to William before
quickly putting it back.

"This, with the duke's signature, took me a week to get."

"I appreciate all you have done to get here, my friend," William
replied, stepping aside so James could enter. "It is good to see you,
as well. Who would have thought four months ago that the prince's
forces would be here?"

James shook his head. "Things change, and quickly. Thank you again for taking the time to discuss the recent issues in our Highlands."

"Please," William said, dismissively, "It is your time that we appreciate! Angus!" he called to his loyal servant. "We will be in the library."

"Aye m'Lord," Angus said, as sourly as ever.

James looked at him as he walked away. "After all these years, you still keep that crotchety old Englishman?"

William smiled. "It's his loyalty that matters most, my friend. I can handle his dour expression." Then, changing the subject, he asked, "Is it true what I've heard about the battle at Culloden?"

"It's nay a battle," James responded. "It's an out-and-out massacre. And to think that the prince has turned his back on the men who fought for him as they did. Rumor has it he is hiding until he can get back to France."

William shook his head. "I've found that many of these rumors are started by the English to lower morale, though I doubt it can get much lower."

"Aye," James agreed. "I doubt it can. Most of the Highlanders are either in jail or running for their lives at this very moment, not to mention the ones who are dead or starving."

Angus interrupted their conversation by opening the library doors. Setting a tray before them, he asked, "My Lords, would you gentlemen care for a wee dram this evening?"

It was William's best Scotch, brought out only for his finest guests. Angus poured both their drinks before setting the bottle between them.

"To Friar John Cor," James said, "who began making this 'water of life' these many years past."

"Aye," the Lord replied. "And to the men of Culloden, of whom many fought for a cause not of their own volition."

William set his drink down.

"James, when I requested your assistance, it was to discuss the Duke of Cumberland and in what direction the crown's goals are in the aftermath of Culloden," he said. "Since that time, I had an issue appear at my very door that I believe must take precedence. Something closer to my heart."

James looked at him, curious.

"It's a woman I knew before I was married, and her daughter, as well."

James looked long at his friend, surprised.

"Are ye looking for trouble now?" he asked.

"Rest assured," William replied, "I have had them checked out and know what they have told me to be true, down to the soldier who got his neck slit."

"They had something to do with that? I heard of this while I was in Inbhir Nis. I thought it was roving Highlanders."

"In a sense, yes," William replied, smiling. He shared what he knew of their travels and how they ended up at his estate.

"You know they are not spies?" James asked.

"To my very life, James, they are not. Their only goal at this point is to make it to Orkney. From there, if I am able, to the colonies. I know they would have taken my son's sailing vessel, aye, and died trying, if I would have given them my blessing."

"Aye," James responded. "That does sound desperate. But what makes their circumstance any different than the other Highlanders in our charge ... the thousands that are trying to leave now?"

"They, as one of many, are no different. Their circumstances, however, are. James, do you remember the story of the young lass reunited by Lady Christian to an heirloom? It was done after the Battle of Culblean. Mothers used to tell it to their daughters, but I still recall it. Think back, my friend."

"Aye, I do," he said, hesitantly. "It was a necklace and earrings?"

"Aye. If you thought you could help those earrings and necklace stay in the rightful owner's hands, as compared to the Duke of Cumberland adding them to the spoils of Culloden, would you help?"

"On my life, you know I would," he exclaimed. "You are telling me it's not a myth?"

William smiled. "On your honor, do I have your word that you won't let this go anywhere but between us?"

"Sir, on my honor as James Douglas, the Fourteenth Earl of Morton, and as a Scot, you have my word."

William thanked him, and began.

"The night before my two charges arrived, I had a visitor. It was Reverend James Hay. He told me there would be two ladies of the Gordon clan coming for my help. After the reverend had warned the women of the imminent danger for all Highlanders, he returned to their home a few days later, only to find it burned out, with no sign of them. It was their father and husband who he had helped that day at Culloden, and then later buried. Before the man died, he told the reverend about the necklace and earrings that were part of his wife's legacy. He knew that if he died, his wife would come to me, the only man she felt could help. So that, my dear James, is why I have sworn you to secrecy. Even though the heirloom will no longer be in Scotland, we know it won't be on display in London as part of their heritage. Can you help?"

"It could be difficult and nigh on impossible," James replied. "Do the ladies know you are aware of their special gift?"

"No, from the moment I saw them, I shared little. Much can

happen in seventeen years. Once they shared their entire story, and it matched the reverend's, I knew I could trust them."

"'Tis true," James agreed. "Much can happen in seventeen years."

"I'd like us to try," William said. "But I don't want to risk another life in the process."

"Aye, but no finer a cause can I think of, outside of Culloden. I will need at least a few weeks or more to contact my friends in France and Norway."

"I understand the Right Honorable Henry Pelham, the prime minister, has been speaking to you about going to the Dutch Republic. Breda, isn't it?" William asked.

James looked at him with amazement. "I've only talked of this once with him. How is it that you know this?"

William only smiled. "This may be the avenue we need. Can you pursue it?"

They laid out plans for his travel to London. For the rest of the evening, they discussed the Highlands's future.

By nightfall, the rain had stopped. William stood outside his door and bid his friend farewell.

"As quickly as you can? None of us can be sure of our circumstances in the near future, and my guests will need all the help we can give them."

It took James longer than the week he had hoped for … much longer. He waited the first week at Cawdor Castle for the return of his servant and the required travel pass. Giving up, he called for his carriage, furious with himself for wasting valuable time. He could have left sooner and already been en route to London. They were just a mile west of Nairn when his coach pulled off to the shoulder of the road.

"M'Lord," the driver called, "you may wish to see this."

James stepped out of the carriage and looked up at the driver.

"What?" he asked, impatiently.

The driver pointed to the side of the road, where, in a heap, was a stack of bodies.

"The fourth one down, m'Lord. I noticed his coat. It's the same one we always wear in your service."

James counted down until his eyes found what his driver had noticed. It was the servant he had been awaiting. A man, who over the last sixteen years had become his dearest friend. They had shared many nights as they watched the skies through James's telescope.

"He looks to be bayonetted," the driver observed. "They must have thought he was a Highlander, sir."

*Damn them!* James thought as he wept. *I will not only help those ladies in Lossiemouth, I will do whatever it takes!*

"Driver, make haste. Once we arrive at Inbhir Nis, I want you to procure a shovel. Our friend will at least have a proper grave. I will not have him exposed to the elements a day longer."

"Yes, sir," the driver said. "I didn't know him that well, but it would be my honor. I only hope someone would do the same for me."

Hearing that, the grief in James's heart lessened. They went immediately to Inbhir Nis, where the Duke of Cumberland had arrived from Fort Augustus two days prior. His driver went for a shovel.

"No, sir," the sentry said, barring James's access to the duke's quarters. "No more passes are to be given, by order of the Duke of Cumberland. 'Tis his word as the brother of the king, and it is final, to be sure. All travel outside of Inbhir Nis has been closed to civilians."

James looked at the young lad, barely sixteen. "You tell Lord Cumberland that James Douglas, the Fourteenth Earl of Morton, is seeking an audience with him, immediately. Tell His Lordship I have urgent business and need to travel."

The young sentry looked dispassionately at the Scot, even with his title, then looked away. "The Lordship is not to be bothered with travel requests …"

James grabbed the young man's red uniform and pulled him close. "You will do exactly as I say. I would hate to report to the prime minister that a young sentry has kept me from getting back to London. Now, young man, I suggest you tell His Lordship that I am here and need to seek an audience with him! Do you understand?"

"Yes, sir," the young sentry replied and ran inside. Breathless, he approached the Duke of Cumberland.

"Sir, forgive my intrusion, but there is a James Douglas, Earl of Morton, outside and wishes to speak to you, sir. 'E says he must travel to meet with the prime minister!"

The Duke of Cumberland's pendulous jowls moved as he raised his eyes from his lunch.

"The Earl of Morton again?" He breathed heavily. "Bring him in, sentry."

The sentry went back outside, leaving the stench of the men, both dead and alive, who were imprisoned there.

"My Lord Cumberland will see you now, sir," the sentry announced.

"Thank you," James growled. He followed him down to a dank office, away from the harshest smells emanating from the rooms down the hall.

"'Ere, sir," the sentry announced. He opened the door to where the Duke of Cumberland was wiping his mouth.

"You have returned, sir," Lord Cumberland said to James. "I can't say it is a pleasure to see you again. What is it you need this time?"

"Your excellency," James began, "I awaited for the return of my servant with a pass that would allow my unhindered travel from here to London. I waited a week, then decided to come myself. Today, I found him outside of Nairn, in a stack of dead Highlanders."

The duke looked at him dispassionately and wiped his fingers of the remnants of chicken. "Sometimes, the wheat is thrown out with the chaff. It's unavoidable."

James looked at the duke, anger flashing in his eyes.

"The battle is over, sir. You have soundly defeated the Jacobites. What you are doing now is nay more than slaughter of innocent people. My servant was one of them."

"You are a Scot," the Duke of Cumberland said.

"You know that I am, sir," James responded, "and loyal to the crown."

"Then what I have done here, you understand, is necessary. One day, all Britain will remember what I have done, and this battle shall be recorded amongst her highest deeds," the duke replied. "Now, if I understand correctly, my sentry states you need another pass, this one to London. Is this true?"

"Yes," James replied.

"Then I must inquire as to what your trip entails."

James looked at the duke. "With all due respect, your excellency, if His Royal Highness deemed it necessary for you to be made aware, then I am certain he would have done so. As it stands, sir, that you do not know, then I must assume it is a matter solely between His Royal Highness, the secretary of state, the prime minister, and myself. I am certain you understand the difficulty of being in the middle of these things?"

The Duke of Cumberland nodded distastefully.

The earl smiled and continued pressing.

"My Lord, if it is not too much trouble, I must get that pass. I would dislike it terribly if I had to explain to His Majesty that I was detained in Inbhir Nis solely for my being unable to obtain one. It would also be greatly appreciated if you could provide me a ship to expedite my travel to London. I have lost enough time already this past week."

The duke relented, and four days later James's ship docked at the Port of London. He hailed a waiting carriage, and the driver jumped down to open his door. Taking his baggage, the driver asked, "Where to, sir?"

"The House of Lords," James said immediately. "An extra shilling to you if you make this a private carriage. An extra two shillings if you can make haste. I must meet with the Duke of Newcastle immediately."

"Then 'tis your lucky day indeed, sir, as I have the fortune to know that the duke is not at the House of Lords, sir, but is hunting a few miles north of London. One o' me mates works for 'im, private like, and took'm there 'is-self earlier this very day."

James smiled. "It is a fortunate day for the two of us, indeed, and an extra shilling as well!"

The driver skillfully wound his carriage through the villages of London until each became farther apart, separated by beautiful green meadows. They pulled up to a circular carriageway that hedged a field, and heard the staccato blast from a shotgun as it searched out its mark among the escaping pheasants.

James paid the driver. "If you can wait for my return, I shall pay you as handsomely for your time."

The driver beamed his approval and, parking his carriage off to the side, pulled out his pipe.

James walked through the fields up to the secretary of state, who had just lowered his fowling piece. Upon seeing James, he gave it to his servant and greeted his friend.

"James, what a pleasure to see you," said Thomas Pelham-Holles, the secretary of state.

"As it is you, sir," James replied. "It is not often that I am able to see you outside your service to England. If I had known of today's agenda, I would have brought my own fowling piece!"

They sat under an oak tree, and Thomas's servant brought the food that had been packed earlier for the day. His dogs, sensing no further excitement, began searching for the squirrels they had smelled earlier.

"Please," Thomas said, pointing to a lunch basket. "Your journey must have left you hungry."

James reached inside the basket and pulled out a small loaf of bread.

"It has been a long time, my friend," Thomas said.

"Too long," James replied, sad that life intervened with the friendships of youth. "But at least we have our work that allows us these occasional visits."

Thomas agreed.

"Then, am I to surmise you have given serious thought to my brother's request?"

"Aye, I have," James replied. "When the prime minister makes a 'request,' it is not something one can take lightly or refuse. Thomas, I would be happy to assist. If a consideration or two of mine could be looked upon with favorable eyes?"

"Splendid!" Thomas said. "I am certain we can make this work. Time is critical, and waiting for the Earl of Sandwich to decide, well ...expediting this issue is critical. What can the crown help you with for your fine assistance?"

James ate his bread slowly, contemplating his words.

"Thomas, your brother's wishes were for me to travel to Breda to act on behalf of England, yes? England's ultimate goal is peace talks with France?"

"Yes. Maybe this time," Thomas sighed, "then, maybe not. I do not expect in our short terms as secretary of state and prime minister the difficulties our countries have endured will be solved within our tenure. What we really need is time ... time to stall until this blasted Jacobite uprising is settled once and for all. What we need first is a slow process and to make the delay look like it is France's decision until we can get the Earl of Sandwich to assist. Timing is our issue, James. We cannot begin these talks and negotiate a peace treaty when England's strength is divided militarily. England can never enter a peace agreement from a point of presumed weakness."

James considered this. "I would be happy to assist. My needs are simple, my friend. I would require the continued use of the English ship the Duke of Cumberland kindly allowed me to use, plus letters of residency for my family so they can travel with me. I'll also need a month to close some personal issues."

"A month?" Thomas asked. "That is fairly quick."

"Aye," James replied. "I have cleared my schedule, but it is still a difficult time for all of us. I need to return to Inbhir Nis immediately to help William, the Lord of Lossiemouth. With any luck, I can assist with his bringing to a close our issue with those stiff-necked Highlanders. After that, it is but a quick trip to Orkney, and then I shall head immediately to Breda."

Thomas listened and then smiled. "By God, the prime minister was right. Give a challenge to a quality man, and he will move heaven and earth to get it done. Do you really feel you can assist up there in those cursed Highlands?"

"More than most would be able to," James replied. "As we speak, the lord is actively removing some of the most troublesome Highlanders. I do apologize about the trip to Orkney, but I am fighting a gentleman in court over a damned land deal. Afterward, I will go to Breda, and," James smiled, "proceed in England's service toward the slowest negotiations anyone could hope for!"

Thomas smiled. "And make it look like it was their request!"

"Without a doubt, my Lord," James replied. "After that, I shall take my family on a well-deserved vacation."

"Then I shall speak to the prime minister," Thomas said. "I am certain he will be able to put in a kind word with His Royal Highness regarding the continued use of the duke's ship. You will keep the same crew to sail her?"

"Yes, sir," James replied. "At least to Inbhir Nis. From there, I shall return his crew to the duke and use the Lord of Lossiemouth's crew to go to Orkney and France. His men have considerable experience with the seas, considering his home is on the firth."

It was a short affair once Thomas had spoken to his brother, the prime minister, and set the wheels turning in James's favor. *Scotland's favor as well,* James thought, *if I can make all this happen.* He shook his head. He knew of no other way to get Elizabeth and Marion out of Scotland, let alone to Orkney. *Everything has to work flawlessly, as it had so far,* he thought. He uttered a silent prayer that it would continue to do so.

James arrived at his home in Edinburgh, and after sharing with his family the realities of what was happening to the clans under the Duke of Cumberland, he laid out his plan.

"It will be the most important thing I have ever done on behalf of the Highlands. Then, after I have completed my trip to Orkney, I shall return with letters of residency for each of you, signed by

His Royal Highness. From here, we will travel to Breda for matters of state that must be attended to, and finally to France for a well-deserved holiday."

The next morning, after James vowed his family to secrecy, he said his good-byes to his family, and departed with ship and crew for the Highlands of Scotland.

Two days later, he arrived in Inbhir Nis. Awaiting him was the Duke of Cumberland, who had in hand four documents that allowed him and his family to "travel as deemed necessary" in the service of England, and stamped by His Royal Highness, the King.

"These documents arrived just before you. It appears you have great influence with His Royal Highness," the duke said, "and I have been chastised for delaying your arrival to London. I understand you will be negotiating peace with France?"

James smiled at the duke.

"It was in a preliminary stage, my Lord, when we last spoke. I apologize for my vagueness at that time or inability to share anything more. One never knows these days whom to trust completely. I am, however, thankful for your wisdom and am sure you understand the position I felt I was in."

"I agree that it is difficult to know whom to trust these days," the duke replied. "However, I am at your service. I understand you are to be traveling with your family. Where might they be at present?"

James smiled cautiously at the duke, knowing he was no fool.

"My family, especially my wife, was taken with a miasma. She feared they would spread it amongst your crew and they, in turn, spread it to your troops. I myself do not know if these things are true, but even at my strongest behest, she remained unchanged in her belief. My Lord, do you think she was wrong?"

The Duke of Cumberland replied slowly, "I do not know. I never understood my own mother, let alone women in general. When you see her next, extend to her my warm wishes for a speedy recovery. And please, feel free to avail yourself of my carriage in your journey to Lossiemouth."

"I shall, my Lord. Thank you for your kind consideration."

James smiled as he left. The duke had extended his well wishes and allowed him use of his carriage? His brother, the king, must have chastised him.

William rushed to greet James as his carriage pulled up to the estate.

"James, how good to see you! I trust your journey went well?" he asked. "I assure you our charges have been equally anxious for your return, inquiring daily for any news."

Smiling, James hugged his friend. "It went better than we could have ever imagined."

"Let me call for Elizabeth and Marion so you only have to tell your story once. Angus, assemble our guests in the library!"

They gathered, excited for the news James would share.

"We shall have an English ship waiting for us at Inbhir Nis. It is the same one he allowed for my passage to London. We can leave any time, but the quicker the better. That is, as long as His Lordship's plans fit into what I was able to provide."

"By all means!" William replied. "Your plans are what we have been waiting for."

"Excellent," James replied. "Now, as soon as we can, we will travel to Inbhir Nis. Elizabeth and Marion, you will accompany me as my sister-in-law and my daughter, using their letters of residency. From there, we will board the duke's ship to Orkney, and I might add, with the blessings of His Royal Highness. Once in Orkney, it should be simple enough to arrange passage for the two of you to the colonies as residents of Norway. Afterwards, I shall gather my family in Edinburgh, and then to Breda in my official capacity as the Earl of Morton and then ultimately to Paris for a well-deserved holiday."

William looked at his friend in amazement, knowing that what he had put together was beyond what any of them could have hoped for.

"No one, my friend, could have accomplished what you have, and in as short amount of time. Each of us can nay thank you enough. We all are indebted to you!"

James bowed modestly, thanking them. "Our only need, kind sir, is if you know of a crew to navigate from here to Orkney and then to the Dutch Republic. I dismissed the one I had back to the Duke of Cumberland."

William smiled and looked up at Angus as he delivered the men a round of scotch. It was Angus's turn to answer, and he saluted smartly, his English accent now completely gone, replaced by a well-worn Highland accent.

"It will be me, sir, your rude Englishman. Me and me friends ... we shall handle your wee ship!"

James was taken aback and then burst out laughing.

"Aye," he said, "I can see the loyalties now!"

Elizabeth translated the English to Gaelic for Marion to understand, watching as the light shown brighter in her eyes with each word. She squealed with delight and hugged her mother excitedly. Marion walked up to James and to William and said in her best English, "Thank you very much."

James looked at her, pleased. He stood up and raised his hands, requesting silence. "Certain things had to be shared, for which I am in debt to William. It concerned these two ladies before us, and their ties to Scotland. Ties, I might add, for which Scotland is, and forever shall be, indebted. What William and I have done, and Angus will soon do, is but a small token of what is due you, and one that can never be repaid. If there were more we could do, we would do so gladly. It is rare that we are given such a privilege."

The two gentlemen bowed before them, and Angus bowed as well.

Angus then held out two packages, one for each.

"At the Lord of Lossiemouth's behest, I went to town and found a few quality dresses for you. It wouldn't be fitting for ladies such as yourselves to arrive in the colonies in your *leines*."

Elizabeth and Marion opened their presents and looked at the dresses that unfolded before them. Happiness beamed from both their faces, and Elizabeth hugged each of the gentlemen before her.

"Oh, Mum, they're beautiful!" Marion whispered.

Angus was pleased. "I wouldna hae the two of ye, coming from the Lord's house, looking anything less than the princesses ye are!"

# TWENTY-EIGHT
## 1746: To the Colonies

Three nights later, they prepared to depart Inbhir Nis. Marion ran to William and hugged him dearly.

Elizabeth walked up and embraced him as well. William looked into her eyes. "These last few weeks have been wonderful. You and your daughter have brought a light into my life that I have not known for a long time. If your path ever finds its way back to Scotland, I would love a second chance."

Elizabeth looked at him quizzically. "William, thank you, but as you know, I have recently lost my husband. May I inquire, where is your wife?"

William, still holding her, said sadly, "My wife passed more than five years ago. Have ye not wondered where she was these last few weeks?"

Elizabeth, almost speechless, said, "Forgive me, m'Lord! I just thought she was handling affairs for your estate, possibly in Aberdeen."

"It is I who must apologize for not sharing, but I knew you were still grieving. If your path does ever find its way back to Scotland," he continued, as he cupped her face in his hands, "would you consider us once more?"

Elizabeth began crying. Through teary eyes, she nodded. "It may take some time."

William nodded, understanding, and then looked at Angus, who went to their carriage, and pulled out a small box.

"This is yours, my love," he said, handing it to Elizabeth. "I received this from Reverend James Hay the night before you arrived. The top was burned, but not beyond repair. I had it restored the best I could for you. I hope whatever it held can one day find its way back inside where it belongs."

Elizabeth looked at the box admiringly, noticing the quality repairs, and handed it to Marion.

"Mum!" Marion cried in amazement, as she gently cradled the ancient box.

Elizabeth wasn't listening. "I promise to keep your offer in my heart, always," she said, giving William one last hug, "and thank the Reverend for me, please."

Elizabeth turned to Marion and readied to board the ship.

James turned, only to see the sudden approach of the Duke of Cumberland's carriage. He quickly walked to Elizabeth, hugging her, and whispered into her ear, "All of Scotland will miss you. Now, quickly, tell your daughter to say nothing. Just hold her throat as though in pain."

"So, this is your family," the duke said as he slowly made his way to the small party at the gangplank. "I am surprised they were able to get here so quickly. I trust their miasma is now better?"

James walked over to the duke and said calmly. "Aye, your Excellency. It was a surprise to myself as well, but as I told you, I hold no high regard for things called miasma. They arrived last night and are ready to take the trip. My wife, Agatha, is still in Edinburgh, not quite well. Hopefully, we can pick her up on our way to Breda."

"And these are your...?"

"This is my sister-in-law, Lucy, and my daughter, Mary. We call her Marion. Sadly, she is still not quite able to speak yet, which in itself is a blessing."

"Quite the wagger of tongue, is she?" the Duke inquired. "And your sister-in-law's name was what? I seem to have forgotten already."

"Lucy, your Excellency."

The Duke walked to Elizabeth and took her hand.

"I am pleased to see you are doing better," he said, as he bowed slightly. "May you all enjoy your trip to France."

He stepped back into his carriage and, attempting to catch the earl in a story he felt was fabricated, called out, "Marion?"

Marion turned quickly to the duke.

"I so hope your throat gets better. Pleasant voyage."

Marion held her throat and smiled, nodding.

The Duke of Cumberland rode off, still feeling something was amiss. But the young lady did answer to her name. He would let it pass. He was frying bigger fish, ones that would guarantee his name a place in history for decades, if not centuries, to come.

The group boarded their ship, showing their residency documents to the soldiers at the dock, and prepared to set sail.

A young man took Elizabeth's bag, then Marion's. He smiled at Marion, whose breathing was still trying to return to normal after the encounter with the duke.

"His Excellency seemed perturbed," he said in English.

Marion shook her head and said, "Gàdhlig." Then recalling the English word, said, "Gaelic."

He smoothly began speaking to her in her native tongue. She smiled, delighted.

"My parents were from the Highlands. Once you get to—is it the colonies?—you won't have to worry about dealing with too many dukes."

As they prepared to pull away from the dock, Angus's voice echoed over the ship, giving orders, and interrupting their conversation.

"I better get going!" he winked.

Marion watched the young man as he began hoisting the sails, his beautiful blue eyes dancing and his auburn hair blowing in the wind.

"My name is Collum, Collum Dirks, my lady!" he hollered out over the wind that was beginning to pick up, and he bowed low.

Marion walked over to her mother. Elizabeth was looking back at the figure still waving from the shoreline, slowly getting smaller as their ship's sails filled completely.

Elizabeth prayed that the kind assistance given by William and James would never be discovered. She was grateful William had accepted the life that had been chosen for him. Without his money and title, she would have had no place to turn. Her mind went to a verse, something from her memory, as she waved one last time to William.

"To those whom much is given, much is expected," she whispered. "This you have done. Thank you, William, my first love. And aye, I shall always remember. And thank you, James. We shall never forget your kindness."

That evening, Marion stood at the deck rail and watched as the waves rose up and then crashed down under the bow of the ship as they headed north.

Collum walked up to her. "Do ye mind company?" he asked.

Marion shook her head. Collum drew close, protecting her against the ocean chill and the occasional splash with his coat.

"Where will ye be going from here?" Marion asked.

"Angus is my uncle," Collum replied, "and I'll be going with him from Orkney to the Dutch Republic, where James has an appointment in Breda. From there, I'm not sure. I would like to stay with him, if he requires my service. If not, I will return to Lossiemouth and then likely home."

"He's a wonderful man," Marion said. "But I did not like him at first!"

"It's all a show, I promise," Collum replied. "Inside, he's like a lovable bear. But one doesn't dare cross the ones he cares for. He'll defend you and your honor to the last breath. He did that for His Lordship's father, at Sheriffmuir. That's why to this day he is part of His Lordship's family."

Marion replied, "What happened?"

"It was towards the end that His Lordship was shot from his horse. My uncle went to him, taking him to a safe place. He continued fighting until the battle was over. He then gathered His Lordship's horse and took him to a doctor. Once he knew he would live, my uncle left, immediately going to sea. It wasn't until ten years later that His Lordship was able to find my uncle and persuade him to come to Lossiemouth. He's been there ever since, now as the servant to his Lordship's son."

Collum continued, "But it was during that ten-year period after Sheriffmuir that my uncle took my father and mother, under new names, to Nova Scotia. We have lived there ever since. They gave up their titles in Scotland, but I know they feel it was worth it."

Marion nodded her head and repeated one of her mother's favorite sayings, "The best things in life are nay things. But why did they have to leave Scotland?"

"It was before I was born. My parents were helping to smuggle weapons from France to the Highlanders, as our family has done for hundreds of years. Scotland has always needed weapons, but their closest neighbor and oft times enemy, England, wasn't willing to give them any. Somehow, the English found out the French were supplying Scotland weapons, and narrowed it down to my parents. They had to go into hiding for more than a year, until my uncle found them and took them to Nova Scotia. By the way," Collum smiled, "I like your words: the best things in life are nay things."

"They are Mum's words, but I am learning to appreciate them more myself. Collum, where your parents live, Nova Scotia. Is it beautiful?" Marion asked.

"Aye, it is, though after seeing Scotland, it can nay compare. But it's peaceful, Marion, and beautiful in its own way. We've no worries about being forced off our land, or a sudden battle happening that our clan leaders say we must fight in."

Marion looked at her companion. "Collum, I … forgive me, as I know how this sounds. Mum always said I was a strong-willed lass. But in some fashion, in some way, I feel I know you. It's as if we have known one another before."

She crossed herself as she looked up at the North Star and said a quick prayer. Collum watched as she did.

"Do you pray?" Marion asked.

"Aye, I do. All my life I have prayed. And aye, I feel as you do. That somewhere we have met or known one another. My mother calls it second sight. That is why, beyond courtesy, I had to help you with your baggage. I had to meet you. You seem ... so familiar to me."

Marion pointed to the North Star. "Ever since I was a wee lass, if ever we were separated from a loved one, no matter where we were, we would look to the North Star and pray before we went to sleep. My father promised my mum and me that he would do this each night while he was fighting for Prince Charles."

The memory of losing her father hurt incredibly. She began to cry and leaned against Collum's chest. It took a few minutes before her tears stopped.

"I'm sorry. It's just that after all that has happened this last month ..."

Collum stopped her. "Say no more. My uncle said you have gone through more in this last month than many would endure in a lifetime."

For the first time in more than a month, Marion felt secure. She didn't know where she and her mother's voyage would end, but so far their prayers had been answered.

"Collum, I don't believe any star has special powers, but each night I'd like to think, as we travel on different paths, we could look up and say a special prayer, for one another."

Collum smiled at her. "I promise that until we meet again, and one day we shall, each night I will be looking at the North Star and thinking of you."

# TWENTY-NINE
## 2005: All Things Revealed

The sun shone brightly through the window of their room. Ian stretched, rolled over, and looked at the clock—almost 11 a.m. He gently touched his wife. "Sweetheart?" Then after a moment, he shook her gently. "Marian?"

Marian's eyes both opened suddenly, and she stared wide-eyed at Ian.

Ian looked at her, curiously.

"Oh, Ian!" Marian exclaimed. "I know!" And then she burst out crying. "I know!"

"Baby ... what is it?"

Marian looked at Ian, uncertain. "I dreamt last night! Did ... Did you?"

Ian nodded his head sleepily, and replied, "Of course. I dreamt of what our lives will be like back in Colorado. I dreamt of our future. It was ..."

"Oh, my God," Marian said, interrupting. "I dreamt of what

happened to the necklace, what happened to my family, and of the knife!" She reached up to touch his face. "And I dreamt of your many times great-grandfather. He was with me, and I learned why your family left Scotland!"

Ian stared at Marian, as she pushed herself up on her pillow.

"His name was Collum," she continued, "and I met him at Inverness when my family left Scotland. Oh, Ian, you and I are so tied together. Our entire lineage is!"

Marian looked beyond Ian, fixating on the castle as she looked out the window, a vacant stare in her eyes as she tried to recall everything. Then suddenly she rose up, excited. "Ian, the necklace is buried here, at Kildrummy! We must go there now! Do you to think Fiona can give us a shovel?"

Marian flung both legs over the edge of the bed and dressed quickly. "Sweetheart," Ian said, trying to calm her down. "Please, baby. I know how you feel. I've felt this same pull for weeks, and I promise I will be the first one by your side. But you know as well as I that there is no way we can go there with a shovel and start digging around for what we *think* is there. It's a historical site, protected by Historic Scotland for the last fifty-plus years. You heard Niall, and you know it yourself. There's no way!" Ian put his arm around her shoulder. "Besides, sweetheart, it's got to have been searched many times over by various archeologists."

Marian looked at Ian, not wanting to accept his answer. "What if they missed it? We can't just pack up and go home. Ian, we've been brought here, through your dreams and mine. We can't leave without trying!"

Ian replied softly, "I know, baby, I know. Don't worry. We will do whatever we have to. These things were shared with us so our lineage was not lost. I can't believe, now that we are here, our search will be left with no answers. There must be more for us to follow, like breadcrumbs on a path. We will get to the bottom of this, even if it takes going back to Niall and the university as well. We will find out all we can, I promise!"

Marian nodded her head, understanding, then wept. It was an hour before they were able to go down for breakfast and to a waiting Fiona.

"I trust you had a good sleep?" Fiona asked, pleasantly enough, then seeing Marian's eyes said, "Oh, I'm sorry. You two seemed so happy last night. I trust it is not our hotel? Should I bring the manager?"

Ian touched Fiona's hand and replied, "It's nothing that you or the hotel has done. Our stay has been exquisite. We're trying to piece together our lineage in Scotland and have come to a roadblock."

"Since last night?" Fiona asked, surprised. "I'm sorry to hear this, but pleased that it's not our hotel. We try to make everything perfect for our guests. Sometimes it's not easy, with a hotel that is as old as this is. And insofar as our guest last night, please forgive him. He meant no harm. He felt terrible afterward, and personally went out and bought you a can of treacle. And I promise I didn't hit him … well, not hard!"

"You didn't!" Marian said, wide-eyed, wiping away at the last vestiges of her tears.

"I did," Fiona replied, "though it were just a wee tap. He's a wonderful guest, as you can see." She handed Marian the can. "Now, *aboot* your search for your lineage. May I suggest the University at Glasgow or Edinburgh? They have wonderful records that go back many centuries."

Fiona looked at each and then inquired, "Can I interest either of you in a Scottish breakfast?"

"Absolutely," Ian replied. "And a cup of coffee... Marian? Yes, a cup of coffee for the two of us."

"Glad to, sir." Fiona replied. "I'll get your breakfasts ordered, and will personally bring your coffee right up."

Fiona left and quickly came back with their coffee. "Now," she said, "is there anything else can I help with?"

Marian thanked her. "I'm not sure there is much you can do. With our search ending here at Kildrummy, our last hope is a gentleman and his wife who will be meeting us this morning."

Fiona reached over and patted Marian's hand. "All the way from the States. I so hope they are able to help you!"

After breakfast was served and their dishes cleared, Fiona came back to their table. "I've been thinking," she began. "May I sit down?"

Ian and Marian nodded, and Ian pulled out her chair. "You mentioned your ties to Kildrummy," Fiona began. "There is someone we know who is a wee bit closer than the universities. He and his wife come here quite often. They run a travel agency and send tourists here throughout the season. So many arrive, curious about Kildrummy, but are unaware of its ties to our King Robert. That's where he and his sweet wife come in. Would you like their number?"

Ian and Marian looked at each other and then at Fiona. "Is it Russell and Hayley?" Marian asked.

"You know them?" Fiona replied. "Is that how you got here, through them?"

"Actually," Ian said, "we only learned of them two days ago, from an archaeologist friend of my wife's. We're waiting for Russell's call now."

"Wonderful!" Fiona replied. "With his knowledge, I'm sure they can at least lead you in the right direction."

Fiona got up, and Ian and Marian thanked her. Ian gently grasped Marian's hand and said softly, "All roads lead to Rome? It seems whatever path we are on, it is still guiding us."

Marian placed her free hand on top of their clasped hands, her spirits raised, and said, "I'm in, wherever our road leads. But this Russell and Hayley. Do you think they are a part of this? Are they the final link to our chain?"

Ian was thoughtful for a moment and then replied, "Baby, many of the things I dreamt I chalked up to coincidence. But nothing as of late seems to be a coincidence any longer. We need to see these people. If they can't help, I'm sure they will point us in a better direction. I hate to think we are chasing clues like a modern-day Indiana Jones, but if that's what it takes, then I'm with you all the way."

Marian hugged him. "I gotta call Momma!"

Ian laughed, "Good idea, we need to check in. I don't think Michael would mind a 4 a.m. call either! Let's do it!"

After spending the next hour talking to very tired family members and friends, Ian and Marian walked from the hotel to the castle.

"I trust you enjoyed your sticky toffee pudding?" asked the ticket seller from the day before. "Fiona serves only the best."

Marian's eyes lit up. "We've never had anything so delicious!"

"Or rich," Ian added. "That and a scoop of ice cream, and it could become our new food group!"

"Sorry you had to make it a two-day excursion, but at least today you won't be rushed. Off the beaten track as we are, it's generally a wee bit quieter than other castles."

Ian and Marian agreed. Admission paid, they walked up the path to the entrance, and stood in amazement.

"It'd be nice to think our new life with our baby starts here," Marian said quietly, as she held Ian's arm. He turned and held her. A gentle mist began to fall as they gazed at the castle.

"I'd like to think that as well. A whole new beginning, Lady Marian."

She smiled, "I like that …Lady Marian. I could have lived here, Ian. Even without the modern things we've become accustomed to."

"Without your microwave?" Ian asked.

"Absolutely," Marian replied. "Especially that thing!"

"To be here when it was constructed, watching it daily. Oh, Ian, my dreams didn't show this. When was it constructed? Do you know?"

"Mine didn't either, but I read inside the ticket office that it was built in the mid-thirteenth century."

A voice from behind them added, "You are correct. And you would have had to deal with the rain then, too."

They turned around and faced the speaker. "Drs. Ian and Marian Dirks?"

"Russell?" Ian asked.

"Yes," he replied, "and this is my wife, Hayley. It's a pleasure meeting you."

They all exchanged handshakes.

Hayley interjected, to Marian, "I apologize, but I absolutely had to come. I hope you don't mind. Are you the same archaeologist who is known here in Scotland and France for your pre-Clovis dig in America?"

Marian blushed. "I had no idea my work had come this far."

"It has," Hayley said. "We've another archaeologist from down south who currently is putting together a documentary on ancient Scotland. Russell used to go to school with him. I do hope while you are here, you get a chance to meet him. He's brilliant."

Marian looked at Ian, then back at Hayley, and said, "I'm sorry, I thought you knew. I worked with Niall at the University of Missouri one summer. We just left him and his family. That's where we got your number!"

"That was my mistake," Russell replied. "In our haste, I forgot to tell her about the referral by Niall. So, from our conversation yesterday, I understand you are interested in learning more about the history of Kildrummy Castle?"

"Yes," Ian and Marian both replied.

"Would this be on a personal or professional level?" Russell asked.

"Our interest stems from a very personal reason," Marian replied. "Ian thinks I may be related to someone from here a very long time ago."

"Really?" Russell asked. "How long ago, do you know? Kildrummy's history ended in the early 1700s."

Ian replied, "It was before then. I believe it was more than six hundred and seventy years ago."

"I see," Russell said, raising an eyebrow. "You've narrowed it down quite a bit. And you believe it was someone from this castle?"

"Yes," Ian replied. "Russell, we know how this is all going to sound, but it was revealed first through my dreams and then Marian's. Accurate dreams, with people, places, everything. We've even tied it to a necklace."

Russell looked at Ian with skepticism, "A necklace?"

Ian replied quickly, "Yes. It's tied to my wife's earrings, likely part of a set."

"That part was through my dreams," Marian replied, "and just last night." She pointed to an area near where the Snow Tower once stood. "Ian's dreams revealed there was a necklace. Mine showed me where it was. I dreamt it was in this area."

Russell and Hayley were quiet.

"We both know how this sounds," Ian said once more. "I know

if you came to me and said the same things, well … I doubt you'd get very far. I've been accused of being more of a realist. I first thought I was going crazy when my dreams began."

Marian quickly added, "And if it weren't for Historic Scotland, I'd be calling Niall to round up a research team to dig every square inch of Kildrummy. Starting within the hour!"

Marian squeezed in a quick wink, but Ian knew she was serious.

"Excuse us for a second, would you?" Russell asked.

They walked away a few feet and were in an animated discussion. Back and forth, they exchanged words, then walked back to Ian and Marian.

"Can you describe the necklace?" Russell asked.

"From what we can surmise," Ian replied, "the earrings and necklace are a matched set: solid gold, with a ruby near the top, and then a gold braid going down to a small diamond, then a ruby at the bottom. It was an heirloom given to Marian's ancestors many years ago.

For some unknown reason, the necklace and earrings were separated. We don't know anything beyond this."

"Actually," Marian said, "I do know why they were separated. I'm just frustrated that I can't use a simple damn shovel to look for it!"

Ian looked at Marian quizzically, and she added, "I'm sorry, sweetheart. I had so much to share this morning that I neglected to tell you this part."

The gentle mist that had accompanied them for the last ten minutes started to let up, but then suddenly, it began to rain hard. Hayley shrugged her shoulders and interrupted. "Welcome to Scotland, where all things can change at a moment's notice. Would you like to go to a favorite pub of ours? It's not far to Cabrach, and we can grab a quick lunch and continue our conversation there."

They arrived at the Grouse Inn, and Russell asked the proprietor for a quiet table off to the side.

"There is a legend that there was a gift from Robert the Bruce to Marion Braidfute," Russell began. "But, as ye can guess, there's a bit of mystery to it, and it's difficult at best to separate myth from truth. I will say that I heard it was jewelry of some sort, but never knew if there was anything more to this than rumor."

"Oh, there was," Marian replied earnestly. "If the earrings I have are of the same set, then my family has had them passed down from mother to daughter for as long as …" She stopped. "I'm sorry. My mother died when I was born, and I'm not sure exactly how long they have been passed down. I'd like to believe it was the six hundred and seventy years Ian mentioned, but I'm not sure."

Hayley reached across the table and touched her hand. "I'm so sorry to hear," she said. "I can't imagine losing one's parents."

Marian thanked her. "I never knew them, so that helps some. But it never takes away the loss." She continued, "Over the last few months, since the time we decided to come to Scotland, Ian has been having dreams. They became more accurate with each dream, and then last night, I dreamt for the first time, and well, here we are. And as I said, I'm ready to grab a shovel. In my heart, I know where it was buried."

"As I told her," Ian added, smiling, "short of donning a black mask and face paint, it can't be done. Besides, we would never go digging around an historic Scottish site, period. Let alone for something we think *might* be here."

Russell nodded his head. "That wouldn't go over too well, especially with it being government controlled. But there were a few sanctioned explorations done here in the 1920s," he added, "and some were done afterward. Some from the area say there were explorations done before then, but that claim, like much of Scotland's history, can't be substantiated."

Russell looked at Ian and Marian and lowered his voice to a whisper. "What I'm about to ask, you don't have to acknowledge. However, if you have the earrings with you …well, no promises. But we may be able to help you in your search for your necklace."

Marian looked at Russell, wide-eyed, and then at Ian. Ian nodded. She reached into her purse and opened the side compartment, revealing a small box. She pulled it out, set her purse aside, and opened it.

"Oh, my," was all Hayley could say, and then exchanged glances with Russell.

Russell looked at the set. "They are beautiful. Do you have time for a story? One that is true?"

Ian and Marian looked at their new friends and nodded.

"Hayley and my family can each trace our ancestry back as far as history can reveal. My wife's family is tied to the Urquharts and mine to the MacDonalds. As a boy, I grew up on a farm just north of here that has been in my family for more than two hundred years. It wasn't until I was nineteen years old that my father showed me a necklace that has been in our family for the last one hundred and fifty years. One of my great-great-grandfathers, I believe five generations back, used to go to Kildrummy and dig as a young man. Most days he never found anything. Sometimes he'd find tiles from the flooring or a layer of charcoal here and there. Once he even found a small cache of coins that were more than five hundred years old. He used those to pay off the farm.

"The most special of all, though, was when he was digging in an area in the middle of the floor, near the old Elphinstone Tower. A tile loosened and after digging down, he came upon what looked like a small clump of pitch. It had hardened quite a bit over the years, and he was ready to throw it away. Instead he put it on a shelf in his barn. Over the next few weeks, he became more curious. One day, he decided to soak it in a tin of turpentine until all the pitch had dissolved. That's when he was able to see it, preserved after all these years."

Russell paused. "What my great-grandfather had found was a necklace like no other. It had strands of gold coming off a gold chain. There were rubies on the top, diamonds in the middle, and rubies on the bottom. Since then, we have had it in our family. We've never shown it, never mentioned it, to anyone. It was something so incredible. That's why I decided to go for a degree in archaeology at the University of Glasgow. I wanted to know more about that era so that I could research the people of Kildrummy Castle. What I discovered, besides my love of Scottish history, is that I truly love sharing our country's history with people. That led to my decision to be a travel guide for the Scotland people rarely see and the stories behind her."

Hayley nudged Russell gently, and he stopped and smiled.

"I'm sorry," Russell said. "I get going on a tangent and sometimes need help to get back on track."

Ian and Marian enjoyed the tangent, and said, "Please, keep going."

"What I learned in my research goes a little deeper than what your dreams have revealed. Your earrings and my necklace go back to a small ceilidh. The set was given to Marion Braidfute in honor of the sacrifice her husband had made for the land he loved. Before Marion Braidfute died, she gave them, as well as her baby, to Lady Christian. En route to Orkney, Christian hid them at Kildrummy Castle. There they stayed, buried, for almost thirty years. After the Battle of Culblean, Lady Christian dug them up and gave them to Marion, who was married to Ian de Airth. The story goes that she presented them to her in front of thousands of men who had just won the battle. However, it becomes more obscure with their daughter, Elizabeth. Back then, many of the families intermarried, kept the same name, and even repeated the same name, so it became harder to separate fact from legend. Apparently, Elizabeth did marry a man and had her only child, another Marion."

Ian interrupted, "See what I mean? The names changing from Marion to Elizabeth and then to Marion again, just in this lineage! At one point, they lived at Kildrummy Castle. That is for certain."

It was Marian's turn to add to the story. "My mother, as I said, died when I was born. My father wrote a letter that said our names alternated back and forth for hundreds of years. Then, when I grew up, I was supposed to name my daughter Elizabeth and pass the earrings to her when she turned sixteen. Ian suggested that my dad had misspelled my name. Maybe that's true?"

Ian continued, "My dream confirms what Marian is saying. The necklace and earrings were both buried in the Great Hall. In 1335, when Marion met Lady Christian, they dug down more than a foot to find the set. That is when my dreams stopped. Since then, we haven't had time to piece our dreams together and had no way of going any further, until we met you today."

Russell and Hayley looked at each other and nodded.

"For whatever reason," Russell said, "I believe we were destined to meet today. I knew I had to find out where this necklace came from. It has held a cherished place in my family for more than one hundred and fifty years. I believe my many-times-great-grandfather, from one hundred and fifty years ago, would be proud to know the true heir had come home to claim the heritage of her ancient grandmother and he was part of it in some way."

Ian was still puzzled. "Why is it, through all the years, with the earrings and necklace separated, no prior owners ever had the dreams

I had?"

Hayley answered, "Ian, this is a guess, but I believe it was due to you. Russell said a Marion from around the 1330s had married a de Airth, yes? Is your name a derivative of this clan?"

Ian replied that they had just had this discussion with Niall.
"My family's name was changed many years ago when we came from Scotland. My best guess is that my great-grandfather combined the two to form 'Dirks' right before they left Scotland. It's been Dirks ever since."

Hayley nodded her head. "From the time Kildrummy was created to the time it was abandoned in 1716, the de Airths, Mars, and Elphinstones played a large part in its history. The jewelry may have been guided in some fashion by an outside hand. But it had to be the right person to receive the dreams. Your marriage may not have been coincidental. Are either of you familiar with second sight?"

Marian replied, "Yes! This was in my dream as well, between Collum and Marion. It's like reading minds, yes?"

"Kind of," Hayley replied. "My entire family has had it for years. But it's more when you can almost sense something … something that needs to be revealed … and often from many miles away. This may be what allowed Ian to be the receptor of Marian's history."

Russell added, "I've experienced Hayley's second sight for years, and from what I'm hearing, I don't believe it could have happened any other way. Ian, I am guessing that you have it, and it took the death of Marian's mother and their lost lineage to trigger everything. As though Lady Christian was called forth from hundreds of years ago, to make sure the lineage she promised Marion Braidfute was maintained. Marian may have been the catalyst, but it was your second sight that allowed the revelations to happen, as well as our meeting you here this very day."

Russell held Hayley's hand. "We would be honored if you would come to our house for dinner, as well as the return of an heirloom to you, Marian, the true daughter of Sir William Wallace."

Marian look dumbfounded. "What??"

Ian laughed, "I'm not sure she has watched the movie *Braveheart!*"

When the laughter died down, Ian repeated Russell's words. "You, sweetheart, are the many-times-great-granddaughter of Sir William Wallace. Marion Braidfute was Sir William's wife, and she bore him a daughter."

"I know who William Wallace was," she interrupted, as she playfully hit Ian in the arm. "I *am* the archaeologist here, and besides, I have seen *Braveheart!*" She looked at her friends around the table. "But you're sure it's me? If so, then I'm at a loss for words."

"Sweetheart," Ian said, "there's not a person at this table who isn't sure. Your many-times-great-grandmother was Elizabeth Marion Wallace, and she was captured at Tain with Lady Christian. They were both taken to the Gilbertine nunnery, where Marion stayed until the day she met Ian."

"Oh, that's got to make Longshanks roll over in his grave." Russell exclaimed. "To know that William Wallace's daughter was raised under the protective care of his son. I don't think I'm going to say a word. Our peace has been too long in the making to add this small bit of history!"

Ian laughed. "I guess our story, or at least our ancestors' story, has come full circle." He looked at Marian, smiling. "I'm glad our Ian and Marion met at the woolery that day. Our being together today, almost seven hundred years later, wouldn't have happened any other way."

They left the pub and went to Russell and Hayley's home. Russell brought out the necklace, as well as a couple of other artifacts from more than one hundred fifty years ago.

"She is the grandest of castles," he said. "My grandfather truly loved Kildrummy, and so do I." He carefully drew out the necklace from a silken bag. "I will miss this necklace and how it's been in our family. But I know now that it was found for a greater purpose."

He handed it to Ian and said, "Marian, I believe you should have had this given to you along with your earrings. I think your mother and all the women in your lineage would be very pleased to know the necklace and earrings have been rejoined, through your dreams and my grandfather."

Ian took the necklace and gently clasped it behind Marian's neck. Then, picking up the earrings, he placed them on her ears.

"I believe they all know," Ian said. "Somehow, I'm sure of this. That each contributed in some fashion to make all this happen."

They stood, each of them, and beheld the Lady Marian Wallace-Dirks.

Hayley said in amazement, "With your mother passing, and no one to know where they came from or what happened to your necklace, to have them re-joined … I've never heard the like."

Russell nodded his head. "Me neither. If anyone ever came to me claiming the same thing, I'd have denied any knowledge of the necklace. But with the proof in your purse, and that they match my grandfather's necklace, I know we did the right thing."

Russell then stood and said to Ian, "With your permission?" Ian nodded, uncertain as to what his intentions were. Russell knelt and kissed the hand of Marian. "All have been returned, my queen," he said.

Hayley gave Marian a kiss and added, "They have come home."

The U.S. customs agent looked carefully at the necklace Marian and Ian declared. "I see you reported earrings when you departed the U.S., but you did not mention a necklace. Is there a reason it was omitted?" he asked.

Both Ian and Marian had a twinkle in their eyes. Ian replied, "Would you prefer the long or short version?"

The agent carefully inspected the matching necklace and earrings. He noted the difference in the patina of the gold, as though aged in different ways.

"They look old. My grandmother used to tell me a story when I was a wee wain," he said, as he looked at Ian, then Marian. "It was about a set of earrings and a necklace that was given by Robert the Bruce to the wife of Sir William Wallace."

He looked closer at the jewelry and handed them back. "Are you Scots?" he asked.

"Yes, we both are," Marian said, proudly.

The customs agent smiled and, waving them through, said, "I am as well. Be sure to tell your children the long version. I'm certain, as Scots, they would like to hear the complete story!

A year had passed since Ian and Marian returned from Scotland. In that time, Marian had hung a picture of Kildrummy Castle in the living room and legally changed the spelling of her name to Marion. Their lineage, after weeks of comparing their dreams, was written down and placed in their safe, never to be lost again. Ian's nights, and Marion's as well, no longer disturbed by dreams, were long and peaceful, disrupted only by the occasional cries of their three-month-old baby, Elizabeth.

Ian knew Marion anxiously awaited the day when she could pass on her wonderful heirloom to their daughter, as well as the lineage of which they were so proud. She would share how their story had been revealed. Then, holding the hands of her daughter, with the pride and intensity her heart truly felt, she would speak the words from long ago.

"You are a Scot!"

# Afterword

In my story, I wanted to stay as close to actual events that occurred at two critical times in Scotland's history. In doing this,
my goal was to make it enjoyable and do so without the incredible burden of detail, even though, after researching for months,
Scottish-English history *is* incredibly detailed.

Only Marian Dirks (the main character); her husband, Ian, and
their respective families; the Lord of Lossiemouth; and a few other
characters are my creations. The remaining characters are true, as
well as the circumstances, such as the battles fought by Robert the
Bruce, the first king of Scotland, and the battle at Culloden ended by
the Duke of Cumberland, with a savagery that decimated the Highland clans and their way of life forever. The inclusion of James Douglas, Earl of Morton; John Montagu, Fourth Earl of Sandwich; His
Grace the Duke of Newcastle-upon-Tyne, Thomas Pelham-Holles,
Secretary of State; and the Right Honorable Henry Pelham, prime
minister, were necessary additions to my story. Each allows my char-

acters to escape Scotland at a time when this was almost impossible. Each of these are real people, taken from history, and weaved into my story. Even the imprisonment of James Douglas and his family, which was not included in my story, actually happened. This was due to their lack of travel documents upon arrival in France, as well as for incriminating papers found on James that revealed a possible connection to the Jacobites.

### Marion Braidfute Wallace

Although many doubt her existence, I do not. Whether she and William Wallace were married is inconsequential; that they had a daughter, especially in the context of this story, is of more importance. Her name was Elizabeth Marion Wallace. Her age at this time would have been very close to what is written, although her mother would not have been found in a hovel, dying. She would have died years prior at the hands of Sheriff William Heselrig of Lanark after she provided William Wallace the time he needed to escape. Is this act by Heselrig one of the deciding factors that drove Wallace to become, as many attest, Scotland's greatest hero in its fight for independence? If not, who knows what would have happened with Wallace? What really happened to their daughter, and who raised her, is for genealogists to research. The rest of us shall let his life continue in legend and folklore.

## Lady Christian

(Christian de Bruce; Christian of Mar;
Christian de Seton; Christian Moray/Murray)

For purpose of clarity, I called her Lady Christian throughout this story, though I placed a "de Mar, de Seton, or Moray" to show the correct period in history corresponding with the deaths of her husbands, her marriages, and her life.

What is true is that she was Robert the Bruce's sister and one who lived through so much. From her youth, she would have been witness to the strong arguments between her grandfather, Robert the Bruce, Fifth Lord of Annandale, and the other contenders for the Scottish throne after the Maid of Norway died en route to Scotland. She would have seen his strong pursuit of the Scottish crown, which I am certain was instrumental in guiding his grandson (the future King Robert I) in his quest to become king.

I chose to make her the heroine in many parts of my story because she was there for it all—from Wallace to the coronation of her brother to the Scottish Wars of Independence. She was imprisoned from 1306 to 1314, and if that wasn't enough, she lost her four brothers and all three husbands by 1338. She personally held and defended Kildrummy Castle in 1335 until her last husband arrived to defend it. In 1349, she saw many of her family and friends die from the bubonic (black) plague. She was an extraordinary lady. She passed in 1357 at more than eighty years of age, incredible for that time.

As a side note, most of the families in this time frame were fighting—if not father with son, or brother with brother, then neighbor with neighbor. A testament to this fact is that Christian the Bruce's daughter married a Menteith who was loyal to King Edward and the one who turned in Wallace to be executed, which is not what was depicted with literary license and freedom in *Braveheart*.

Also, in my research, I found certain statements that put doubt on Lady Christian the Bruce's marriage to her first husband, Garnait, (or Gartnait, as historians may write) of the Mar family. One can only wonder, however, if she was not a Mar, why then was she such an integral part of Kildrummy Castle? Certainly she was not given as much freedom in its control out of kindness. Marriages at this time were done for political advantage for the combined families. It is without doubt that Domhnall mac Uilleam arranged for the marriage of his sons and daughters to Scotland's higher ranking families, most notably Isobel to Robert the Bruce, future king of Scotland; Marjorie to Sir John of Strathbogie (Earl of Atholl); and son Garnait to Christian, Robert the Bruce's sister.

### Robert the Bruce

One of the challenges I faced in writing this story is that there are many versions of what happened to King Robert the Bruce after Methven. Stories, many passed down from one family to another, and others written as fiction, were later taken as fact. Even if certain things are true, such as the skirmish at Loch Tay, it becomes difficult to use in a story without more substantiation. Some modern historians state that after Methven, Robert went west to Dalry, a name that means "King's Field." One can easily assume that this town's name came about after 1306, not before. Others state he went north to Aberdeen, where he picked up the royal family, went to Kildrummy, and then down to Loch Tay, and then to Strathfillan, where, after losing this battle, he decided to split his family apart, and send them back to Kildrummy. All this ambiguity becomes a challenge when attempting a historical novel, without having more knowledge of a time frame that is known for its lack of written history. Even a noted historian of the time, Barbour, who was a child when Robert the Bruce was alive, has written accounts that have been proven to be subjective, and very pro-Scot, many of which have since been discredited.

Finally, another possibility for this period is this: If Robert the Bruce had not returned once more to Scotland when he did, in pursuit of the crown, then the job that Lady Christian's son-in-law, Alan Menteith had, of finding William Wallace and betraying him to King Edward, would likely have been given to Robert.

Such were the times. So, interspersing twenty-first century views on fourteenth-century realities adds an additional layer of difficulty, especially when it comes to Robert's vacillating between the English and the Scots. It is recorded that Robert said, "No man hates his own flesh, and I am no exception." Yet fight he did against the Scots on more than one occasion. As no one alive today was there, I hope the descendants of the characters I brought to life will allow for any variations in my writing from what they believe to be true.